THE COLLECTION

by

SARAH STEEL

CHIMERA

The Collector first published in 2000 by
Chimera Publishing Ltd
PO Box 152
Waterlooville
Hants
PO8 9FS

Printed and bound in Great Britain by
Omnia Books Ltd, Glasgow

THE COLLECTOR

Sarah Steel

This novel is fiction – in real life practice safe sex

'Not too fast. Punishment must not be rushed. Pace her pain so that both her body and mind can savour it slowly,' Dr Stikannos whispered. The wheelchair rattled as he inched his metal mask towards her whipped cheeks. 'Four more,' he pronounced. 'But slowly, my dear. The pleasure of pain is a feast. But it is a banquet,' he added darkly, 'that must be taken leisurely, by both the punisher and the punished.'

Chapter One

The doors closed with a hiss as soft as a honeymoon cane across the eager bride's bare bottom. The train slid out of Paddington, gathering speed as it nosed out of London and headed west.

In her deserted first class carriage, Emily settled back into her seat, dimpling the cushion with her rounded buttocks. Shielding her eyes from the afternoon sun, she glimpsed half-remembered, almost forgotten landmarks – a green water tower, the teetering scrap pile of a breaker's yard, the crooked church spire – in the suburban sprawl.

It was several years since she had taken this, or any, train journey. Now, at twenty-two, she drove everywhere in her black Audi. The car was her bonus from the directors of the Knightsbridge art gallery where she specialised in authenticating minor masterpieces. Up to her eighteenth birthday, she had taken the train out of Paddington to Birchwood Hall, the notoriously strict Wiltshire boarding school for privileged – if wayward – young ladies.

Emily squirmed at the sudden memory of Birchwood Hall. With her parents in Hong Kong and only a frail aunt to supervise her increasing delinquency, Emily had been consigned to the boarding school for the discipline she sorely needed.

Birchwood Hall.

The steel wheels seemed to be whispering the haunting name. Lulled by the rhythm of the train's sleek progress, Emily dozed, forgetting the purpose of her journey – to catalogue the private collection of Dr Stikannos in his rural lair – and slipped into a reverie of her former boarding school days. And nights.

Her days there had been dominated by the presence of a strict games mistress who was also Emily's head of house. Images of the hockey field flooded back: of pony-tailed schoolgirls in short, pleated navy skirts scattering after the shrill blast of a whistle had signalled the bully-off. Ripening breasts bouncing within their firm bondage of tight cotton vests, knuckles whitening as they gripped their hockey sticks, the cavalry charge of squealing schoolgirls would dash across the shaven sward. The chill wind mottled their exposed thighs, impudently whipping up their skirts to reveal panties stretched tightly across pink, plump cheeks. Emily hated hockey and often hung well back from the sphere of play where the tackling was fast and furious – only to be hounded by the games mistress who scolded her for slacking and promised punishment after the match.

'See me in the changing room immediately after your shower, girl.'

Half time. Perspiring, mud-splashed girls collapsing onto the pitch, wriggling their bottoms as the spiked grass stubble prickled their exposed flesh. Biting greedily into quartered oranges and sucking hard, juicing their dry throats and mouths, the girls eased their aching torment.

A long whistle blast signalled the second half. Instantly gathered into their team huddles, the girls bent over, thigh to thigh, tugging up their white ankle socks. Rising, bottoms bumping, they plucked away the cotton of their panties from their hot clefts. A short, sharp whistle blast. Play began. Thrills and spills for the squealing girls – but not for Emily, loitering in the goal-mouth, hating hockey and hating even more the appointment with the games mistress after the shower.

In the showers, the delicious sting of hot water on her breasts and buttocks, raking her nakedness and teasing her erect nipples. Stumbling from the sluice, her feet slapping on the wet tiles, Emily would grope blindly for her towel. Dabbing at her bottom, belly and outer thighs, she would

6

attempt to scrabble into her school uniform – desperately hoping to be discovered fully dressed by the slipper-wielding mistress. Her frantic haste was always futile. Emerging through the clouds of steam, the grim mistress would pounce upon her anxious prey and order Emily to undress.

'You know I want you bare-bottomed. Bare-bottomed and bending, girl. At once.'

Crimsoning with shame and squirming with burning resentment as she obediently stripped, Emily would pluck at her knotted tie, shrug off her crisp white blouse and peel off her panties with trembling fingers. The games mistress always stood, thumbing the smooth sole of the leather slipper, gazing dominantly down upon the struggling schoolgirl. Burning with indignation as her breasts were bared, Emily would attempt to cup and cover her dark nipples.

'Now stop being silly, girl,' the games mistress would warn, raising the slipper menacingly above Emily's soft cheeks. 'Panties down, please.'

Emily dreaded the moment when her blonde pubic snatch peeped out as, inch by inch, the tight elastic was thumbed down over the swell of her buttocks and firm thighs.

The speeding train rattled across the points and lurched as it thundered through Slough. Emily opened her eyes, blinking away the disturbing memories. The late summer sun blazed directly down. Emily blinked again, squirming in the fierce heat. Heat. She shivered suddenly, remembering the hot kiss of the slipper across her bare bottom.

The games mistress would approach Emily, tapping her open palm with the slipper.

'Bend over. No, further. Bottom up a little more.'

Emily, biting her lower lip, could not but obey, her blonde mane curtaining her blushing face as it spilled down. Inching her thighs apart, her breasts would bunch between her straightened arms, which stretched down to where her

7

fingers splayed across her tiny toes.

'Feet a little more apart, girl.'

Emily would shuffle obediently, closing her eyes tightly as she felt her pussy becoming more exposed to the stern gaze of her punisher.

Then came the admonishing words, frequently emphasised by light taps of the cold slipper upon her upturned cheeks. Emily would bridle under the reprimand, hating the absolute authority of the games mistress gazing down upon the buttocks she proposed to beat.

A brief silence – before the slipper spoke.

Crack, crack.

The harsh, swiping strokes snapped out aloud in the echoing changing room.

Crack, crack.

The leather soon grew warm, but not as hot as the peach-cheeks it punished.

Crack, crack.

Straining up on tiptoe, Emily suppressed her squeals.

Crack, crack.

Then the controlling hand of the strict mistress pinioning Emily's neck in preparation for the final, stinging flurry. A triple echo of snapping leather across the crimsoned cheeks – and Emily would squeeze out the tears welling up to cloud the shine of her grey eyes. Her teardrops would sparkle like diamonds as they spilled.

Moving closer, so threateningly closer, to her bending, hot-bottomed victim, the games mistress always angled the slipper upwards, caressing the stubby nipples of Emily's bulging breasts with the warm leather. It was almost like a private ritual; after the searing swipes the domination of her captive breasts, causing Emily to gasp aloud as her nipples, peaked with a pleasurable pain, kissed the tormenting hide.

8

Jolted into wakefulness, Emily discovered that her brief dream had rendered her nipples stiff. The speeding carriage swayed slightly. Emily felt her breasts joggle – and noticed how swollen and heavy they seemed in the cool satin cups of her brassiere. The painful memories of her schoolgirl days at Birchwood Hall had disturbed her. Deliciously. Her pussy had become moist and warm, the labia peeling apart like petals to kiss the tight lace of her panties. She squirmed in her luxurious seat, grinding her buttocks into the first class comfort of the soft upholstery. Dropping her right hand upon her thigh she inched her fingertips towards her pubic mound. Moments later, her thumb was pressing firmly down upon her clitoral bud.

'Tickets. All tickets ready, please.' The approach of the inspector broke into Emily's spellbound self-pleasuring.

'Miss?' He was at her side, eyebrows raised.

Flushing deeply, she withdrew her hand from her lap and fished out her ticket.

'Change at Swindon, miss,' he murmured, staring down intently.

Grinning to herself for almost being caught red-handed, or rather it would have been sticky-fingered, Emily eased back into her luxurious seat and closed her eyes once more. The rhythm of the train seduced her mind back into a reverie or Birchwood Hall.

Memories of punishments in the dorm.

There had been a particularly predatory dorm prefect who was jealous of Emily's blonde mane and beautiful grey eyes. Tossing her own dark curls imperiously, with a cruel glint in her cat-green eyes, the jealous dorm prefect would seize every opportunity and excuse to dispense discipline – rapidly coming to regard Emily's bare bottom as her own to punish at will. Emily was frequently spanked and sent to bed hot-bottomed.

Lipstick was forbidden to the girls at Birchwood Hall,

but craving the sweetness of forbidden fruits, the more rebellious among them frequently broke the rules. One November evening, when the rest of the dorm were sitting at their desks tackling their Latin prep, Emily had sneaked up to her deserted dorm to dry out a candy pink lipstick. Plying the sticky shaft to her lips, she paused to study the result. A soft noise behind her froze the glistening shaft at her mouth – but it had only been the wind-whipped wisteria scratching at the rain-spangled windowpanes. Emily sighed and giggled as she glimpsed her own reflection in the looking glass, the pink lipstick once more unsheathed and poised at her pouting lips.

'Got you, little bitch.' The venomous hiss of the dark-haired dorm prefect, creeping up behind Emily on nylon stockinged tiptoe, caused the lipstick to veer wildly from Emily's startled mouth, leaving a deep pink stripe across her left cheek.

Resistance to the authority of the dorm prefect would have led to further, possibly more painful, consequences. Probably a stinging twelve strokes of the cane administered by the Head in front of all the assembled girls. So Emily dropped the lipstick and submitted to her doom.

Emily moaned softly as she slept – and remembered. Remembered the ambiguity of her delicious confusion when being punished by the predatory dorm prefect. The heat of her mounting excitement suffusing her face and breasts as the mixture of fascination, dread and reluctant desire churned within her. The promise of sweet pain drowning her dismay at the threat of impending punishment. Punishment, which was for Emily increasingly becoming a strangely perverse pleasure. In her dreams, she licked her dry lips. Lipstick. She tasted the sticky sweetness. Tasted and remembered that dark November night in the dorm. That dark November night when her awakening sexuality had surrendered its innocence and submitted to experience.

'You know this is forbidden,' the dorm prefect had

snarled, snatching up the lipstick and jabbing it accusingly at Emily.

Emily had bowed her head and nodded: acknowledging her crime and the punishment to follow.

'Up.'

Emily obeyed, rising unsteadily from the stool before the looking glass. Her fingers tugged nervously at the hem of her white uniform vest.

'Across the bed,' the prefect ordered sternly.

Emily eased herself down across the bed, nestled her hot face and soft bosom into the eiderdown. How it had prickled and tickled her nostrils and nipples. Soon, cruel fingers were lifting up her pleated uniform skirt, exposing her proffered buttocks. Those same fingers, as strong as they were slender, peeled her panties down. Slowly. A loud heartbeat hammered in Emily's brain as her panties inched down. Her soft cheeks wobbled as the tight elastic tightened into a restricting band just above her knees. Squirming on the bed, face down, bottom up, she had been bared and prepared for her pain. Pain she anticipated with delicious dread. A delicious dread attested to by her tightly clenched cheeks and thighs – squeezed together in anxious, eager expectation.

'Peccadillo Pink,' the dorm prefect pronounced disdainfully, reading the black lettering on the golden case of the lipstick. She held the bullet-like shaft at arm's length between fingertips and lowered it in front of Emily's sorrowful gaze. 'Peccadillo. The Latin for sin. Wickedness. And of course you should be doing Latin prep now, shouldn't you. Hm?'

Emily acknowledged the fact, burning with shame.

'Double punishment. Bottom up.'

Emily, whimpering, obeyed. She jerked her hips up a fraction. Her tummy left the eiderdown as her bare bottom rose, the perfectly rounded cheeks held ready, and Emily gasped aloud as the dorm prefect applied the lipstick dominantly across her naked cheeks.

'See?'

Slowly, Emily strained to peer over her right shoulder. The dorm prefect held a small mirror just above the panties binding Emily's lower thighs. In the oval of silvery glass Emily glimpsed her pink striped buttocks.

'What do you see?' came the cruel command.

'Pink stripes,' Emily had whispered into the eiderdown.

The dorm prefect dropped the mirror on the bed and started to unbuckle her thin leather belt. 'I am going to punish you with my belt until your bottom is pink all over. Understand?'

Burying her face into the eiderdown, and gripping it tightly with her taloned fists, Emily tensed – holding her breath for the first lash. It came almost instantly, followed by seven more in searing succession, the swipe-strokes exploding across her satin smooth cheeks with loud snap-cracks.

After the final lash of leather across soft skin, there had been a pause. Emily burned with shame. Her secret shame. The shame of her tingling nipples. The shame of the wet heat at her sticky labia – sticky labia that had peeled apart and were pouting as they kissed the eiderdown.

'Peccadillo Pink,' the dorm prefect whispered, finger-tracing each darkening weal across the softness of the double domes of punished flesh. The tremulous horizontal strokes became a single dominant gesture. Then the fingertip tapped the rosebud of Emily's tight little anal whorl. Tapped inquisitively. Dominantly. The fingertip probed. Urgently.

'Turn around. Look.' The earlier cruel tone had softened slightly. The voice of the punisher now spoke with a softer severity.

Emily twisted. In the mirror held above her blazing buttocks she saw the finger being removed from her sphincter. She saw her own whipped cheeks spasm and clench to retain it. Heard her carnal gasp of pleasure as the winking lipstick's shaft was brought to her anal whorl. Felt her slit bubble and soak as the hard, waxy length slid between her cheeks.

'Peccadillo Pink,' the dorm prefect whispered.

Grinding her hips down into the eiderdown and squeezing her punished cheeks fiercely, Emily had started to come.

Emily opened her eyes. The pulse at her hot slit was almost intolerable. Juiced and enflamed by her intimate memories of pleasurable punishments and delicious discipline at Birchwood Hall, she yearned to ease her torment. Too risky to finger herself here, even though her carriage was deserted. Rising unsteadily, she weaved her way down between the seats towards the toilet.

Inside, with the narrow door safely bolted, she dragged her pale blue leather miniskirt up over her hips and then palm-pushed her panties down to her trembling knees. Squashing her buttocks up against the cool porcelain sink, she parted her thighs as wide as the stretched panties at her knees would permit and dipped her fingertips into her liquid heat.

Her soft buttocks rode the sink as the train lurched. Her cheeks spread themselves, the flesh dragging slowly against the smooth surface. Her cleft yawned. Stretched with a pleasurable pain, it ached sweetly. With her fingers she peeled the outer lips of her sex apart, exposing the darker flesh of her glistening fig. The perfume of her arousal rose to her nostrils. She grunted impatiently, returning her wet fingertips to play with the ultra-sensitive inner lips. She stroked them firmly with her fingernails, buckling helplessly as a fierce paroxysm ravished her. With her thumbs tormenting her clitoris, she strummed herself ruthlessly, with increasing ferocity, summoning up the climax she urgently desired.

She closed her eyes tightly. The sun blazing down through the opaque window drenched her in its golden light, the bright gold burning crimson behind her eyes. Trees and telegraph poles flickered by as the train hurtled onwards, each sharp shadow fleetingly registering in her brain like the flickering frames of a silent film. Concentrating hard, she filled the frames with vivid images fresh from her dreams of Birchwood Hall. The games mistress pressing the warm sole of the punishing slipper up against Emily's peaked nipples. Yes, the soft rubber sole raking her stiff nipples. Oh God, *yes*.

Her fingers worked furiously. Her belly tightened and her hot hive wept sweet honey. The silent film flickered on – now showing snatch-shots of the dorm prefect, probing Emily's whipped cheeks with the golden bullet of the forbidden lipstick. Probing her anus as the puckering crater of her sphincter opened to receive the cold shaft. Emily clenched her buttocks, acknowledging the delicious memory as her fingers straightened and slid between the glistening labial folds.

She was coming. Any second now. Up on tiptoe, her splayed cheeks grinding rhythmically against the cold sink, Emily rapidly approached her violent orgasm. *Yes*, almost there. She punished the flesh-thorn of her tingling clitoris beneath her thumb. *Yes*, one more image would spill her over into liquid ecstasy. One more.

And it came to her, suddenly, like the stroke of a cane across her bottom. The elusive image she needed to make her come. The music teacher. Emily shuddered and groaned as she remembered being spanked at Birchwood Hall across the music teacher's knee. The pale hand, the slender fingers. The scarlet fingernails. As the slightly cupped spanking hand swept down across Emily's bare bottom she had wriggled across her punisher's lap, deliberately rasping her pubic nest against the bristling warmth of the music teacher's dark bronze stockinged thighs. Yes… oh hell, *yes*…

A Dalek voice broke into her sweet suffering. 'Swindon,' its disembodied nasal tone droned eerily. 'Swindon.'

Oh shit.

The train lurched as it decelerated, jolting as it braked.

Emily opened her eyes wide. Another lurch and jolt shook her into alertness. The braking carriages collided gently – but with enough force to thrust two fingers deeper into her muscled warmth. Emily whimpered in frustration – but failed to come.

Frantically dragging her panties up in her haste to get out of the toilet and off the train, Emily winced as the stretch of satin bit deeply into her humid cleft. Plucking her torment away, she smoothed down her miniskirt and dashed out of the toilet without bothering to rinse her feral-fragrant fingertips. On the platform, in the warmth of the evening sunset, she struggled to recover her customary poise: the South Ken stance, chin tilted up and blonde mane swept back. But her breasts rose and fell as she battled to breathe more evenly. Ignoring her burning pussy, she waited for the blood singing in her ears to fall mute.

Milton Parva. Upper Follingham. Steeple Rising. Emily traced her destination with a trembling fingertip on the spiderweb of branch lines radiating out from Swindon. A car would be waiting for her at Steeple Rising. Emily hoped it would be a Rolls. She wondered what Dr Stikannos would be like as a host. A notorious recluse, she had discovered, who had persuaded her Knightsbridge gallery to send Emily down on a consultancy basis for a very fat fee. Bored with the stale heat of late summer London, she had jumped at the chance. Cataloguing and authenticating minor masterpieces would tweak up her slightly limp c.v. and lead to greater things. Paris, perhaps even New York.

'A week or so in Wiltshire, my dear,' the director of the gallery had purred gently, his sibilant vowels as discreet as the fat tyres of the Bentleys straddling the double yellows outside in Hans Crescent. 'And of course, my dear, you'll keep a copy of your discoveries for me, won't you.'

Emily agreed. She had no choice in the matter. Her director had thinly veiled the instruction as an invitation.

Standing on the empty platform, watching the shadows

lengthening, she wondered if it had all been a mistake. Rusticating in Wiltshire could prove very dull indeed. And she'd miss the Notting Hill Carnival for which she had a commanding view from her Ladbroke Grove flat.

Her train arrived, a miserable little three-carriaged bone-shaker with no first class seating. She would have no opportunity to continue – or complete – her self-pleasuring. No, setting aside the pressures to masturbate and climax, she concentrated on preparing for the moment when she met Dr Stikannos. First impressions and all that. He'd probably be deaf, over seventy and as distrusting of her youthfulness as of her being female. These crusty old eccentric art lovers always were, she mused. Better have a few appropriate phrases ready. Chiaroscuro. Quattrocento. It would be easy enough to convince him, she felt sure.

The lazy train trundled along the branch line through the heat haze towards the distant purple smudge of the gathering dusk. Emily grew hungry, having had nothing but an expresso and an extremely jammy doughnut all day.

At last a familiar name appeared in the glimmer of a yellow platform light. Two more stops.

Sixteen minutes later the train slowed for Steeple Rising. With the maddening prickle of her dormant orgasm smouldering in her panties, Emily prepared to alight.

There was no Roller glinting in the station car park. Not even a Saab Turbo or Range Rover to whisk her off to her mysterious destination. Emily stood pensively in the tiny glazed brick entrance. She could smell disinfectant of industrial strength and mice. She stepped out into the darkness of the station car park, and the fragrance of sweet peas from hanging baskets rewarded her. The night had the chill of sudden summer sunsets. She shivered. Up in the violet light, a huge moon shimmered. In the tall elms surrounding the tiny station rooks were roosting noisily. Further away, an early owl hooted. From a distant coppice a vixen barked her longing for a mate.

A dancing single yellow beam lanced the darkness, then Emily caught the approaching snarl of a motorbike. Probably a plough lad heading for the local pub, she surmised. The bike, a big heavy machine, slued into the station yard. The engine crackled angrily then abruptly died, and a lithe, leather-clad girl dismounted.

'For Dr Stikannos?' she drawled, her Sloane accent surprising the dark Wiltshire night air.

Emily nodded, slightly stung by the curt question which only defined her in relation to the mysterious art collector – not in her own right. She redressed the balance spiritedly.

'He's expecting me. I'm Emily—'

'Put this on,' the leather-clad girl broke in, taking her shining helmet off and tossing it across.

'I – I can't…' Emily stammered. 'I mean, I've never—'

'Come on,' interrupted the bored voice.

Struggling with the heavy helmet in the darkness, Emily flushed angrily. The rider tucked her long raven hair and twisted it into a ponytail. Emily, now juggling with her leather shoulder bag, hesitated.

'Best be quick, Dr Stikannos doesn't like to be kept waiting,' the girl observed, straddling the heavy bike expertly and sinking her shining leathered buttocks down onto the saddle.

'Can't he manage to run a proper chauffeur… I mean a car…' Emily added hastily, covering up her unintended insult.

Ignoring the remark the rider kick-started the bike, and a twist of the throttle drowned out the possibility of further conversation.

Emily, having rearranged her bag and donned the helmet, approached. She was angry. No, not angry. Disappointed. The bike and its rude rider were certainly an anticlimax. She had expected something grander. Something more impressive.

The rider waggled her bottom impatiently, and Emily

17

wanted to spank the leather buttocks very, very hard. Suppressing her grin, she mounted, and her miniskirt rode up alarmingly, exposing her thighs. Dipping her head, the girl in front opened the throttle and released the brake. The heavy bike lurched, spat gravel and shot forward, its yellow beam flooding the narrow lane ahead.

Emily, perched daintily on the pillion like a freshly spanked schoolgirl balancing her scorched bottom on a hard wooden stool, wobbled violently and clung on desperately to the girl in front. Her encircling arms found, and hugged, the rider's leather-bound breasts. She squeezed their soft warmth fiercely, and terrified of the hot metal between her legs, she opened her thighs even wider, crushing her pubis into the rounded, leathered cheeks.

The rider twisted the throttle wide open and launched the roaring bike along the twisting country lanes. Moths danced for a split second in the sudden blaze of the headlamp. Fleetingly, Emily saw the jewel-eyes of a rabbit or a fox flash, sparkle, then vanish. Speech was impossible. Her eyes were blinded with tears. Hanging on tightly, she gulped for air.

Nodding fronds of creamy cow-parsley whipped her thighs as the bike roared down the narrow lanes, skimming the sedge of the looming hedgerows. Crushed up against the supple warmth of the leather-clad girl, Emily shuddered as the bike hit a rut. The back wheel bounced, sending a shock wave straight up into her pussy. The throbbing engine's pulse had already peeled her wet labia apart, and now they were kissing the rounded buttocks before them, through her delicate panties. Emily groaned, dreading the moment when the bike braked to a final halt and the rider found her rump to be slippery.

Suddenly the bike did brake, growling softly as it came to a brief halt – only to roar again as the rider took a sharp left and shot between two granite gateposts and across a rattling cow-trap. They were now charging up a narrow drive, flanked by scented lime trees on either side. Emily caught brief glimpses of the manicured lawns. At last, she thought, easing her grip around the other girl's breasts, they'd arrived.

But they hadn't. There was another three minutes at over seventy mph before the dark mass of the mansion glinted in the moonlight. Brilliant arc lights flooded their arrival as the bike scrunched to an expertly braked stop on the gravel at the foot of steep stone steps. Blinking as she adjusted from the darkness to the sudden brilliance, Emily noted that the entire forecourt was floodlit. Security conscious, she thought. Perhaps this mysterious Dr Stikannos had something to hide – or guard – after all. If she was cataloguing his treasures for an eventual sale, she could be in for a percentage.

When she dismounted she realised that her legs were like jelly, almost as if she had just orgasmed. She wobbled unsteadily, struggling once more with the heavy helmet. Her panties were soaking. The thrilling bike ride had softened her up as if she had been knuckling her slit.

At the top of the stone steps, one of the dark blue double doors opened wide, revealing a woman in the strong light. Then the floodlights suddenly expired. Back-lit, the woman in the doorframe was merely a svelte silhouette to Emily as she shielded her eyes from the glare.

'Good evening. I am Ursula, PA to Dr Stikannos. And you must be Emily.' The tone indicated cool efficiency. The greeting was perfunctory.

Handing her helmet to the leather-clad rider, who took it with a curt nod, Emily shook her blonde mane loose and shrugged her bag down onto the gravel. Her legs had almost stopped trembling but her belly was still knotted with suppressed excitement.

'Get that round to the back at once, Chloe,' Ursula snapped waspishly. 'Why didn't you take the car?'

Chloe unzipped her leathers down to her navel. In the

shaft of light from the open door above, the upper swell of her bosom gleamed.

'Needed the ride,' she retorted sullenly, trundling the heavy bike over the gravel into the dark shadows beyond the pool of light.

Emily skipped up the stone steps and allowed herself to be ushered into the bright entrance hall. 'Is Chloe the chauffeur?' she asked brightly.

'Secretary,' Ursula answered, locking and double-bolting the doors. The tone was stern. 'You won't have much to do with her.'

A bit rude and unnecessary, Emily thought. The remark had all the velvet venom of a warning. The woman didn't want her to have anything to do with the girl, Emily suddenly realised; years in an all-girl boarding school had fine-tuned her sixth sense to the undertones of jealousy and possessiveness.

Ursula glanced at the newcomer sharply. 'This way.'

Emily was allowed a brisk wash and a glass of chilled Chardonnay before being presented to Dr Stikannos.

'There's something I must attend to immediately,' Ursula had announced, disappearing immediately.

Sitting very comfortably at a seventeenth-century dark oak table, nursing her frosted glass of deliciously refreshing wine, Emily suddenly wondered, for the third time that day, what the hell she was doing in this isolated fortress. They were all so rude. And where was everyone?

Out in the garage, fashioned out of eight loose boxes that once stabled hunters, Chloe trod out of her clinging leathers and stood utterly naked under the single light bulb.

'Get across that saddle, bitch.'

'No, Ursula, please. I didn't mean to—'

'Wait,' thundered the dominant PA. Bending, she lowered her face to the warm leather of the bike's saddle, sniffing

20

intimately at the gleaming hide. Her pink tongue-tip quivered then darted out, lapping at the wet patch where Emily's tiny slick glistened.

'Please…' the shivering nude whined. 'Don't—'

'Took the bike deliberately, didn't you, my precious little bitch. Hmm? Got her all fired up, I'll bet. Hug you tightly all the way here, did she?'

'No,' Chloe protested unconvincingly.

'Down across the saddle. I'll teach you, my girl,' Ursula snarled. 'My girl,' she sternly emphasised, reaching up to take down a short riding crop from its nail in the whitewashed brick wall.

The tip of the crop, an inch of ox-blood leather, quivered as Ursula tap-tapped the proffered buttocks of the whimpering nude. The wicked little loop of leather gleamed as the crop was levelled dominantly down to depress the curved cheeks.

'I'm sorry,' Chloe whispered. 'Please don't whip me—'

Having judged the distance, Ursula flicked her supple wrist, raising the whippy crop up and above the naked buttocks below.

'No…' the naked girl squealed, grinding her breasts into the leather saddle as she squirmed in mounting dread.

'Keep your sticky fingers away from our little blonde art expert, Chloe. Understand?'

Chloe opened her mouth to reply. The crop whistled down, and Chloe was surprised by the shrillness of her scream.

Sitting at the dark oak table, Emily tossed back the last of her wine. A faint cry – a shrill squeal of anguish – caused her to drop the glass. It rolled on the thick carpet, luckily still intact. It was a nice example of Genoan, worth at least two hundred. She scooped it up, sighing with relief. Breaking the glass would not have been a very impressive start. Another faint scream – a muffled sob of sorrow. What the hell was that? Accustomed to the urban throb of Notting

Hill Gate – late night sirens and the rumble of the last tube to Hammersmith – she supposed it to be a fox taking something soft and feathered. Nature red in tooth and claw, and all that. Yes, a vixen taking a pheasant. Or being taken brutally by a midnight mate.

Red in tooth and claw.

Emily remembered the red nails on the spanking hand of the severe music teacher.

She ached for a climax.

In the garage, writhing across the leather saddle, her juice now smeared into Emily's across the supple hide, Chloe parted her dry lips, now capable only of deep sobs, to receive the gag Ursula was forcing her to accept. Silenced, she shivered beneath the shadow of the whippy crop that had already kissed her bare bottom fiercely.

'You belong to me, darling bitch,' Ursula whispered softly, lashing down the crop once more with vicious tenderness. 'To me.'

They should have told her. They should have *bloody* told her. Emily was angry as she struggled to recover herself. The shock had been brutal. Talk about Phantom of the bloody Opera!

Before her, in his wheelchair, the gloved and masked art collector twisted awkwardly and spoke to his PA.

'Where are our manners? Ursula, show the young lady, and may I say what a most charming young lady she is, to a chair.'

They were in the library. An apple log fire, sunk into a grey heap of perfumed ashes with a few winking embers, slumbered in a magnificent Adam grate. Four Faberge eggs delicately mounted guard above on the cast iron mantelpiece. The chocolate brown walls were busily crowded with collector's pieces – representing the cream of every recorded culture. Emily saw items from the Chinese

Tang dynasty, artefacts from Mayan idolatry, and a pair of golden sandals from a Janissary seraglio. She glimpsed the rare folios, bound in pale cream leather, the spines stamped with rich gold lettering. Some rare prints – erotic Flemish originals – graced the far wall. The furniture was sparse – to allow easy access for his wheelchair – but expensive.

Scowling slightly at the gentle rebuke, Ursula guided Emily to an Italianate chair of gilded yew Dante himself might once have owned. She sat down gingerly. 'This room is beautiful,' she sighed, taking it all in once more and complimenting her host.

Across the swathe of deep Bulgarian carpet, Dr Stikannos struggled to propel his wheelchair with his useless, gloved hands. Ursula was at his side in an instant, suavely repositioning the chair to her master's satisfaction. He nodded his contentment to her and turned to gaze upon his guest. From behind his dull steel facemask his dark eyes glistened. His face was, according to the outline of the mask, quite square. Probably heavily jowled, Emily thought. She imagined the thick, sensual lips. The patrician, slightly hooked nose. At his temples, she noted that the thick black hair was streaked with silver. Not a weak man. Out of his chair, with his hands restored to their strength, a formidable specimen. The crippled hands and wheelchair did not render her host a spent force; they gave him an enigmatic mystery.

Dr Stikannos. Emily considered the name. Lebanese? Greek? His voice, when he had spoken briefly, had given no clue to his race or creed, and those impeccable vowels had been more Eton than Aegean.

'You come to me highly recommended, Emily,' Dr Stikannos murmured, lingering on her name as he would over an excellent claret.

She imagined his wet tongue protruding through the metal slit – and shivered.

'Emily,' he repeated, savouring the sound.

First name terms already. And with a seriously rich client.

23

She began to relax, until she realised that she didn't know his full name.

'Your duties, which I am sure you appreciate, will be to produce a catalogue for a little private viewing I am arranging. You will authenticate, and price, certain items from my collection.'

'Settling all questions of provenance and attribution,' Emily replied. Her voice sounded a little strained. Tense. Stay cool, she told herself. Relax. He was just a rich guy in a metal mask.

'As you say,' he echoed appreciatively, 'provenance and attribution. I am relying on your expertise,' he purred softly.

Emily smiled, but already her thoughts were wandering. How did it happen? A car smash? A bungled kidnapping? The ravishes of some tropical disease?

'It was a fire,' his precise voice said.

Emily looked up guiltily – becoming slightly annoyed at having her mind read so easily. 'But I wasn't—'

'No, no lies, Emily. Do not ever lie to me.'

That was all he said. No direct threat. But the menace of the warning was almost tangible. Emily squirmed.

'You were wondering about these.' He twitched his leather-gloved hands. 'And this.' He struggled to paw his metal mask. 'Everyone who meets me wonders, Emily. And you are no different. It usually takes them three minutes before they begin to speculate. I calculate that it took you two minutes and forty-two seconds. I am right, am I not?'

Emily blushed and nodded. She felt a confusing mixture of sympathy for the crippled connoisseur and resentment at his ability to invade her private thoughts. Did he have ESP powers?

'No, not ESP,' he chuckled, 'just a deep knowledge of people.

'I expect you will be with us for several weeks,' he continued suavely.

Weeks? But the Director at her gallery had said ten days

– tops. Emily, distracted by this unexpected possibility, failed to notice that the full reason for the gloves and metal mask had gone unexplained.

'I don't think I'll be able to—' she started to say, countering the length of stay Dr Stikannos had proposed.

'As for remuneration,' he cut in, 'let us say a percentage of the final sale, hmm?'

Thousands, Emily thrilled. Thousands. He was talking—

'Thousands,' Dr Stikannos whispered. 'I'm talking many thousands of pounds.'

Emily avoided his shrewd gaze, hating being so transparent to him.

'Ursula, before you conduct Emily to her quarters, be good enough to bring me my collection of miniatures, my delightful selection of mirabile vidu.'

Emily studied the svelte PA as she sprang to her master's command. Ursula was slender, heavily breasted and plump buttocked. Ripe and firm, but athletic, with a supple, graceful strength. Thirty-four? Thirty-six. Certainly in the early summer of her womanhood. And green-eyed, like a cat. Like the dorm prefect who had made Emily's bare bottom her own. Emily thought Ursula's closely cropped dark hair gave the lithe PA an appearance of sharp severity. Yes, an older version of the dominant dorm prefect: only more feline, more menacing, more powerful.

'Ivory. An exquisite piece, don't you think? Japanese,' Dr Stikannos pronounced, offering Emily a thimble sized kondu, the sacred seal of an emperor.

She palmed it, conscious of their gaze upon her face, her response. Accordingly, she became wide-eyed and wondering. Better please them in this collector's feast of egotism. Then her heart skipped three distinct beats as she suddenly truly appreciated what it was she held in her trembling hand. There was, to her certain knowledge, only one other example like it in the world – currently on loan to the—

'Smithsonian Museum in Washington,' Dr Stikannos supplied.

Emily nodded. 'They probably don't even know of its existence,' she smiled, returning the ivory seal.

'Yes they do,' he whispered. 'This,' he continued, his unblinking eyes studying her reactions, 'came from the dead hand of Peter the Bald. I have the hand, taken after his execution. It is in formaldehyde.'

Emily winced as the heavy silver ring plopped into her waiting palm. She held her breath as she examined it. It was not so much priceless as quite simply without price.

'You have his hand?'

'That must be our secret. If those barbarian scientists were to subject the tissue to DNA testing it would—'

'Change the face, and fortunes, of European monarchies,' Emily rejoined, thankful at last to be able to complete one of her host's sentences.

And how did he manage for sex? she suddenly wondered. Blushing at the prurient thought, she returned the ring to its owner, avoiding his dark eyes.

'I manage,' Dr Stikannos said softly. 'I manage.'

Ursula frowned, not understanding.

Emily flushed scarlet in her confusion. 'I'm sorry,' she whispered. 'I didn't mean to—'

'And this,' her host continued, ignoring the momentary diversion, 'is a… but I'm sure you know.' He produced a small silver mounted lozenge from its purple velvet pouch. 'You do know, don't you?'

Emily knew it was not a compliment, or a tribute to her expertise. It was a challenge. An open test of her knowledge, judgement and commercial sense.

She peered down at the artefact. The silver mounted gem was a pale cornelian cut with a slightly convex upper face. Etched into the glittering surface was the tiny naked figure of a young woman. The nude, bound to a whipping post, twisted in her agony as minutely etched winged cupids flayed her naked buttocks.

Emily swallowed softly to lubricate her dry mouth. Her tongue felt thick and swollen.

'Does it suggest anything to you, my dear?' The wheelchair creaked as Dr Stikannos bent forwards, his crumpled gloved fists almost – but not quite – brushing her knees.

Emily took a deep breath, desperately trying to banish the image of his gloved hands cupping a whore's breasts. Concentrate. This was the test. She must come through.

'It's an intaglio. From the Allectus period. Certainly no later. The pale cornelian had expired by then.'

Dr Stikannos inclined his head, but did not comment.

'Silver mounted. Carpathian silversmiths would have done the framing and delicate chasing.'

Her host nodded. Slowly. Twice.

'It depicts the punishment of Lexa, an early lover of the poet Lesbia. Lexa betrayed Lesbia with a vestal virgin, for which transgression—'

'Good, yes, transgression,' Dr Stikannos whispered. 'I like that. Whipped for her transgression…'

'For forty days,' Emily concluded.

'And the creator?'

'Constantius Caius,' she answered promptly. 'Price?' Emily tilted her head, conscious of the glitter in his dark eyes behind the mask. Price. Keep cool, calm and professional. Every word counts.

'It should never be sold. It is too beautiful to ever leave your possession, Dr Stikannos.'

He remained silent. A shadow in his eyes told her of his fleeting doubts. She saw his eyes flicker for the very first time since their encounter. Why? Did he really doubt her acumen and ability in that vital area – price?

'No. It must not be sold, but,' she paused, for maximum effect, 'for insurance purposes only, two million.'

That had got him. Game, set and match, Emily thought.

'Yes,' he murmured. 'Exactly right in every particular.'

Behind the mask, Emily saw his eyes widen appreciatively. If that was a test, she had passed, she comforted herself.

'You understand the mind, the very soul, of the true collector, Emily. You understand very well. And what do you really think of my little collection? Apart from my vanity and egotism, hm?'

Emily smiled, relaxing. 'You have an appetite for that which is most precious, most beautiful,' she replied.

'Yes, my dear. You are, once again, perfectly right. I have an appetite.'

'This is your room. Rooms.' Ursula nodded. 'The shower is through there.'

Emily buckled slightly at the splendour of her bedroom. A canopy of gilded lawn draped the capacious four-poster William & Mary bed. Her toes were tickled by the sensual depth of the Chinese silk carpet. Pale velvet curtains at two huge sash windows banished the darkness of the Wiltshire night beyond.

'Thank you, it's wonderful,' she gushed, suddenly feeling shy and slightly overwhelmed. 'Dr Stikannos is—'

'Depending on you do to a good job on the catalogue,' the stern PA replied crisply. 'Be sure not to disappoint him.'

Emily, more taken aback than stung by the waspish retort, nodded meekly.

'He rewards failure as generously as he rewards success. Goodnight.' Ursula left as abruptly as she had spoken.

Alone, Emily explored her sumptuous quarters like a child abandoned in a deserted sweet shop. Bouncing on the bed, she slid with a soft squeal down the silk coverlet and landed with a soft bump on her bottom, her cheeks cushioned by the deep silk pile of the carpet. It tickled her inner thighs. She squirmed, giggling. Kicking off her shoes, she scrunched her toes in the delicious silk. Seconds later, she rose and bounded across to a white fridge fitted into a recess. Opening it, she discovered a supper of salmon mayonnaise, raspberry sorbet and a pint of chilled, sec Krug.

She ate the sorbet first – it reddened her lips and tongue – then stripped down to her bra and panties for the more serious business of the salmon. Stretched out on the carpet she started to eat, savouring each mouthful as if it were a wicked sin.

Uncorking the Krug, she sipped it straight from the ice-cold bottle, exploding into naughty giggling as the bubbles prickled her nose.

Down in the converted butler's pantry, Dr Stikannos stared impatiently. In front of his wheelchair there was a bank of eight large screens. Small red lights winked at the base of each grey, inert monitor.

'Number six!' he barked.

Ursula leaned over his wheelchair and jabbed the control panel with her index finger, her breasts bunching as they pressed into his left shoulder. One of the monitors snapped into brilliance, its tiny red light now green. Up on the screen they saw Emily, thighs splayed to receive the empty champagne bottle, then thighs clamped together to hold the icy glass to the heat of her exposed sex.

'Excellent,' purred the masked voyeur. 'Zoom in. Quickly… no, not the face. Give me her breasts!'

'Patience,' Ursula murmured, twiddling the joystick deftly and bringing the breasts into close up. She captured and held them as expertly as the La Perla brassiere had done. The lens lingered. The wheelchair creaked. Up on the screen the undulating mounds of soft flesh rose and fell rhythmically. The nipples, visited by the cold champagne bottle, were fierce little peaks of pleasurable pain.

'The face. Let me see her face.'

Ursula's slender finger stroked the stubby knout of the

joystick. In the monitor, Emily's moistened lips parted in a widening smile.

The Chinese silk tickled the cleft between her peach-cheeks. She wriggled. The Krug bottle twisted, rasping her outer labia apart, and raking her clitoris. She screamed softly. Stretching down, she grasped the bottle by the golden foiled neck and pumped it against her slit, concentrating hard on her tiny love-thorn. The wet glass dragged against her clitoris: re-igniting the fire that had been smouldering there all day. A fire that had yet to be quenched. A fire first fuelled by the memories of delicious punishments at her boarding school, then fed by her furious fumbling in the lurching train's toilet. Fires further enflamed by the thrilling bike ride, and the raw smell of leather, the soft buttocks and the softer bosom of Chloe.

'She'll do it there, on the carpet, using the bottle,' Ursula remarked clinically.

'Too crude,' Dr Stikannos whispered excitedly. 'No, the girl is an exquisitely refined specimen. An exotic.'

Ursula's eyes narrowed. For the second time that evening their green light betrayed her jealousy of the newly arrived young blonde.

'Put number seven on,' he hissed. 'Quickly!'

'The shower?' she countered, doubtfully.

'The shower,' he repeated, his helpless gloved hands twisting in feverish expectation.

Emily suddenly sat up, propping herself on her elbows, her breasts swaying deliciously as she rose. The sweet ache at the base of her belly clamoured with a loud silence for relief. Tossing the empty Krug bottle aside, she scrambled to her feet. Her breasts felt tender, the darkened nipples engorged. She thumbed them, shuddering at the cruel stab of pleasure. Slightly tipsy after the Krug – and increasingly dizzy with lust – she stumbled towards the shower. Dragging aside the curtain, of opaque gold decorated with red herons spearing fat carp in their bills, she reached up and twisted the tap. Under the instant jet she offered her face, breasts and belly to receive its delicious, raking sting. Turning, she cupped her buttocks and dragged them apart, squealing as the cascade sluiced her spine and drummed down into her exposed cleft.

'A big close up of her fingers,' the connoisseur insisted. 'I want her fingers, no, her fingertips, in shot at all times.'

Remaining silent, Ursula tweaked the stubby joystick, thumbing the knob until the lens relinquished its unblinking gaze on the nude in the shower – in medium close up – and focused on the frenzy of fingertips busy at her exposed slit.

As the shining fingernails scrabbled at the darkly fleshed labia, the wheelchair rattled in response.

Crushing her buttocks against the slippery tiles with such force that her anus puckered up to kiss their stern glaze, Emily spread her legs apart and strummed herself rhythmically, taking care not to neglect her clitoris with upward strokes of both thumbs. A single image blazed behind her tightly shut eyes. The tiny naked figure etched in the cornelian intaglio. Lexa being whipped for her sinful betrayal of Lesbia. The image of pain and suffering, guilt and punishment, haunted Emily's imagination. She could almost hear the whistle, then the stinging crack, of the cruel thongs lashing the rounded buttocks of the writhing nude. The nude, bound and helpless at the whipping post, her shrill screaming silenced for eternity in the frozen cornelian.

And Emily knew the secret etched into the erotic cameo: knew that even as she was suffering, lewd Lexa was thrusting her thighs into the post to which she was bound, grinding her delta frantically as the whips cracked down. Punishment and pleasure. The sweet sorrow of delicious pain. In the intaglio the face of Lexa was unseen. In her erotic imaginings, Emily saw the face of the bound nude: it was her own.

No, she shuddered, struggling to deny her deepest, darkest desire. No, never. Not that. She shook her head, her wet blonde hair scattering pearls of glistening light. But the image of herself being bound and flayed across the bare buttocks slowly strengthened and, inexorably, dominated her seething brain. Yes, it was she who was being whipped. Not Lexa. It was she who writhed as the cruel thongs striped her naked cheeks.

Bowing down in submission to the fierce fantasy and surrendering to its dark delight, Emily came. It was an exquisite orgasm.

Pounding her wet buttocks against the tiles as she collapsed into the vortex of a second climax, Emily continued to squeal as she suffered the velvet violence of a third.

Downstairs, Dr Stikannos pawed helplessly at the bulging erection trapped within his trousers.

'Please,' he whispered hoarsely, jabbing Ursula's thigh beseechingly. 'Please.'

'It's not good for you,' she murmured, caressing his metal mask. 'You must save your strength for a complete recovery.'

'I beg you,' he gasped, twisting in his wheelchair.

'Well, just this once, as she's new,' Ursula relented, kneeling down against the wheel and, snapping on the brake, unzipping her master deftly.

Dr Stikannos raised his helpless hands like an infant being changed by its nanny as she fingered out his rigid length. Encircling his throbbing erection within the gentle strength of her slim fingers, she started to pump slowly, deliberately.

Emily grunted, twisted on her whitened toes and collapsed down on her knees, crushing her face and breasts against the wet tiles. Flattening her tongue against the shining wall, she lapped eagerly, jerking her hips and buttocks as the final orgasm ravished her kneeling nakedness. Stretching her arms up she pressed her wrists together, echoing those of Lexa tied to her pillar of pain.

'On the face or breasts?'

'On her bottom,' Dr Stikannos gasped. 'Let it be her bottom.'

Ursula thumbed his glistening glans ruthlessly. Her chairbound captive gasped again, then gulped and held his breath as he approached the moment of explosive release.

'On her bottom it will be,' Ursula whispered excitedly, suddenly infected by her master's frenzy. Fisting his erection firmly, she aimed it up at the monitor then pumped vigorously: directing his squirt of hot seed upwards.

The splatter of his liquid release splashed the image of Emily's wet, shining bottom. The cloying semen slithered slowly down the surface of the screen, following the dark gape of Emily's cleft between her splayed cheeks. On the screen, at that precise moment, the lens caught her squeezing her cheeks in a final climactic paroxysm. It appeared to Dr Stikannos that she was trapping his silver stream of seed: trapping and containing it between her clenched buttocks.

'Her eyes,' he grunted. 'Let me see her eyes.'

Ursula rose, wiping her semen-sticky fingertips on her thigh, before adjusting the joystick.

Up on the CCTV screen, Emily's grey eyes gazed out blankly, lust-dimmed and drained.

Behind the steel mask, darker eyes burned intently as the watcher drank his delicious fill of the watched.

Chapter Two

Emily woke and stirred luxuriously in her huge four-poster bed, stretching her toes into the furthest corners of the sensual silk sheets. Thirsty, she bounded out of bed and scampered, naked, across to the fridge. There she found orange, pineapple and cranberry juice, together with stubby little half litres of Belgian lager and bottled mineral water to choose from. She selected the carton of chilled pineapple juice, opened it and drank deeply.

An eerie sound outside brought her to the window. It reminded her of French taxi klaxons in grainy black and white movies. A rising, shrill metallic note with a soft echo. Puzzled, she peered down into the grounds, pressing her naked breasts against the cold glass pane and causing her nipples to prink and peak.

The pale mists of early dawn drifted across the horizon. Within the grounds surrounding the mansion, beech trees loomed and thrust up proudly, but the manicured lawns remained shrouded in the shallow mantle of undulating silver cloud.

Turning back into her room, Emily fished out a black velour jogging top and trousers. After snapping on her brassiere and tugging up her panties, letting the cotton kiss her pubis, she dressed quickly and slipped out of her room.

Tiptoes took her down to the imposing front door. An earlier riser had already unlocked it and drawn the bolts. It opened silently, allowing Emily to skip down the stone steps and tread the mist shrouded lawns.

The chill made her shiver. The eerie calling cry broke the silence again. Emily turned. On the low wall skirting the paved terrace along the west wing she saw eight peacocks.

The birds were perched precariously, flashing their finery in the first rays of the red, rising sun. Up above in the beeches, squat black crows screeched down jealously. The peacocks were breakfasting on crumpled slices of blackened toast.

Emily paused, silently admiring the splendid birds as they continued to dine with a delicate elegance. As the sun turned to gold, promising another hot summer day, her footsteps took her around to the back of the imposing mansion. There, standing on the cobble stones just as the stable clock chimed seven, she glimpsed the green door of a redbrick outhouse swing silently shut. Wondering who was up so early, Emily approached the door. She paused at a window, peering in.

A former dairy and buttery, the building had been converted into a gym. No expense had been spared. It was a neon-lit hi-tech temple dedicated to the perfection of the human body. Aluminium and steel apparatus gleamed under the harsh lights above. On the polished wooden floor, squares of dimpled rubber matting formed a perfect geometrical pattern.

Then she saw her.

She saw her and shuddered.

Chloe, stripped naked, was sitting in the lotus position, her squashed buttocks spread across the dimples of a black rubber mat. Emily's fingertips stroked at her throat as she imagined the rubber dimpled thorns piercing the soft satin of the curved cheeks, no doubt teasing the outer labia and prickling Chloe's exposed slit.

Early morning yoga, Emily supposed, as she gazed through the window at the nude's dark hair spilling down in a frozen cascade, curtaining her slender back down to where the supple spine swept into the opening of the dark cleft between the superb cheeks. Emily watched furtively as Chloe raised her arms for the third time, joining the palms of her hands together above her head as if in silent prayer.

At the window, her breath clouding the glass, Emily peered

into the gym, savouring the sight of the exquisite nude poised in her graceful meditation. Then the spell was broken as Chloe suddenly lowered her hands. Emily realised the leather-clad girl who had taken her pillion on that beast of a bike was now cupping and squeezing her breasts. The warm breath at the clouded pane misted the glass opaquely as Emily's excitement increased. Inside the gym, squatting bare-bottomed on the dimpled rubber mat – Emily imagined the heat of her cleft dulling the rubber and moaned softly – Chloe was clearly pleasuring herself. It was unmistakable. The nude's angled elbows betraying the gripping, squeezing action of the unseen hands.

Emily gasped softly as she saw the hands drop as Chloe nestled her knuckles at her pubic nest. Emily imagined it crisp and as shining black as the crows up in the beeches.

Or was she shaven? Emily felt a sudden rush of confusion, a burning delight and a delicious shame as she yearned to see if the squatting nude's pubic delta was cleanly shaven. Twisting the toes of her trainers into the cobblestones, Emily tiptoed up, straining to glimpse Chloe as she masturbated. Then to her surprise, the nude rose up.

Emily smothered her grunt of pleasure, ducking down instantly in case the involuntary sound betrayed her presence at the window. When Chloe had risen from the rubber, peeling her buttocks from the dimpled mat, she had exposed her bare cheeks completely, revealing to Emily's shocked delight the stripe-bites from the crop.

Carefully inching back to the glass, Emily risked a quick peep. She saw Chloe. She saw the whipped cheeks, supple and rubbery and softly bunched. The nude stood, thighs wide, her feet planted apart. Her left hand, palm in against the swell of the striped buttocks, massaged the punished flesh rhythmically. Emily took a deep breath, then realised what Chloe's unseen right hand was doing: it was working between her thighs. The slow, masturbatory movement of the hand when Chloe squatted on the rubber was now a frenzied self-pleasuring. Head tossed back, her shining stream of black hair spilling down wantonly, Chloe rose up on her toes. Emily, seeing the knees of the nude beginning to bend and buckle, knew that the climax was imminent.

She held her breath, transfixed in her accidental voyeurism, frozen and afraid to move, as she watched the nude in the gym drag the starfish splayed fingers of her left hand across her reddened weals. Emily flinched as Chloe's fingernails sunk into the satin globes, raking and rekindling the crop's lines of pain. Chloe shuddered and spasmed, her left leg twisting, its knee nuzzling its twin in an arabesque of ecstasy.

As her thin squeal of delight split the silence of the gym, Emily slunk away, one question burning in her brain. Who? Whose hand had gripped the crop so fiercely, raising it up only to lash it down.

Who?

In the warmth of a large, rambling kitchen, its glazed tiled walls gleaming with sparkling coppers and saucepans, the far wall dominated by a huge Aga, Emily discovered a pert young girl, a couple of years younger than herself, busily preparing breakfast. Poached eggs seethed in a small pan alongside a larger skillet in which succulent sausages and crisp rashers sizzled. The air was heavily perfumed with the aroma of freshly ground coffee and the more acrid smell of blackened toast. Several slices, charred and slightly twisted, had been rescued from the toaster and set aside on a large green plate.

'The peacocks adore it,' the girl grinned infectiously. 'I crumble it up and soak it in milk for them. But don't tell Ursula. She counts everything as if this was a pauper's house.'

Emily found herself returning the conspiratorial grin, instantly liking the pert little minx. 'I won't.'

'Susie,' the pretty girl smiled, drying her hands on a cloth.

'I'm the maid.'

It was a simple statement. *I'm the maid.* Emily, introducing herself, picked up a small dish of raspberries and ate them one by one as she studied the girl who had returned to the Aga to rescue the sausages from incineration. Dressed in a very fetching short black skirt, black blouse, frilly white apron, black shiny stockings and black lace-up shoes, she was the perfect picture of a pretty, mischievous maid.

Emily wondered – and Susie answered the unspoken question.

'Daddy got into some sticky financial mess with Dr Stikannos, and so I came here to work. I'm cordon bleu – well almost. And, well, I sort of stayed.' Susie shrugged then returned to fork the sausages into a deep dish, which she slid into the belly of the Aga to keep warm. As she bent down, Emily had a brief glimpse of the darker bands of her black stocking tops and of the snow-white panties stretched across deliciously plump little buttocks.

Sinking her lips into the final raspberry and sucking hard, Emily continued to wonder. Daddy's sticky financial mess had brought the minx here – as what? Bonded labour? Was the delightful little maid here in servitude to Dr Stikannos until some huge debt had been repaid? Emily swallowed the tiny sweet berry and shivered.

'Kippers?' the maid suggested. 'Grilled trout?'

Emily said she never had anything in the morning. 'Just coffee, thanks.' But Susie proved so attentive, so solicitous, that Emily found herself tucking into a delicious sausage and two poached eggs. They had been deliberately arranged on the willow pattern plate in a rudely suggestive design; the long glistening sausage flanked at one end by two quivering eggs.

'Spinster's comfort,' Susie giggled, placing the lewd breakfast down. 'Keep your strength up.'

Despite herself, Emily giggled too.

Chloe, still perspiring slightly from her rigours in the gym, joined them, sitting next to Emily and tucking into melon frosted with ginger and brown sugar.

Ursula appeared, her stern face immediately upon the maid. Sharp questions were asked about the blackened toast. Emily heard Susie's mumbled apologies, and realised that the maid was afraid of her strict mistress. Chloe and Emily had reached the marmalade stage, and beneath the scrubbed pine table their thighs almost touched. Ursula, nibbling fastidiously at an unbuttered slice of crispbread, switched her green gaze from the maid to Chloe. Emily noted that the eyes held a predatory, possessive glint.

Susie sidled into an adjacent pantry, juggling with an armful of plates. Emily ignored the coarse-cut marmalade and picked up a stone jar of clover honey. Spearing the golden ooze with her knife, she spread a generous smear across her toast. The honey ran, coating her thumb instantly.

A sudden crash from the scullery announced a broken plate. Ursula sprang from her chair and strode across to the scullery door. Looking in, she barked angrily at the maid.

'Careful,' Chloe warned gently, alerting Emily to the honey inching down to the palm of her hand. 'Here, let me.'

Emily had expected a napkin, but instead, lowering her face, Chloe took Emily's thumb in her mouth. Closing her full lips, she sucked hard, and Emily's nipples tightened in response. She wriggled as she felt the warm wet mouth tighten around her captive flesh. Then she felt the muscled tongue. Chloe glanced up, and their eyes met.

The sound of a sharp spank broke the silence, immediately followed by a soft squeal from the punished maid.

'And if you break another plate it'll be the cane!'

Emily's heart fluttered at the words. The cane. Would Ursula really bend Susie over, drag the white cotton panties down over the taut black stocking tops and ply a yellow whippy bamboo cane across the minx's cheeks? Chloe, softly nibbling Emily's thumb, glanced towards the scullery doorway, and her eyes clouded with fear and guilt. Emily glanced over her shoulder, and met the stern stare of Ursula's green eyes. Chloe's mouth loosened, releasing Emily's wet thumb from its inner warmth.

Lowering her eyes and blushing, Emily shuddered again. At the sound of the harsh spank as the firm tongue licked her imprisoned thumb; and at the jealous flash of anger flickering across Ursula's narrowed eyes.

Emily sat in the soft leather chair listening attentively to Dr Stikannos.

'And so before I turn my treasures over to you for cataloguing, I want to hear for myself how you view, and respond to, a powerful image. I am sure you can list the salient details perfectly well. You have already demonstrated that to my complete satisfaction, but what I want to see, Emily, is your reaction. Your reaction to the inner meaning, the message, of a great painting. You do see?' he added, spreading his useless, gloved hands wide. 'Provenance and a price do not fully capture the glory of a great work of art.'

He paused. Sensing a need to respond, Emily nodded. 'I will be careful to include an appreciation—'

'Exactly,' he broke in. 'It is an appreciation I seek so that my potential buyers, after the private viewing, will burn to buy and own the piece.'

'Whet their appetites?' Emily said softly.

He nodded. 'But there is an art in seeing into the inner meaning of a painting. This morning we will examine two masterpieces and you will tell me not only what you see, but what you feel.'

'Give you an appreciation?'

'Yes.'

Emily twisted in her leather chair, her velour-sheathed buttocks rasping against the dull hide, as she followed his gesture to the wall opposite. Apart from some pedestrian, dark Dutch engravings – worth no more than eight thousand each – there were no paintings on view. At his desk, in his wheelchair, Dr Stikannos jabbed at a panel of silver buttons. A large white screen unfurled down against the wall, and the lighting in the room dimmed. A soft click sounded and a strong beam punched the gloom, filling the white screen with swimming shapes and colours. Dr Stikannos, pawing at his controls, brought the image into sharp focus.

'The paintings themselves are hung in air-conditioned and properly lit surroundings. You will be able to see them, in the raw, later. What you see now are thirty-five millimetre slides. Observe, Emily, then tell me what you see and feel. Give me a full appreciation.'

Emily felt her throat tighten and her tongue thicken in her dry mouth. She tried to steady her trembling palms by pressing them down into the leather arms of her chair as she gazed up at the image projected on the screen.

After many minutes' silence Dr Stikannos spoke softly. 'I'm waiting, Emily.'

Without taking her eyes from the haunting image – without even blinking – she answered him in an excited whisper. 'It is wonderful and quite without equal. An example from the school of Pforr, from his Lukasbund primitive period. But wait, it's not a Pforr, is it? I mean, the subject matter, the composition, yes, they are his and they are all there. No, it is not his entire work. I've got it,' she half rose from her chair, 'it was finished by his closest friend, Overbeck.'

Dr Stikannos remained silent, but in the glimmer of the projector his metal mask flashed as he nodded appreciatively.

'Painted in eighteen-eleven. Certainly no later than eighteen-twelve. But…'

'But?' came her host's purring echo.

'I thought, I mean I'm sure that this work was in the Staedelinstitut.'

'It was indeed, until nineteen forty-five. The Russian lorries beat the allied tanks to the gates of the gallery. Lorries are better designed than tanks for loot. We may omit the boring details, Emily, but all you need know is that the painting resurfaced in Minsk. It now hangs in my collection.'

'But…'

'Another but, my dear?' he countered suavely.

'You simply can't just… I mean, you'll need an export licence—'

'You have correctly identified who painted it, when and indeed where it was painted,' Dr Stikannos murmured, glossing over certain legal issues Emily had raised, 'now I want you to look again. Forget about its provenance. Tell me what you see. What you feel.'

This was the moment Emily dreaded. She would much rather discuss the Lukasbund school's theories, but her eyes were drawn up to the image as if she was under hypnosis. The erotic painting projected onto the screen was powerfully arousing and she was already quite excited. She squeezed her thighs together to contain her dampening panties.

'I'm waiting,' he whispered.

'The Lukasbund school depicted the darkly oppressive religious themes of the fifteenth century primitives. Themes of punishment and atonement. Of strict chastisement of the sinner and the stern mortification of the sinful flesh. Their motto was, translated from the original, wantons must be whipped, the lustful must suffer the lash. This painting,' Emily continued in a feverish whisper, 'comes from a series entitled Contrition and Penance. The painting entitled Contrition was destroyed by a crazed nun in eighteen ninety-four. Penance, the surviving picture, was removed from the public gaze shortly after.'

'Details, details. No more mere facts, Emily. Tell me what you are feeling.'

Emily swallowed uncomfortably before continuing. 'It depicts the flagellation of sinners – sinners who have owned and confessed their wickedness. They are nuns. Nuns being punished for indulging in the forbidden pleasures of the flesh.'

'The flesh,' Dr Stikannos echoed.

Emily's voice quavered. She took a deep breath. On the screen she saw the blues and greys of a shadowed crypt. The deeper shadows were executed in purples. Tiny silver and gold points of fragile light from winking candles illumined the darkness, making shapes and their shadows visible. She counted five beautiful young women, three of whom were stripped naked, the remaining pair garbed in the crow-black habit of their strict order.

'The two nudes dangling from the gibbet have been questioned. The questions, and their answers, were of an intimate nature. They continue to deny their sinfulness and so must remain upon the gibbet, naked and in painful bondage. See how the silvery rope tied fiercely at their bound wrists has been threaded down across their breasts, burning into the swollen mounds of defenceless flesh, continuing down across each belly then biting up between their parted thighs.'

'Continue,' Dr Stikannos whispered, fisting his leather gloves into his erection in the darkness.

'They will hang from the gibbet in their burning ropes of bondage until they utter their full and frank confessions. See, at the breasts, where the rope causes the tamed bosom to bulge, the delicate brushwork. The fine tracery of crimson stippling. That is where a thonged whip has lashed their breasts to force confession from their stubborn lips. The candles are marked. The hour is midnight. They will dangle, whipped and bound, till dawn.'

'Excellent. You are bringing the picture to life, Emily. Narrative account is most stimulating.' In the darkness, his sheathed knuckles trapped and tormented his aching erection.

'The third nude, the kneeling, naked nun, has confessed. The two robed nuns dominating her are her punishers or flagellants. Having whipped her confession from her, they have cut her free from the torments of the gibbet and forced her to kneel. To kneel, naked and in shame, as true penitents must. Her knees kiss and suffer the hard flagstone floor. Dominated and in dread of her impending pain the penitent cringes, but a cruel hand forces her to bury her face into the thighs before her. And there, gazing down pitilessly, stands the second flagellant. She is holding up aloft the thonged lash, splaying the supple tongues of leather out across her open palm. A dozen strokes have been administered. Already the bare buttocks are criss-crossed with seething lines of fire. A dozen remain to be dispensed.'

'More context,' her host hissed. 'Tell me the story the mute paint cannot fully proclaim.'

'The nun who is dominating the kneeling penitent seems almost lost in thought.'

'Why?'

'As she crushes the weeping face of the whipped nude into the dark robes at her pubic mound, she remembers receiving her own penance.'

'Go on.'

'Her own searing stripes. The whistle and crack of the leather across bare swollen cheeks, torments with delicious dread and sweetly savage memories.'

'Excellent. And?'

'The whipper, the stern flagellant who palms the instrument of pain meditatively before returning it to the reddening cheeks, is…'

'Is what? What of the whipper?'

'Is fingering the thongs of pain as gently as she would finger her own forbidden flesh.'

'And what of the whipped?'

'She kneels, sobbing, crushing her face between the thighs of her dominant chastiser. The black robes smell of candle grease and pungent, female arousal. The penitent's arms encircle her punisher, her hands clasping the robed nun's broad buttocks. When the whip cracks down across her bare bottom she will squeal aloud, then talon the heavy melon-

44

buttocks with spasming fingers as she mouths her anguish into the black robed pubis.'

'You spoke of her confession in the gibbet. Her sin? What was her sin?'

Emily had the sudden urge to mount and ride the leather arm of her sumptuous hide chair. Ride it, raking her sex lips against the sheen between her clamped thighs, dragging her clitoral thorn up into a pleasurable peak of exquisite agony.

'The sin?' Dr Stikannos insisted, a dark stain spreading at his knuckles, leaving the gloves wet and shining as he came.

'The stripes she bears, and the pain to come, are for her grave sins; for her surrender and submission to carnal desires and pleasures of the flesh. She purloined a thick, beeswax candle after vespers and stole out to the carp pool in the moonlight. They found her there, cowering in her sin and shame, squatting astride the tool of Satan fashioned from the wax. Too big to penetrate her virgin hole, she sat astride it, forcing its thick snout up between her painfully splayed buttocks, the white wax buried in the pink rosebud of her anus.'

'How do the sisters term that forbidden part?'

'The Gate of Hell,' Emily gasped. 'Sodom's postern.'

'Why so the Gate of Hell?'

'Such is the heat between the buttocks when carnal desire is kindled and enflamed there, the dark robed sisters deem it to be certain that hellfire awaits those who enjoy the devil's dance there.'

'The devil's dance?'

'When the muscles spasm and forbidden juices flow, scalding the flesh thereabouts…'

Click. The image on the wall vanished.

Click. Soft lights suffused the room. Emily collapsed in a perspiring slump, her heartbeat hammering as the blood sang in her ears. When she looked up, her host had gone. She shuddered and moaned softly, crimsoning in sudden shame.

Where had all that come from? From what unacknowledged depths of her yearnings and dark perverse desires had that torrent of sado-masochistic delight poured? The painting was of two robed nuns punishing a kneeling penitent, while two more naked sinners dangled in their torment. There was no beeswax candle in the picture – no hint of anal masturbation. No clues suggesting that the penitent was sniffing the feral heat of her dominant's weeping arousal.

'An excellent appreciation, Emily,' Dr Stikannos announced, returning in his wheelchair. He was, she noticed, now wearing a robe of white towelling. 'I have the full provenance of the piece. I know it well. It is indeed an Overbeck, after Pforr. Entitled *Penance*, it was completed in eighteen-twelve. It was banned from the public gaze by the Bishop of Magdeburg in eighteen ninety-four, after its sister piece, *Confession*, was attacked and destroyed by a disturbed nun. That much is all on record. Yes, the provenance is sound,' he concluded.

His voice was as dry, as detached, as any of the white-haired professors at the lunchtime lectures on art history at the V&A, Emily thought.

Then a sudden urgency entered his voice, a vibrancy, as he continued. 'But you,' his metal mask glinted as he turned to face her, 'have given such a compelling account of the painting's story, fleshing out the faded tones with such a…' he hesitated, adding, 'fervent and intimate appreciation.'

Emily blushed, shy and confused. She palmed the arms of the leather chair, drying her perspiration on its sleek hide.

'The nun is unknown. Her sins, mild or grave, go unrecorded. And yet under your discerning eye, she lives. Lives again to suffer the cruel stripes of her penance. You detail her punishment, her thoughts and feelings, as if you had been there. As if you had been her punisher. It is as if you had discovered the nun by the carp pool, burying the beeswax in her sinful flesh. You even enumerate the strokes her bare buttocks have received, and those she has yet to suffer. And you explore the minds of her two dark robed dominants, her flagellants, bringing to life the landscape of their dark desires. The tall one, who lingers over the fond remembrance of her own sweet pain. And the other, who weighs her whip judiciously before swiping it down across the bare buttocks below.'

Silence fell between them. Emily, ashamed and astonished at the wealth of lubricious detail she had drawn up from the well of her feverish imagination, avoided his eyes – eyes that now glittered behind his steel mask.

'For the sale, I was thinking of a guideline price of half a million, Emily.'

She gazed down at the carpet, squirming under his scrutiny. Squirming, and hating his knowledge of her; knowledge she had unguardedly revealed in her erotic narrative.

'But with your interpretation in the catalogue notes, I can safely start the bidding at eight hundred thousand.'

Startled, she glanced up at him. 'Really?'

'I will certainly hope to get a million by the close of bidding, my dear. Thanks to you. Be sure to include every detail. Especially the beeswax candle.'

Emily looked away. God, he must think her really peculiar.

'Yes, the beeswax candle, an inspired touch,' he grunted, straining slightly in his wheelchair as he tossed her a box of tissues. 'Here, dry yourself.'

Emily caught the box clumsily, extracted three pastel tissues, and then froze. What was he suggesting?

'Your hands.' His words broke the uncomfortable silence. She looked up and gulped. Her host was gazing intently at her through his metal mask, the eyes glinting with amusement.

Biting the softness of her lower lip, Emily wiped her palms. The wet tissues perfumed the room, and to her instant relief he returned his gloved hands to the buttons on his desktop. The lights dimmed once more, and in the gloom

Emily heard the wheelchair creak as he jabbed at the controls.

Click. A second image filled the screen on the wall opposite.

'Attribution first, Emily, and then I think you know what I want you to do. Every picture tells a story, does it not? I want you to tell me the story.'

The painting was brutal in every aspect. A boldly executed work with shouting colours that hurt the eye. Reds, oranges, ochres and browns crowded the canvas in a fusion of socialist realism and magical surrealism. In essence, it was a painting of a fully clothed businessman, pig-faced and pinstriped, kneeling dominantly behind a sprawling nude. Face down and bottom raised, she hunched on all fours in his shadow.

'Mexican,' Emily pronounced. 'A political statement. Mid-twenties. Nineteen twenty-six. Probably an early Orozco. Very collectable, and so the price guide should be around three hundred thousand. Surprising how the rich chase these examples of revolutionary art.'

She had managed a matter-of-fact, almost prim tone.

'An excellent summary, my dear. Facts, names and dates. But it is your feelings I wish to hear.'

She paused, marshalling her riotous thoughts. She stared at the violent image steadily, unblinkingly. The dapper pinstripe suit and polished patent leather shoes of the businessman. The sheen of his top hat clasped to his groin with white knuckled fingers. The naked beauty, her melon-breasts spilling loose and lovely, the dark nipples engorged.

'It is symbolic. An excellent example of Mexican revolutionary art. She, bending submissively to his lust, represents the people. He is a figure of rapacious capitalism—'

'No, no, no,' Dr Stikannos broke in impatiently. 'These are facts. Facts available in any good treatise on socialist art. I want to hear what it is you feel. Give me your deepest responses.'

Emily nodded. She focused intently on the image, immersing herself in its vibrant daubs completely. Then she heard her own excited voice give a narrative account. 'He has used fruit on her. His power is spent, his moment of dominant supremacy is passed. See where it has rolled under the cane chair, the glistening orange he raked between her parted thighs. And there, by her crumpled dress, is the banana he used to ravish her. Her bottom is raised submissively, her head hangs in burning shame. A silver dollar winks from her cleft. He wedged it between her cheeks after enjoying her. She is the wage slave. But the hour of capitalism is over. He is empty, quite useless. In his impotent fury he has had to take his own hand to his tired flesh. When he comes, he will empty himself into the top hat. The artist has created a powerful visual joke. The brutal master ends up coming into the symbol of capitalism.'

'Superb,' Dr Stikannos murmured. 'The fruit. I saw it as merely spilling from the table in an amorous tussle. You see it differently, still glistening from her ravished flesh. Excellent. Be sure to include that narrative in the catalogue notes, Emily, and we will commence the bidding at nine hundred thousand.'

Emily worked alone in the library all afternoon, but found it difficult to concentrate as she started the task of cataloguing the collection. So many thoughts distracted her. So many images returned to torment her. She was both ashamed and excited by her session with her host, ashamed and excited by her responses to the erotic paintings. Where had all those feverish imaginings sprung from? What deep dark unfathomed well lay dormant within her, from whose unsuspected springs such deliciously disturbing fantasies flowed?

She remembered her invention of the beeswax candle probing the buttocks of the naked nun. The kneeling businessman, who may have just pleasured the whore like hundreds before him, picking up his top hat and preparing to go: no, she had him masturbating into the topper having used fruit on the nude. Emily shivered as she remembered her excited description of the orange raking the wet slit and the fat banana thrusting between her clenched cheeks.

Emily suddenly grinned. She told herself she had done it to shock Dr Stikannos out of his suave complacency. Make him see things in his private treasure trove of art he had never seen before. But her grin faded as she acknowledged a deeper truth. The crippled man in the steel mask had exercised a compelling force over her. He had successfully willed her to submit to his desire, squeezing her obscene thoughts, longings and yearnings, from her despite her squirming reluctance. She sensed his power and blushed as she realised that she had performed like a puppet. It was as if he had turned a key, unlocking and exposing her true sexual being; her deep desire for sweet suffering and pleasurable pain.

Other thoughts plagued her as she sat at the desk, pen in hand. How had he come to acquire these works? His entitlement to have them, let alone sell them, was questionable to say the least. Emily suspected she was getting out of her depth. Dr Stikannos was operating beyond the law. His multi-million pound activities were shrouded in criminality. She must be very careful. Emily knew full well the penalties and pitfalls of rogue trading. She wanted no part in dodgy deals, private viewings or clandestine sales. No VAT, no export licences. No questions asked, but plenty to be answered should the Art Fraud Squad become inquisitive.

And there were other disturbing questions to be answered. Chloe sucking hard on Emily's honeyed thumb at breakfast. Ursula's green eyes glinting with sudden jealousy. The sound of Susie the maid being spanked. That single, crisp blow. But what made Emily most uneasy was her memory of the moment when Dr Stikannos had tossed her the box of tissues to dry her perspiring palms. She burned as she remembered almost instinctively dabbing her wet pussy with the tissues – then looking up quickly to see his eyes sparkling behind the stern metal mask.

Dinner was a formal affair. Sitting in his wheelchair at the head of the elaborately decorated table, Dr Stikannos raised the tiny silver bell. He glanced at Ursula. Ursula inclined her head. He tinkled the bell.

Susie entered promptly in response, placing delicious pâté and baskets of warm toast before the diners, serving Dr Stikannos first, Ursula, Chloe then Emily. A chilled Hock accompanied the pâté. The talk across the table linen and winking silverware was a polite exchange of polished opinions, encompassing the fate of the euro, West Bank politics and the decline of the French film industry. Dr Stikannos seemed well briefed, his gloved finger firmly on the global pulse, Emily reflected.

A salmon mousse followed the pâté. Dr Stikannos declined, nursing his frosted glass of Hock between gloved knuckles. Emily felt slightly unreal. As he talked, dominating the conversation, her host displayed a knowledge of the wider world his self-imposed exile from it in seclusion denied. Chloe, Emily noticed, only spoke in direct response to a question from Ursula.

A muffled crash outside the double doors brought the exquisite meal to an abrupt halt. The doors parted and Susie's face peered in timorously. Emily thought she saw fear in the maid's eyes.

'I'm sorry,' she whispered. 'I've dropped the grouse.'

Rising quickly from her chair Ursula snarled softly, but Dr Stikannos quelled his assistant with a raised glove.

'No matter, girl,' he purred.

Ursula resumed her seat.

'We will continue with a sorbet. Mint, I think. Then some

cheese. And perhaps Emily would like a little fruit?' he added.

Emily, haunted by her enthusiastic interpretation of the Mexican painting, avoided the glint of the metal mask and twiddled with her napkin. In her confusion she did not forget Ursula's suppressed snarl of fury at the maid's mistake – or how the urbane tone of Dr Stikannos had failed to conceal his anger, betrayed by the twisting, gloved hands.

Trembling slightly, Susie served the sorbet, a sweet course, good English cheese and delicious Egyptian coffee in golden demitasse cups Emily instantly recognised as once having been the property of Mussolini. As she sipped and savoured the aromatic coffee she thrilled to the possibility that her lips touched the eggshell china once kissed by the doomed lips of Ii Duce.

'I'm sure Emily has had an exhausting day,' Ursula suddenly announced.

'Yes,' Dr Stikannos agreed. 'An early night, I think.'

'I'd like a walk in the grounds before—' Emily began.

'That, I'm afraid, will not be possible,' Ursula snapped, folding her napkin with an air of finality. 'Security measures,' she answered Emily's startled look. 'Infrared alarms. No,' she continued, drawing a firm line under the issue, 'I think you'll be much more comfortable up in your room.'

Emily was being sent to bed like a child. She bridled with angry resentment, but Chloe, saying her goodnights softly, rose and left the dining room, so consoled by the thought of her digital television waiting for her up in the sumptuous bedroom, Emily also folded her napkin and rose from the table.

Upstairs she found herself ignoring the television and selection of books and fashion glossies. Why had she, and Chloe, been so firmly dismissed from the dining room? And what did those angry leather gloves twisting the napkin mean? Was Susie, the clumsy little maid, to be scolded for her carelessness? Chastised, even?

Emily's pulse quickened at her throat. Acutely aware of her host's keen response to images of punishment and suffering, and suddenly remembering Chloe's whipped cheeks revealed in the gym earlier that morning, it occurred to Emily that she was in a house where the practice of correction and discipline was a distinct possibility.

Against her better judgement, and with a thumping heartbeat, Emily stole down the darkened staircase and stealthily approached the double doors of the dining room. With her ear pressed against a wooden door panel, she strained to overhear. All was silent. The doors were fashioned from seasoned oak – dense and solid. She knelt, bending and drawing her eye to the keyhole. She peeped inside – where all was dark and still.

They too had gone to bed, she realised.

The idea of Susie being punished was a product of her overheated imagination. The dining room, like the darkness she crouched in, was deserted. Emily breathed out slowly, sensing a certain disappointment, an anticlimax to her feverish expectations.

Rising from the floor, and feeling very foolish, she wondered what was happening to her; imagining all this intrigue of punishment and discipline after viewing a couple of erotic paintings. But there had been Chloe's bare bottom bearing the reddened stripes of punishment. She had seen that. And the sound of a spank when Ursula had swooped upon the maid in the scullery. But Chloe could have administered those stripes to herself, with her own hand – with a coat hanger or a leather belt. Emily remembered whipping her own naked buttocks lightly with her sports bra. Most young ladies with pert, spankable bottoms probably did the same. And that sharp smack in the scullery? Just Ursula clapping her hands together impatiently on discovering yet another broken plate. That was all.

Somewhat relieved, yet stubbornly disappointed, Emily

turned in the darkened passage and made for the stairs.

Her soft foot was treading the fourth step when a shrill squeal froze her toes to the carpet. She span round, peering into the darkness. At the end of a long corridor she spotted the bar of golden light beneath the door of her host's private office.

She was at the door in seconds. Again she found it too dense to hear through. Again she knelt, peeping through the keyhole. Through it she glimpsed Dr Stikannos in his wheelchair. His velvet dressing gown was opened, the lush folds peeled across his thighs. Emily gasped softly. At the base of his pale belly, the gloved hands knuckled a proud erection.

Swish, crack!

The unmistakable hiss of a cane cut the silence. Emily shivered. A gasp of suffering and a deep sob followed. She knew it! She just knew it, she exulted, forgetting her fear of discovery in her triumphant excitement. This was a house where the pleasures of pain held sway!

But from her kneeling position at the keyhole Emily could only glimpse Dr Stikannos in his wheelchair, not the drama of domination and discipline unfolding beyond her line of vision.

Then she saw it.

Above the wheelchair, on the wall, there was an oval Flemish mirror suspended from a golden chain. In its clouded glass Emily could just make out the figure of a partly uniformed maid – naked but for her apron and black stockings – bending and bare-bottomed. It was Susie, and she was squirming under the menace of a raised cane.

Swish, crack!

The gloved knuckles pawed at the flesh-spear throbbing between the useless hands. Dr Stikannos grunted, but it was the sharp squeal that caught Emily's ear. Unseen, except for the blurred image in the aged mirror, the maid was responding to the cruel cut of the cane. Emily narrowed her eye, concentrating hard. In the glass, across the whipped cheeks, a thin red line was darkening into a bluish weal to join four other livid stripes. Susie's cheeks were clenched tightly together, her cleft a mere flesh-crease, as if she were squeezing out her pain. Emily counted the five red weals, then watched in the glass as the cane flickered up once more.

Ursula spoke. 'How many?'

'Eight,' Dr Stikannos growled. 'She must learn.'

The glass showed Ursula lowering the tip of her yellow cane to the punished rump to tap-count the tally of the slicing strokes.

One. Two. Three.

The rounded buttocks squirmed.

Four. Five.

The cane rested lightly across the soft curves, depressing them dominantly for a brief moment before sweeping up to quiver above.

Swish, crack! *Swish, crack*! Emily winced and blinked as the two withering strokes sliced down, lashing the proffered cheeks vehemently. In the glass Emily saw the punished maid rise up on her toes and teeter tipsily. Ursula snarled and ordered the snivelling maid to remain perfectly still.

'Thighs apart. No, more… better. A little more. No, bottom up, girl. And keep touching your toes.'

Emily could not see – but could imagine – Susie's trembling fingertips scrabbling to brush her scrunched toes; toes sheathed in the sheen of black nylon stockings.

'Final strokes,' Ursula announced crisply.

Susie mewed like a kitten in a cloudburst. The sound of the bare-bottomed, cane-striped maid whimpering in fearful expectation brought a warm wet bubble to Emily's labia. The cane lashed down, twice, in a blistering staccato. Emily felt the bubble burst, drenching her pubic nest. Pressing her thighs together to contain the hot soak, she hugged her knees to her breasts. In the room Susie sobbed softly, but was dominantly silenced as the punisher brought her glinting length of yellow cane to the lips of the punished.

'And straight up to bed,' Emily heard Ursula instruct the whipped maid. 'And no playing with yourself, understand? I will personally inspect your bed sheets tomorrow morning and if they are stained, your bare bottom will receive the same all over again.'

'Excellent,' Dr Stikannos whispered excitedly, his engorged shaft thick and erect, his hands helpless at the sides of the wheelchair.

Clutching the rest of her maid's uniform, abandoned brassiere and forlorn little white cotton panties up to her breasts – leaving her pubic mound utterly exposed – Susie stumbled towards the door. Ursula flicked the cane, and Emily heard the squeal escape the maid's lips as the thin whippy wood lashed the outer curve of her pert left buttock.

In the darkness Emily sprang up and flattened herself against the wall, dreading the consequences should she be discovered. The door opened, flooding the corridor with a blaze of light. Emily shut her eyes tightly. The door closed softly and darkness returned. Susie, whimpering softly, scampered away. Emily was safe, and she let out a long silent sigh of relief. On the point of sneaking back up to her own bedroom, the sudden thought of the urgent erection between the pawing leathered gloves detained her.

What was happening now? Was he masturbating?

Compelled by her morbid fascination, Emily knelt and pressed her eye to the keyhole once more.

'Please…' Dr Stikannos gasped, jerking in his wheelchair, his crippled hands jabbing the empty air above the red snout of his cock.

'I think not,' Ursula murmured primly, ignoring his anguish as she inspected the tip of her cane. The yellow wood was slightly stained where she had tapped Susie's wet slit between the third and the fourth stroke. She kissed the wet wood fleetingly.

'I beg you…'

'Too much excitement is not good for you,' Ursula replied crisply, lowering the cane along her lithe leg and tapping it against her flesh impatiently. 'You have had enough for this evening, doctor. I caned the girl's bare bottom very strictly, didn't I?'

'Yes,' he whispered thickly.

'And gave her an extra stroke?'

The wheelchair creaked as he slumped, nodding his silent agreement.

'And you saw everything, didn't you, doctor?'

'Yes,' he grunted, his metal mask flashing as he tossed his head back in a frenzy of frustration.

Shouldering her cane, Ursula strode towards the wheelchair and stood before it, planting her feet wide apart. Emily was taken aback to witness the reversal in the balance of power between employer and employee. It was now Ursula so absolutely in control. Emily could not actually see the cane tip worrying the glistening glans, but she knew from the angle of Ursula's elbow, and from the smothered cry of delight from the partially obscured wheelchair, that Ursula was now mistress of her master.

'I beg you…' he pleaded.

'You beg, do you? You beg for relief in release, hm? It is not enough for you that I bare the maid's beautiful little bottom and then stripe it with my cane? Hmm? Now, like little Oliver clutching his empty bowl, you ask for more?' she taunted.

'Oh please, please,' he moaned, adding soft obscenities in an unknown, foreign tongue.

'Very well, you can use my breasts,' she whispered.

Such was the excitement in his response Emily, cowering at the keyhole, thought he would come there and then. Her right hand sought out and quickly found her pussy. She tweaked the outer labia through the wet cotton of her panties, rubbing the juiced lips together brutally between finger and thumb.

Back in the room, she saw Ursula kneeling a few feet away from the wheelchair. Dr Stikannos was struggling. Emily saw his feet grinding into the metal footrests.

'Get up out of that chair,' Ursula commanded dominantly, unzipping her sheath dress and shrugging it down from her shoulders. The exposed skin gleamed. The white brassiere straps bit deeply, suggesting to Emily – who could not see the exposed bosom – the fullness of the breasts and the delicious depth of their cleavage. 'You know you can. Up, doctor, and approach.'

Dr Stikannos was on his knees, shuffling towards his prize. Ursula cupped her tightly fettered breasts and squeezed them, moulding their soft warmth together.

'Come and empty your seed onto them,' she whispered, her words both an invitation and a silken challenge.

Emily gasped softly as she watched his thick cock nodding pliantly as he neared. Her thumb concentrated on her clitoral bud, pleasure-punishing the erect little love-thorn with firm, rhythmical sweeping strokes. The hot scald of her arousal soaked her. All the pent up excitement of the day gathered in a tingling peak, erupting as a sudden spasm, ravaging her. She came, jerking her hips into the empty darkness. Collapsing silently against the door she crushed her flattened tongue to the wood and lapped frenziedly. She ached for something stiff and severe up inside her – something to grip with her contracting muscled warmth.

Moments later, shuddering slightly as the final paroxysms ebbed away, she pressed her eye back to the keyhole. Her vision was blurred. She blinked. Focusing, she saw Dr Stikannos collapse onto the carpet inches in front of Ursula. He curled up, writhing in frustration. He cursed her long and loud.

'Temper, temper,' Ursula teased, her tone one of mocking disapproval. Then the tone sharpened to a crisp command. 'Stay exactly where you are.'

Rising sensuously, she plucked a red velvet cushion from

an Adam chair and returned to the spot where her employer lay in his delicious anguish on the carpet. Positioning the cushion under his shaft, she rose to stand over him, straddling him dominantly. Emily smothered her carnal grunt of pleasure as she watched Ursula position her nylon stockinged foot down upon his upturned buttocks, after flipping away his dressing gown with the tip of her cane, then tread the pale cheeks imperiously.

Dr Stikannos cried out aloud as the stockinged foot on his buttocks drove his glans into the velvet; gouging his glistening snout into the softness below.

Emily and her host came together, her softly whimpered gasps of delight drowned in his shrill scream of satisfaction.

'Now just look what you've done to that cushion,' Ursula cried out, her feigned severity sounding real. 'That was a very wicked thing to do, wasn't it? Hmm? You should be made to lick it clean.'

He writhed, his metal mask glinting as he struggled to twist around and gaze up at her. Were his eyes clouded with a fearful dread, Emily wondered, or were those eyes hidden by the mask sparkling with devotion?

Ursula raised the bamboo aloft. 'And I suppose I really should punish your bare bottom while I watch you lick the cushion clean, hmm?'

Up in her bedroom, after rinsing away the juices of her orgasms from her pussy, Emily slid into the cool sheets of her capacious bed. Her heart was still beating and her brain swam giddily. Half formed thoughts began to crystallise into fragile certainties. One of them became uppermost: she was leaving tomorrow. Returning to London. To her job at the gallery and her Notting Hill flat. To the normality of crowded tube trains. To her familiar round of cautious pleasures and tame little indulgences; champagne, a dildo, sexy undies.

Back to London.

Sinking into her lace pillows – and into the half conscious

state just before sleep – she shivered with pleasure as her nipples rasped the sheet. Palming and then squeezing her naked breasts tenderly, then with a sweet savagery, she allowed her hands to stray down across her belly. Her fingertips found the fringe of her downy pubic bush. She plucked the tiny coils gently, then more firmly, groaning at the delicious pain. One image dominated her sleepy brain: Susie's bare bottom.

As her breathing slowed and deepened, Emily half imagined, half dreamed of the bending maid offering up her plump little rump for the cane.

The punishing cane. The short supple length of cruel bamboo.

Behind her closed eyes the image of it glinted as it swept down, slicing then swiping the soft cheeks. Bequeathing their plump curves with a thin red line of pain.

Swish!

Emily shivered in her troubled dream. A crimson flash exploded behind her eyes. It was as though she herself had just been lashed. Pressing her bottom down into the silken sheet she squeezed her cheeks together, sensing a sudden crimson agony. Again her sleeping brain witnessed the bamboo rising, quiver, and then flash as it whistled down. Another bright flash exploded behind Emily's closed eyes. Again she grunted softly in her dreams as her bottom blazed beneath the cane's fierce kiss.

Moaning, Emily tossed in the expanse of her enormous William & Mary bed. Something was disturbing her delicious dreams. Ursula was caning a bare bottom. Emily found the experience deeply satisfying. Unseen, she watched, thrilling to the red lines searing the defenceless cheeks. Ursula's green eyes sparkled in triumph as her fingers tightened around the bamboo cane.

Swish!

Another blistering stroke across the soft, suffering cheeks. Automatically, though sleeping fitfully now, Emily's fingers dabbled down at her wet sex. But something – some dark shadow – stirred deep in her tired brain. Something, it understood, was not quite right.

Ursula was caning a bare bottom. That much Emily's brain fully understood – and took pleasure in the knowledge.

Susie. It was Susie, the mischievous maid.

Ursula was caning Susie. But in her dreams, Emily's voice rose in muffled protest. Susie was kneeling – and watching. No, that could not be right, not right at all, the molten logic of the sleeping brain reasoned. If Susie was watching, whose bottom was being whipped?

Emily whimpered softly as her kaleidoscopic dream froze into a single, sharp image: Ursula was raising the whippy wood once more. Raising it high above a shivering, naked bottom.

Emily's bottom!

Chapter Three

Dr Stikannos sipped his early morning cup of Gunpowder tea, carefully avoiding any inelegant clinking of the Sevres teacup against his metal mask. His dark eyes flickered down to gaze at the wafer of lemon floating in the pale gold liquid. As he brought the delicate teacup up to his lips once more savouring the citric tang, his eyes flickered up to the screen. His wet lips pursed into a thin line as he savoured the second delight: the image of Ursula inspecting the maid's rumpled bed linen.

'Rewind,' he whispered.

Ursula, who had joined him downstairs in the butler's pantry after her early morning visit to Susie, obeyed. She jabbed her finger down on the control button. Up on the screen she saw herself jerking backwards like a drunken marionette until she magically disappeared behind a door that slammed silently shut.

'Play.' The Sevres teacup rattled expectantly in its eggshell-thin saucer.

Ursula's straightened forefinger jabbed down once more. The screen showed the door to Susie's bedroom opening. Ursula watched the replay of herself storming in – snatching up and dragging down the sleeping maid's duvet.

'Fast forward.'

Ursula, smiling grimly, deftly rescued the imperilled Sevres from the quivering gloved hand of her master. Standing beside the wheelchair, her thigh brushing his shoulder, she followed his gaze up to the screen. On it, she saw herself inspecting the sheet between the naked maid's thighs, then roughly gripping each of Susie's wrists and sniffing suspiciously at the captive fingertips.

'No, fast forward to your masterstroke,' he whispered. 'A devilish piece of cunning.'

Returning to the control panel, her mouth twisted into a cruel smile. Yes, it had been a devilish piece of cunning. She watched Dr Stikannos nodding judiciously as, on the screen, Susie squirmed in Ursula's fierce grip – both wrists held in a dominant left fist while Ursula's free fingers explored the maid's slit for the moistness. A cane lay lengthways alongside the cowering maid.

Ursula jabbed the fast forward. Seconds later the screen showed Susie alone in her bedroom. With the imminent threat of punishment over, the maid scrambled to the end of her bed and knelt. Naked, her belly and inner thighs thrust up against the corner of her mattress, Susie began to masturbate – lasciviously raking her sex down against the edge of her bed.

'Foolish young lady,' Dr Stikannos chuckled, clapping his gloved hands together excitedly in eager anticipation.

Just as Susie's mouth opened wide, signalling her mute ecstasy as she came – jerking herself into the corner of the mattress – the bedroom door burst open once more and Ursula strode in.

'Big close up.'

Ursula obliged, zooming in to capture the maid's face frozen in terror as she twisted her head over her shoulder and stared up into Ursula's unblinking green eyes.

'Medium long shot. I want you both in frame.'

Ursula's eyes sparkled as they watched the naked, kneeling maid being arranged for her punishment. Watched as the girl's face changed from the brief distort of orgasm to the pale mask of fear.

'Delightful,' Dr Stikannos murmured as, up on the screen, Ursula dominantly buried Susie's face into the mattress, the mattress Susie had just been using to help herself come.

Trapped and helpless, her bare buttocks raised, the maid shivered as Ursula flexed the whippy length of her supple cane.

'How many?'

'You know how many,' Ursula countered. 'You've watched this bit twice.'

Dr Stikannos grunted impatiently and twisted in his wheelchair.

'Want an early morning peek at your little art expert?'

The metal mask glinted as he nodded. Ursula's fingers stroked the control panel fleetingly. Up on the screen, the image of the cruel cane lashing down across the upturned buttocks of the helpless maid switched in a clean cut to an image of Emily, up and dressed, packing her bag.

'Up with the lark,' Ursula murmured. 'Looks as though your little bird's about to fly.'

The wheelchair creaked as its occupant twisted restlessly. Ursula saw the gloved hands clench into impotent fists of fury.

'Relax,' she whispered soothingly. 'I'm full of devilish cunning, remember. Full of little surprises.'

Up on the screen, they both watched as Emily zipped her bag shut, rose up, shouldered it and looked around her sumptuous quarters with an air of finality. Of finality and farewell.

'Nothing to eat?'

Emily smiled and fingered her cup of coffee. Next to her, Chloe was tackling a brace of trout with unconcerned gusto.

'Surely some toast?' Ursula pressed solicitously.

'I'm fine,' Emily replied. 'Besides,' she added quickly, glad of the opportunity, 'my taxi will be—'

'Taxi?' purred Ursula. 'You have arranged for a taxi?'

'Not yet,' Emily shrugged. 'But I'm afraid I have to go back to London this morning.'

'Does that mean one less for lunch?' Susie inquired, emerging from the larder with a tray of Dover sole she had just skinned and boned.

'Get on with your work, girl,' Ursula snapped, her green eyes remaining steadily upon Emily.

Emily, conscious of the penetrating gaze, squirmed uncomfortably. She attempted a bright voice. 'I'll phone for a taxi and then say goodbye to Dr Stikannos. I'm sure he'll be able to get another—'

'That will not be possible,' Ursula cut in brusquely.

Catching the waspish tone, Emily looked up, while beside her Chloe put down her knife and fork and kept her eyes carefully lowered.

'Not possible?' Emily echoed. 'Is he – is he unwell?'

'The taxi. Not possible, I'm afraid. We do not encourage unscheduled visitors here.'

'Could Chloe take me to the station?'

Ursula ignored the direct question. Her answer was oblique. She said that Dr Stikannos was waiting for Emily in his study.

'Leave your bag here.'

It was impossible to gauge his reaction. Inscrutable, he had continued to sit impassively behind his desk. The metal mask remained perfectly immobile. The wheelchair had not even creaked.

And the gloved hands remained out of sight beneath the desk. Emily squirmed, breaking the silence in the study following the declaration that she proposed to return to London. She spoke rapidly.

'You'll be able to engage someone quite easily to catalogue the works for sale.'

Dr Stikannos remained silent. Emily pressed on doggedly, apologising once more and adding some gushing praise for the collection he had amassed.

'I am disappointed.' The three simple words, spoken softly, managed to convey a menace of malice.

Emily bowed her head and blushed.

'I had hoped you would become of some assistance to

me, Emily. I am disappointed.'

'There are plenty of others, more expert than I…' she replied lamely, her voice fading as she gulped.

His dark eyes glistened. He was staring directly into her own. Shyly, her grey eyes fluttered down – only to be drawn back up to meet his stern gaze. Reluctantly, but as if compelled to do so.

'This is a unique moment, Emily. Soon you will leave this room, and we will never meet again. And yet, in the brief space of time we have shared together, I have come to know, to know and understand you intimately.'

Emily's face blazed bright red.

'Intimately,' he whispered again. 'A unique moment. A moment denied to so many. In the few minutes remaining to us, we can say what we would otherwise never dare to say.'

'The Overbeck – you had it smuggled out of Minsk?' Emily blurted suddenly. 'I promise I'll never tell.'

'I do not speak of my art or of anything in my collection, Emily. I speak of you and I. Of what I have glimpsed in your nature. Of what you have revealed of yourself to me. I speak of your needs, your longings and of your deep desires.'

Emily, standing before his desk, blinked in the strong sunlight streaming down through the oriel window behind him. She shuffled, acutely conscious of the flame of shame suffusing her face.

'Your desires,' he whispered fiercely. 'Come here.'

She stepped around the desk, trailing the splayed fingertips of her left hand along its polished surface, and positioned herself behind his wheelchair.

'Over to that chest of drawers.'

She propelled the wheelchair across the study to a rosewood chest, late seventeenth century, English, with curved stiles, a delicately scrolled plinth and canted cornering. Emily concentrated on the exquisite piece intently, enumerating its features – anything rather than dwell on the man in the metal mask's words.

Dr Stikannos raised a gloved hand, motioning his desire for her to position his chair alongside, not facing, the rosewood chest. Emily inched the wheelchair into the desired position.

Scrabbling slightly, and with some effort, he managed to slide open the second drawer. Obedient to his leathered fingers, it opened silently. From its green baize depths, his gloved hand withdrew three items: a diamond-studded gold collar; a tiny golden ring and a coiled, glistening strap. He laid them in his lap, closed the drawer and nodded his desire to return to his desk. Emily obeyed, repositioning the wheelchair behind the desk before treading softly back to her spot before it.

Head bowed, her blonde mane curtaining her grey eyes, she drew her hands together behind her back. Her fingers wriggled into each other, then interlocked, resting above the swell of her buttocks.

Dr Stikannos had carefully arranged the three objects on the polished surface of the desk. The diamond-studded collar and the tiny golden ring were reflected in the depths of the gleaming wood. The coiled strap – half an inch thick and some eighteen inches long – slowly unfurled. Emily watched it. Dark brown, almost purplish, rather than the black she had at first thought it, the length of supple hide uncoiled like a sleeping snake awoken at sunrise.

'Submission and surrender,' she heard him pronounce, tapping each of the three objects in turn with his leather-sheathed index finger. The fingertip paused to caress the diamond-studded collar. 'Submission to the pleasures of pain.'

Emily's mouth dried. She swallowed with difficulty. Her left shoe prinked, the kitten heel rising a fraction from the carpet. She dug the polished toe-cap into the softness at her feet. Behind her back, above the swell of her leather mini-skirt rounded by her pert rump, her fingers splayed out in a sudden spasm.

'Emily, we have so little time. Let us at least speak openly, candidly, of our acknowledged and unacknowledged desires. These,' he continued suavely, 'are little toys once used for the training of a Sultan's favourite. I managed to secure them for myself, for my collection, after some not inconsiderable inconvenience and expense. I traced them to a brothel in Budapest. Their provenance,' he continued conversationally, 'will, I know, interest you. The Sultan captured and consigned into his harem the daughter of a Nubian necromancer. The girl was a proud beauty, wise in lore and languages. A prize for any collector of the esoteric and the exquisite to obtain. The girl,' he continued seamlessly, his tone urbane and silken, 'proved difficult, however. The Sultan was disappointed—'

Emily flinched at the word.

'She had to be removed from the harem where her disobedience had threatened to provoke rebellion and sedition. But the Sultan, knowing the true value of his latest acquisition, refused to trade her into servitude. No,' Dr Stikannos remarked, nodding approvingly, 'despite his disappointment the Sultan saw in her the spirit and the mettle of an Arab steed. Unbroken and untamed. But he meant to ride her, Emily. He meant to ride her. And how does one break the spirit of a mettlesome steed? Hmm?'

'The bridle. The bridle and the whip.' Her whispered response sounded strange to her ears, as if the reluctant admission had been forced from the lips of another.

'The bridle and the whip. Precisely so. This collar,' he toyed with it affectionately, thumbing the glinting diamonds, 'he had fashioned for her. The Sultan made the slave girl wear it as a sign of her submission to his will. He would visit her tent, at night, and attach a golden chain to it, then lead her – often dragging the protesting girl belly down across the cooling sands – to a whipping post. There, with this,' he weighed the recoiled length of hide in his gloved palm, 'he would lash her soft nakedness until she submitted to his lustful longing. It is the penis of a bull camel. I believe it bites the female buttocks more viciously than Malayan clouded bamboo.'

Emily moaned softly as she swayed before the desk.

'Broken under the nightly scourge,' Dr Stikannos continued, 'the Sultan's favourite could not but submit. As a further sign of her surrender to his absolute mastery over her, the Sultan had this golden ring forged by his most experienced craftsman. Measurements were taken from her little finger for which it was honed out of molten gold. But so utter was her submission, after the cruel visitation of the lash, the Sultan's favourite willingly wore it there...'

The gloved hand spasmed, and Emily grunted as the camel's penis flickered and lashed out, the tip of the oiled hide licking her pubis. She staggered backwards, both hands clamped at her stinging pussy.

'There can be nothing more perfect than when a born master meets a true slave, Emily. He must be patient. Firm. Cruel, perhaps. But patient. Her surrender and submission, however long and painful that journey may be, leads to sweet delights for both.'

'No,' Emily mumbled sullenly, flouncing her blonde hair defiantly. 'You are wrong. I do not—'

'Don't lie to me, Emily. Remember, I have seen into the core of your inner being. I know the secrets of your yearning.'

'No, you're wrong. I'm not like that.'

He held up a gloved hand imperiously. 'The pleasures of pain and the sweetness of suffering are your true appetites, your burning desires.'

'No, never!' she shouted.

'Trust me. I know.' His words were whispered softly; so softly, their velvet menace both sobered and frightened Emily into silence.

Neither spoke. Panting, Emily returned his gaze defiantly.

A loud silence filled the study. Dr Stikannos slowly coiled up the length of supple hide, knotted it expertly, then gathered up the diamond-studded collar and tiny golden ring into his gloved hand.

'It is a pity you choose not to stay and serve me.'

'Goodbye, Dr Stikannos.'

Stumbling in her confusion, Emily made a less than convincing show of self-possession as she left his study. Closing the door firmly behind her, she paused, her hand at her throat. Her head swam, her knees felt like jelly. The pulse at her jugular plucked fiercely. Emily closed her eyes and shook her head in an effort to rid herself of the blood singing in her ears.

But there were other telltale symptoms; symptoms she could not deny. Her panties were wet from the warm seeping of her sex – a seeping conjured up by the encounter with Dr Stikannos beyond the study door. A warm seeping awakened by his words – and hastened into quicksilver by the brief kiss of his whip at her labia.

But he was wrong; she couldn't be like that. She couldn't be. He had her completely wrong. She didn't crave the cruel lash of a master's tongue, or the fiercer stroke of his cane. She was no submissive waiting to be awoken, then broken, by the brutal touch of a dominant. There could be no solace in submissive servitude—'

'Emily?'

It was Ursula, emerging swiftly from the shadows into the bright sunlight flooding the far side of the hall. Her green eyes squinted into the strong sunbeams. Her cropped hair shone.

'Come with me, please. There is something I need to discuss with you most urgently.'

'But I didn't. I don't even know what you mean.'

'Letters,' Ursula repeated. 'Where have you hidden them?'

Emily shrugged, throwing her hands out wide.

'They were in the Louis XV ormolu escritoire,' Ursula insisted. Emily blinked uncomprehendingly.

'The writing desk at which you compiled your catalogue notes.'

'Yes,' Emily nodded, 'I know. It's one of a pair made in the Corderey workshops in Nantes.'

'There were four letters penned by Voltaire to his mistress in that escritoire. Two are missing.'

'But that's not fair,' Emily protested hotly. 'I didn't even know about them and I certainly—'

'Knew the value of the two you stole. Come with me.'

'Where are we—?'

'Shut up and follow me.'

Angry at the outrageous accusation and eager to clear the matter up, Emily strode after Ursula out of the mansion, across the cobblestone courtyard and into the converted gym.

Chloe, dressed in a tight-fitting white vest and tiny, buttock-sculpting shorts, was already there, standing directly beneath a neon strip-light, her breasts firm within the vest. She was caressing the scuffed hide of a vaulting horse with her flattened, smoothing palm.

Ursula closed – silently locking – the gym door, then strode past Emily and joined Chloe at the horse. For a fleeting moment their fingertips kissed across the swollen flank of dull leather.

'Strip,' Ursula barked. 'I'm going to search you thoroughly.'

Chloe grinned, patting the hide impatiently, her fingers drumming their eagerness for the feast of Emily's flesh. Emily shook her head and stepped back. Turning, she scampered to the door. Her hand grasped the handle and twisted it down, then shook it vigorously. It was a futile gesture. She glanced over her shoulder. Chloe's sneer was triumphant. Her fingers were still busy at the hide.

'No,' Emily shouted, her shrill protest echoing eerily around the gym. 'You wouldn't bloody well dare…'

'I'm waiting,' Ursula purred, her flattened palm now on top of Chloe's: fused into a single flesh, their splayed fingers palmed the leather rhythmically.

'Look,' Emily blustered, rattling the door handle violently, 'there's been some dreadful mistake.'

'Which you made when you stole those two valuable letters. Private sale, was it? Suppose so; you've got the contacts. Or,' the green eyes narrowed accusingly, 'were they for your private collection?'

'Look, I didn't touch them—'

'Strip! At once. Chloe,' Ursula snapped, 'assist her.'

Chloe abandoned the vaulting horse with a resounding slap and paced swiftly across the polished wooden floor. Her pumps squeaked sharply beneath her purposeful stride. Emily shrank away from the locked door and, sidling, backed up against a set of wall bars. As Ursula joined the advancing Chloe stride for menacing stride, Emily rose up on her toes and crushed her soft buttocks into the smooth bars behind.

They caught her and stilled her wriggling, in a cruel pincer of gripping talons.

'Hold her,' Ursula hissed.

'Got the bitch,' Chloe grunted, her raven hair tossing tempestuously as, thighs splayed, she grappled with her struggling captive.

They pinioned Emily with brutal efficiency, forcing her arms up behind her back. They stripped her naked with cruel economy, leaving her top, leather miniskirt and panties in a puddle on the polished gym floor.

'A natural blonde,' Chloe hissed, her fingertips straying briefly across the rasp of Emily's pubic nest.

'Cut that out,' Ursula snarled, her green eyes flashing angrily. 'Give me a hand getting her across the horse.'

Moments later, Emily was forced belly down across the

apparatus, her naked breasts squashed and bulging into the harsh hide. The gym echoed to her ringing shrieks of protest. Chloe, pinioning Emily's wrists in a fierce grip, held her wriggling captive securely by dragging Emily's out in full stretch. Emily twisted and jerked as Ursula approached her from behind, standing between her splayed thighs.

Emily squealed as a firm palm cracked down viciously, instantly reddening the swell of her right cheek.

'Keep still, bitch. You are entirely at my mercy now and will suffer unless and until you confess to the theft.'

'But I didn't,' Emily wailed.

A second severe swipe of flesh upon flesh seared down across the writhing nude's upturned bottom. And then two more in swift succession.

'Unless and until you confess to the theft and return the letters, understand?'

Silence reigned for long seconds. Then Emily sobbed aloud.

'Stop snivelling,' Ursula hissed, and four crisp spanks followed in a sharp staccato. The punished buttocks blazed beneath the onslaught.

'No, stop, please – I didn't—'

'Hold her down,' Ursula ordered. 'She needs a little persuasion.'

Emily screwed her eyes tightly and squirmed against the leather, shivering as the departing footsteps paused then slowly returned towards the horse. What had Ursula meant by persuasion? What had she picked up from the table over by the far wall of the gym? Emily's mind was a whirlpool of torment. Into that anguish stole the sounds of Ursula's slow but certain tread. Unhurried, but utterly assured. Emily panicked, the full horror of her helplessness brutally vivid. She was bare-bottomed across the vaulting horse. Bare-bottomed, pinioned and helpless before her cruel tormentor. A cruel, closely cropped tormentor whose green eyes had flashed jealousy – and jealously – at Emily since her arrival.

A cruel, green-eyed tormentor who was now gripping an instrument of persuasion; an instrument of persuasion designed and destined to bring pain to Emily's naked cheeks.

Ursula's voice was calm. Calm and reasonable. It betrayed nothing of her devilish intent. 'Can you tell me what this is?' she inquired politely.

Emily felt the cool kiss of dimpled latex alight upon her left cheek.

'Hmm?' The dimpled latex depressed the curved buttock beneath its weight.

'N-no,' Emily whispered uncertainly, her lips mumbling into the hide, her tongue-tip shrinking from its feral tang.

Ursula depressed the table tennis bat more firmly, almost flattening the ripe swell of the naked buttock beneath. 'Oh, come along now,' she bantered, cajoling her victim teasingly. 'Have a guess.'

'I don't know.'

'Then I'd better tell you, mm? It's a table tennis bat.'

Emily groaned.

'It has a beautiful, red rubber surface. I am going to beat your bare bottom, bitch, until your cheeks are as red as the rubber. Hold her,' Ursula warned, swiftly raising the bat aloft.

Emily squeezed her cheeks, tightening the rounded hillocks of naked flesh in an automatic reflex against the imminent pain. Ursula snarled, and keeping the cruel bat aloft above the bunched buttocks below, forced the tip of her left thumb down into Emily's cleft. Cupping the outer curve of the cheek with her fingers, she slowly squeezed. The swollen flesh in her grasp whitened where the fingertips dug deeply.

'Open.'

Despite the pain, Emily did not obey.

'I said open up, bitch. I want your bottom big and round for the bat. Unclench your cheeks this instant.'

Sinking her belly and upper thighs into the horse across

which her nakedness was stretched, Emily loosened her muscles, unclenching her cheeks as instructed. She whimpered aloud as she felt Ursula's thumb bullying her sphincter; dominantly worrying the wet pink of her puckering anal whorl.

'That's better.' The thumb stroked the anus with a savage tenderness, dragging the hot flesh from side to side. 'You'll find that obedience is best.'

The words chilled Emily's heated brain – but it was Chloe's cruel laugh that froze her heart behind her ribcage. For a split second, Emily forgot about the bat.

Crack! *Crack*! The bat splatted down twice in vicious succession, blistering her bare bottom. The dimpled latex left twin crimson blotches across the curves of each quivering dome. Emily howled as she writhed, wriggling and struggling frenziedly in a frantic bid for freedom. At the end of her painfully outstretched arms, she felt Chloe's grip tighten at each captive wrist.

Crack! *Crack*!

Emily yelped as four scarlet flashes exploded: two behind her eyes, two upon her helpless cheeks.

Crack! A single, searing swipe. Emily's stubby nipples rasped the leather horse.

'Ready to confess?' Ursula murmured.

Emily moaned deeply as her tormentor plied the surface of the bat across the crowns of her scalded cheeks, smoothing the buttocks she had just blistered.

'I didn't steal,' Emily whispered, tossing her golden mane free from her tear-jewelled eyes. 'I swear I didn't.'

'Silence,' Ursula barked. 'Silence until you wish to confess. I'll have no more lies.' She cracked the bat down harshly, twice, once across each shiny-sore cheek. 'You've had your chance, bitch. You chose not to do so. And now you must suffer the consequences.'

Chloe giggled, a perverse squeal of dark joy.

Crack! *Crack*! Two more withering swipes of the red

rubber-skinned bat barked out as the dimpled latex savaged the naked bottom of the helpless, outstretched nude. Twisting and jerking in her pain and shame, Emily ground her belly and breasts into the hard hide. To her alarm, dismay and shocked confusion, her labial lips rode the leather, lubricated by the juice weeping from her hot slit.

Crack! *Crack*! Emily bubbled and grunted as her liquid heat popped silently, soaking her inner thighs.

'I'm waiting.' Ursula whispered the words, then deftly flicked her wrist to angle the thin edge of the bat down between the punished cheeks. Emily moaned.

'So, do you wish to speak? Speak, and confess?'

Ursula forced the edge of the bat down into her victim's cleft.

Bending her face down closer, as if to inspect her handiwork, Ursula narrowed her eyes into fierce slits of concentration. She plied the bat with subtlety, raking it firmly between Emily's hot cheeks. A second silver bubble winked at the dark lips of Emily's pouting pussy as the thin edge of the bat ravished her sensitive cleft. Ursula paused, withdrew the bat a fraction and rested it face down upon the reddened left buttock, and instantly jabbed the bubble of liquid arousal with her right thumb. It shivered and burst, soaking the scuffed hide of the horse below, the wet stain as dark as velvet.

'More,' Chloe shrilled, her cruel lust tightening her throat, giving her words a strangled excitement. 'Give her more.'

'Yes, she needs further persuasion,' Ursula nodded, weighing her words carefully as she now weighed the rubber-sleeved bat upon her upturned palm. 'Further persuasion.'

Emily tensed, her twin cheeks suddenly moulded into rounded hillocks of firm, fearful expectation. Squeezing her eyes shut, she nuzzled the pungent hide of the vaulting horse.

Then the curt tones of Dr Stikannos broke the silence of the gym. Emily opened her eyes in surprise. She had not heard the key in the door behind her. Or heard the door open. Had not heard the wheelchair's creak.

'I need to speak with you. In my study, please.'

Emily strained, twisting her face upwards a fraction. She saw the speaker box; an internal intercom system. The man in the metal mask was still behind his desk in the study where she had left him. He was summoning Ursula to his side.

'Tie her hands tightly and bring her along to the study. He'll want to question her,' Ursula instructed, lowering the bat once more and squashing the punished buttocks dominantly.

Emily, still naked, squirmed between her captors as they flanked her, pinioning her firmly between their thighs. Behind her back, above crimsoned cheeks, her bound wrists writhed. Dr Stikannos, behind his desk, gazed steadily up into the nude's frightened eyes.

The sun had passed its zenith and no longer flooded down through the oriel window behind him. But Emily still blinked as she tried to avoid his piercing eyes; blinked because of the tears of shame swimming in her downcast eyes.

'The Voltaire letters,' he repeated, pressing his gloved fingertips together beneath the chin of his metal mask. He switched his gaze to Ursula. 'Has she confessed?'

'Not yet. I was questioning her when you called for me. I was persuading—'

'Persuading?' The word came quickly – greedily.

Ursula grappled Emily roughly, twisting the naked girl around, proffering the reddened bottom to her master.

'Ah. And did she respond? To your persuasion?'

'It depends what you mean by respond,' Ursula replied enigmatically, spinning Emily around to face the desk once more. 'Little was forthcoming from these lips,' she continued, fingering Emily's lower lip, 'but these lips spoke quite eloquently,' Ursula laughed, dropping her hand down to briefly knuckle Emily's moist slit. 'Quite eloquently.'

Chloe giggled. Dr Stikannos quelled her instantly with a flash of his upturned metal mask.

'There can be, of course, absolutely no mistake?' he asked. 'The two Voltaire letters are missing?'

'No mistake,' Ursula snapped testily. 'Except hers.'

Emily appealed directly to her host. 'Search my bag,' she blurted, her voice shrill with both fear and anger.

Behind his mask, his dark eyes glinted as they raked her squirming nakedness. 'That is exactly what Chloe is about to do,' he replied.

'I've looked,' Chloe said simply.

'I'll take a closer look,' Ursula barked, gripping Emily by the nape of her neck and forcing her down before the desk. 'Untie her.'

Chloe obeyed the strict command, bending, her bosom crushing into Emily's shoulders as she loosened the cords at the kneeling nude's wrists.

Emily winced as she drew her freed hands together to modestly shield her pubic mound.

'Anything?' Dr Stikannos asked.

Ursula was rummaging briskly through Emily's bag, tossing the contents onto the polished surface of the desk.

'I've done that,' Chloe insisted impatiently.

'Cunning little vixen, this one,' Ursula snarled. 'She'll have hidden them well. What's this?'

Ursula had extracted Emily's dildo. Her cropped head lowered as, twisting the base, she peered suspiciously into the hollow phallus.

'Think there's something…' she grunted, inverting the dildo and tapping the base on the desk. 'There,' she exclaimed as two cylinders of ivory-grey paper slipped out.

'What's this?' The two gloved hands pounced eagerly. Clumsy, leathered fingertips scrabbled to unfurl the tightly rolled letters.

Emily stared in horror as the fingers prised open the two letters, carefully smoothing and flattening them out on the polished surface of the desk. The spidery writing had been penned in a sepia ink and had faded with age.

Dr Stikannos read out aloud, his French pronunciation crisply impeccable. 'Most certainly these are from my collection of Voltaire's juvenilia,' he concluded.

'But I didn't take them, I swear.'

He ignored Emily. 'Leave us, Chloe,' was all the man in the mask said. The tone was mild, almost weary.

Chloe departed as softly as a shadow.

'Stand up, Emily.' Again, she noted no anger in his voice. Just a flat, dull weariness.

Rising, and steadying herself at his desk, she made a final and desperate bid to establish her innocence. Her grey eyes grew wide as, head tossed back defiantly, she denied the theft.

'She's lying,' Ursula said calmly. 'You have seen the evidence. You have all the proof you need.'

'No, she's wrong. I didn't—'

'Be quiet, bitch!' Ursula tugged the nude's blonde mane, forcing Emily to kneel once more before the desk.

'Leave her; she is free to go.' Dr Stikannos had spoken so softly his words were barely audible.

Emily, despite the pain of Ursula's grip, raised her head and gazed across the desk. 'I'm – I'm free?' she faltered, her sudden disbelief stronger than her sense of relief. 'I can go?'

'But…' Ursula began, protesting.

'Free to go,' Dr Stikannos nodded. 'Free to go back to London. But to what, Emily? Consider carefully.' His voice was now a silken purr. 'To disgrace, certainly. To prosecution, possibly.'

Emily gasped. Ursula grinned.

'I shall of course communicate my displeasure to your gallery. Whatever they decide to do with you I cannot say,

79

but of this be sure. Within a few days every gallery door will be closed to you, Emily. Cork Street, Mayfair, then the entire West End will be closed to you. No gallery or art house will ever think of employing you.'

'She'll be lucky to get a job serving up burgers and fries,' Ursula laughed.

'No, you can't... I didn't—'

'However, there is a way,' he broke in suavely, 'to solve this unpleasant little matter.'

'A way?' Emily whispered anxiously. 'I don't understand.'

The metal mask flashed up at Ursula. 'Tell her.'

'Stay and take your punishment,' Ursula said.

'No...'

'Your punishment,' Ursula repeated, 'then remain to complete the payment of your debt by completing the catalogue.'

'But that's...'

'The choice, such as it is, is yours,' Ursula rasped. 'Which is it to be? Choose.'

'And choose wisely, Emily,' Dr Stikannos hissed.

Emily bowed her head. She was burning with indignant fury. She had been tricked and trapped by a cheap ruse, and was being forced to accept both punishment and servitude in the lair of Dr Stikannos. But the alternative, total disgrace in London, was unthinkable.

'Have you chosen, Emily?' he demanded. 'And have you chosen wisely?'

'I-I will...'

'Yes?' he prompted, relishing her anguish.

'I will stay. Stay and finish the catalogue,' she added quickly.

'And?' Dr Stikannos insisted, savouring the approaching moment of his sovereignty over her.

'I will complete the catalogue for your sale. That is all. You must not—'

'Must not? My dear girl, you are no position to dictate terms. You have decided to remain here – to remain here and to be dealt with for your crime. Your crime,' his voice suddenly rose sharply, 'the guilt of which has been well proven. For the theft of the letters.'

'Might I suggest the whipping post?' Ursula interposed softly.

Dr Stikannos chuckled darkly, apprehending the cruel pun instantly.

'The whipping post, for *whipping* the *post*. Yes, excellent,' he laughed. 'So be it. But first,' his amusement vanished as quickly as it had come and his voice suddenly hardened, 'you must accept this.'

Emily, legs trembling, approached the desk. Shamefully conscious of her utter nakedness, she attempted to cover her breasts, crushing her forearm up against her nipples, and covering her blonde nest below.

'Arms down by your sides,' Ursula snapped.

Emily hesitated, protecting her modesty against the eyes behind the metal mask, and a sharp swipe of Ursula's flattened palm scalded her naked left buttock. The cheek wobbled and crimsoned – as did Emily's face. Reluctantly, fearful of another brutal smack, she lowered her hands obediently against her thighs. Dr Stikannos turned his mask directly on her, as if discovering her nakedness before him, her helpless nakedness, for the very first time. Emily could almost feel the heat from his piercing glare. The glare of his penetrating, merciless gaze.

'Bring her here, to me.'

Ursula roughly propelled the nude around the wide desk, forcing Emily down upon her knees before the wheelchair.

'Remember?' he purred.

Emily averted her face, avoiding the outstretched glove, the leathered fingertips of which fleetingly grazed her chin.

'Emily.' The voice was stern – dominant.

As if spellbound, Emily focused on the gloved palm, and

upon it she saw the jewelled collar.

'Remember?' he whispered. 'I gave you its provenance. And purpose.'

Emily clamped her trembling thighs together.

'You will wear the collar.'

'No... not that... never—'

Ursula quelled Emily's outburst with a double swipe of her hard palm down across the fleshy cheeks below. Emily squealed her torment.

'Silence, bitch. The master is talking.'

The master. The word exploded silently with a crimson blaze behind Emily's eyes. Dr Stikannos was the master. And Emily? Not his mistress, or consort. No, his slave. His to punish for pleasure and pleasurably punish as he chose. Master. Master and slave. Emily swayed gently on her knees as the dread delight of her dark, delicious doom swept over her. Terrifying, yet thrilling her. Haunting her brain with a sweet sorrow.

'You will wear this collar. It is my wish. And in a moment you are to receive the lash.'

'No. Please, no...'

'Yes, Emily, the lash. We will explore the pleasures of pain together – mutually. And later, when you have become accustomed to the whip, you will become eager for the ring.'

'The ring?' Emily remembered. 'Never.'

'Believe me, my girl, you will come to beg to wear the ring.'

'No, not that. You may beat me—'

'May I?' he mocked, then his tone became brutal. 'I do not need or seek your consent, Emily. Bear that in mind as you kneel before me.'

Emily glanced up directly into the eyes behind the mask, and the gloved fingertips at her tilted chin dominantly checked her fragile display of insurrection.

The soft leather stroked her face firmly, then, splayed out over her golden mane, forced her head down into

82

subjugation and submission.

'You must learn to listen. Listen and obey. Accept the collar.'

Emily, shuddering, bowed her head even further down, and moaned softly as the leathered fingers of Dr Stikannos placed, then secured, the bejewelled collar around her soft, white throat.

Dr Stikannos – now her master.

'Your badge of servitude, Emily. Wear it with due humility. It marks your first faltering steps along the path of submission that will lead you to the bittersweet delights of—'

Slavery. Emily silently completed his sentence. And in completing his sentence, she realised that she was about to commence hers: her sentence to servitude. To suffer and submit to his whip. But, her heart hammered wildly, would there be more? Was she to become the plaything, the sexual toy of Dr Stikannos? His, utterly, to do with as he pleased? Unless she could escape. Yes, that was it; suffer a whipping to appease them. Then engineer her escape.

'All foolish thoughts of escape,' he murmured softly, 'must be abandoned, Emily. You must surrender and submit to my will completely. Do not struggle or strive in futile bids for freedom. More importantly, surrender your mind to me. I wish to own you totally. I do not, like the Sultan, have to take a stubborn and rebellious girl to the whipping post. But I will if it is necessary to do so.'

Emily choked on a dry sob. His fingers found her chin and tilted her tear-streaked face up to meet his stern gaze.

'No tears or self-pity, my girl. Remember, I know your true nature. Trust me. Although you do not fully realise or accept the fact, I know that your spirit and your flesh yearn to be enchained. Body and mind, you ache for the tender dominance of a master. A master who can be gently cruel, a master who can and will be brutally kind. Trust me.'

The gloved fingers squeezed her face until it ached,

forcing Emily to gaze up submissively into the metal mask.

'I know. You yourself have revealed it to me. You yourself have told me so.'

'The whipping post?' Ursula urged, her green eyes flashing impatiently.

Releasing Emily's chin from his grip, he nodded.

'And do you wish her to taste that?' Ursula asked, pointing to the coiled camel's penis on the desk.

He shook his head, scooped up the lash and thumbed it firmly, squeezing a pearl of oil from the supple hide. It glistened on the leather of his controlling glove. 'No, not yet. Later. Take her to the whipping post and bind her tightly to it. See that the cords bite. And use a cane. Take a silver Sumatran bamboo from my collection.'

Emily moaned.

'This,' Dr Stikannos whispered, clenching his gloved fist over the camel's penis, 'must be a delight to be deferred.'

Emily shivered. Her mind was haunted by his earlier words. Had she really revealed a servile nature, a desire to be dominated, to him? A tiny pinpoint of golden light illumined a crimson corner of her mind. In her turmoil of confusion, fear and delicious dread, the pinpoint of light flickered and flared, burning with an intense blaze. Was it the hot shame of her reluctant self-knowledge? Or was it a glimpse of the blistering heat about to be bequeathed across her bare bottom by the impending bamboo?

Desperately trying to avoid confronting her true nature – for what he had said could just possibly be true – Emily allowed herself to be frog-marched by Ursula out of the study and down the corridor. The creak of his wheelchair following behind broke into her trance. She blinked, suddenly alert and anxious. What was happening? Where was she being taken? She planted her feet stubbornly down on the floor. Ursula swivelled about, grimaced, and grasped Emily's elbow painfully.

'No, no force. Leave her,' Dr Stikannos purred. 'She must

take these steps of her own accord. The girl must walk unaided to her painful pleasure. Remember, Emily,' his voice softened, 'remember the fate of the Nubian? She too wore that collar, that badge of shameful pride. You now wear it. Her fate has become yours.'

Emily closed her eyes and shivered as she recalled the account of the rebellious Nubian being dragged across the desert sands to her punishment, as she vividly imagined the naked slave girl struggling and writhing at the end of the tightening chain. Yes, in the desert at midnight. But here, in gentle, gentrified Wiltshire? On a late summer's sunny morning? Surely not. Wiltshire, teeming with pale yellow sandstone manor houses peopled with pedigree and privilege. This wasn't happening. It just wasn't true…

'Emily?'

The sound of her name being insistently repeated drew her out of her reverie.

'Do you really wish to have a chain attached to that collar? Do you, Emily? Must we be forced to drag you in such an unseemly manner to the whipping post?' he reasoned.

Emily shook her head in mute resentment.

'Well?'

She bowed her head and started to walk slowly, hating her capitulation and ready acceptance of his words, but hating even more the threat of being ignominiously chained.

'Excellent,' he whispered. The wheelchair creaked.

'Move.' The crisp command came from Ursula.

The sombre procession left the mansion by a side door and made its silent progress towards the gym. Out on the shining cobblestones a tomcat padded up, whiskers twitching inquisitively. Ursula's green eyes flashed, and the cat turned tail and scuttled off into the shadows.

It was eight feet high, two feet in circumference and padded with a hessian cladding of sacking. Ursula took careful pains to arrange the naked girl securely at the whipping post, tying

Emily's ankles down at either side of its base and then binding her wrists high above her blonde mane.

'Perfect,' Dr Stikannos approved. 'Now get the cane.'

Emily squirmed, instinctively testing her bondage. But Ursula had been brutally efficient, rendering her captive immobile at the post. Bound naked and helpless in her burning cords, all Emily could just about manage was to nuzzle her nipples into the coarse hessian and press her hot pubis against the itchy sacking stretched around her pillar of pain.

Ursula, echoing the techniques of Persian slave traders centuries ago, had deliberately arranged her victim's feet at either side of the post so that they were forced to curl slightly inwards, their soft soles curved to kiss the hessian, their tiny toes whitening as they scrabbled to grip.

Utterly helpless in her bondage, Emily squirmed to ease the tension in her neck and across her straining shoulders, but all movement and attempt at ease was impossible. And to her horror and shame, the stricture of her bondage was already kindling a tiny flame of delight deep down in her belly. A tiny flame of delight that flickered and danced as Emily struggled and wriggled once more, ravishing her breasts and peaked nipples painfully into the post.

Swish!

A single note from the silver Sumatran's song of sorrow. Ursula had returned, cane in hand. She stood behind and slightly to one side of the bound nude.

Swish!

The whippy cane sliced down once more, cutting the empty air with an evil hiss.

Swish!

The third practice stroke filled the silence with its eerie thrum.

Above her blonde head Emily's bound wrists writhed. Her fingers spread out like startled starfish. Against the ticklish hessian, her labia, already sticky, peeled apart. Emily almost swooned as her wet slit kissed the harsh sacking into which her pubis was pressed. No, it wasn't happening. Was Dr Stikannos not mistaken? Had he read her true nature so correctly? To her shame, she realised that she was indeed responding to the burning ropes that bound her so tightly. And to the haunting swish of Ursula's singing bamboo, which was about to burn her bottom so blisteringly. She was responding to the promise of pain as though velvet caresses awaited her nakedness, swollen with the promise of pleasure. Her wet labia dragged open against the hessian. Emily grunted. Eyes tightly shut, gritting her teeth, she fought desperately to deny the terrible truth. No, she was not like that. He was wrong…

Ursula levelled the cane against the curved swell of her victim's bare bottom. A slight, supple wrist movement inched the thin wood inwards, dimpling and indenting the crowns of the satin cheeks. Emily shivered at the cool kiss of the wood. A spasm of dread rippled across each buttock, joggling them deliciously.

'Commence,' growled Dr Stikannos, his excitement thickening his normally controlled voice and treading his customary composure. 'Give Emily her stripes.'

She tensed, but nothing could have prepared her for, or protected her against, the first dreadful stroke. The silver Sumatran rod swished down at an angle, lashing the upper quarters of her poised peaches. Emily squealed shrilly. Ursula jerked the tip of the cane down against the swell of her victim's left thigh. Above, the dancing globes of whipped flesh bore a reddening weal.

'Again.' His voice had risen half an octave in his tightened throat.

Swish!

As the bamboo sliced down Emily's toes dug frantically into the sacking, and above her flounced mane her fingers splayed out in an arabesque of anguish.

'Again.'

Ursula administered the third: another cruel stroke. It whistled in horizontally to bite into the buttocks with mathematical exactitude, leaving a fresh thin red line across the naked cheeks. Above, the precise stripes planted by the unerring rod were darkening slightly into purpling pain-made-visible.

Against the post her peaked nipples ached viciously. At the base of her belly, her hot slit seethed. The seeping of her juices scalded her inner thigh flesh. To her horror, Emily felt the first vague rumour of an orgasmic pulse plucking deep within her wet heat, felt the merest ripples of those muscular convulsions that heralded eventual climactic paroxysm.

'Not too fast. Punishment must not be rushed. Pace her pain so that both her body and mind can savour it slowly,' Dr Stikannos whispered. The wheelchair rattled as he inched his metal mask towards her whipped cheeks. 'Four more,' he pronounced. 'But slowly, my dear. The pleasure of pain is a feast. But it is a banquet,' he added darkly, 'that must be taken leisurely, by both the punisher and the punished.'

The punisher. Emily imagined damp patches under Ursula's armpits where the sweat of exertion darkened the white cotton vest. Within that vest, Ursula's breasts would be swollen, rounded and heavy with arousal, the nipples fierce points of dark desiring.

The punished. Emily was the punished, silently mouthing the syllables like a spanked schoolgirl resentfully learning her Latin verbs. The punished. A hot spindle of liquid lust wept from her inner labia. Her clitoral bud raked into the hessian. She screamed aloud.

Ursula, examining the tip of her glinting cane, bowed her cropped head, acknowledging her master's instructions. 'As you so rightly say,' she murmured, briefly licking the bamboo, 'the pleasure of pain must not be rushed. Let her naked flesh dwell for a spell in fearful anticipation.'

The wheelchair groaned as he writhed pleasurably. God,

Emily thought, the woman was giving him a verbal wank. Talking up the whipping to make him come. And she was their plaything. But, she suddenly realised, it was a deliciously disturbing sensation: to be bound and striped before him, causing his shaft to thicken and stiffen. To be helpless and at his mercy, but inflaming him and arousing him to come. She closed her eyes, shrinking from – but reluctantly compelled by – the image of his stream of hot release splashing her scalded cheeks as he spurted over her caned bottom. No, not that. Please not that…

Emily drowned in the depths of her confusion. She slumped against the whipping post, rasping her clitoris once more against the coarse hessian. She tossed her head back as she squealed – a loud, long paean to savage joy.

'Stripe her,' Dr Stikannos barked.

Swish!

The bamboo spoke, obediently answering the instruction. Emily hissed her anguish. The wood had whipped down savagely, searing her clenched cheeks with a withering stripe. Rigid in her bondage, her spine arrow-straight, she sobbed brokenly.

Behind her the wheelchair tyres squeaked on the polished gym floor. Suddenly, Emily felt the coldness of a silk shirt against her hot flesh. It was Dr Stikannos. Up close and very, very personal. She sighed aloud at the cool silk as his shoulder snuggled up to take the soft weight of her naked buttocks, and sighed again as his silken shirt sleeve encircled her clamped thighs. Then the ice cold of his metal mask as it pressed fully into both buttocks. Emily shrieked like a lapwing taken in flight by the talons of a falcon.

'Again,' he whispered, his command muffled as his mask nestled into her soft cheek's curve.

Emily felt, fleetingly, the butterfly of his whispered breath at her flesh. So intimately invasive. So delicately dominant. Then the brutal lash of the bamboo across her trapped, bulging buttocks.

'Again.'

His encircling arm tightened expectantly as his shoulder bunched her bare bottom up for the cane. The metal mask crushed devotedly into her outer thigh. The silver Sumatran, competently plied by the cruel chastiser, struck once more, the fierce tip landing less than an eighth of an inch from the edge of the mask.

Emily sobbed aloud, but was silenced almost immediately by the touch of his leathered fingertip forced up between her clamped thighs into her pussy. She moaned as she felt the leather probe her sticky heat.

'Wet,' he pronounced. 'Wet when whipped, Emily. I believe our journey has well and truly begun.

'Leave us now,' he commanded, his cold mask grazing Emily's hot flesh as Dr Stikannos ordered Ursula to depart.

Rigid and helpless at the whipping post, her bare bottom ablaze after the administration of the blistering bamboo, Emily wept softly. Softly and silently, her grey eyes awash with her shame and sorrow. Just as softly, her sex wept its warm arousal. Her face shone with the salt of her sorrow. Her inner thighs shone with the scald of her sweet shame.

She felt the metal mask full upon her buttocks, felt its cool surface pressing in against her caned cheeks. The gloved fingertips, at each hip, steadied and stilled the quivering globes within their controlling grasp. The mask pressed more dominantly, then Emily felt the wet tip of his probing tongue, flickering out to lick and lap at the burning weals where the cane had kissed. She tensed. The darting tongue retreated behind the cold metal, and Emily unclenched her tightly bunched buttocks.

'Lexa… Lexa at her post of punishment and pain.' His whispered words, curdled by a dark chuckle, caused Emily to juice furiously as the memory of the tiny figure frozen in amber flooded back to sear her imagination.

She burned at his intimate knowledge of her private, secret

thoughts. Lexa, at her whipping post. Dr Stikannos knew every twist and turn of her mind, Emily thought. Damn him. Damn him to hell. Dr Stikannos had known; known, seen and understood. Was there no escaping his dark wisdom, his awareness of hidden sexual psyche?

'Lexa,' he murmured, raking his thumb down her cleft between the whipped cheeks. 'My own little Lexa.'

She started to come.

Oh God, no. He'd know. He'd see her. Smell her. Finger her shameful wetness.

Emily squeezed her cheeks together as she struggled to deny that which could not – would not – be denied. The welling climax was implacable. Her sex dripped, as if drooling over the delights to come. She strove vainly, twisting in her taut bondage, to postpone the inevitable.

The cold metal of his mask crushed into her hot cheeks more fiercely. She sensed him sniffing deeply, savouring her feral essence. Spasming as she writhed in the violence of her orgasm, Emily jerked her hips back as far as the restraining cords would permit, grinding her bottom into his face.

His tongue became busy at her spread cleft, licking and probing at her tight anal whorl. The rosebud sphincter opened its petals and puckered to the wet tongue. Emily shrieked, renewing her jerking and rolling her buttocks frenziedly. He grunted. She felt the tongue retreat instantly. He cursed viciously. Something strange, which her mind could not comprehend, was happening. The mask, loosened and dislodged by her joggling buttocks, slued across his face. The cold metal, now clouded by her anal heat, slithered down across the swell of her clamped thighs. Emily squealed, and the wheelchair groaned as he twisted in its confines. Emily heard the mask fall harshly down onto the polished wooden floor. Glimpsing down instinctively she saw the gleaming surface below, and then looked directly into her own contorted features: reflected back up to her from the shining mask that had kept the damaged face of Dr Stikannos hidden from her gaze. Peering intently, she saw her mouth twisted in dismay, then she saw her own grey eyes widening in alarm. In the top half of the shining, upturned mask, she saw the twisted blackened features of her host and master. The scarred and scorched face of Dr Stikannos, unmasked, revealing the ravages of the fire.

Emily shrieked. The whipping post seemed to crumble and collapse within her grasp. The bright neon lights of the gym burned bright crimson, silver and then black: Emily fainted, dragging down into the depths of her unconsciousness the terrifying image revealed in the mask at her bound feet.

Chapter Four

Emily awoke but kept her eyes shut. The soft sounds, and softer light, at her bedroom window told her that it was a full hour before dawn. Wood pigeons murmured to themselves up in the tops of trembling elms. Higher up in the violet light of retreating night, a nightingale spilled down its cascade of liquid delight.

Her brain kicked in, calculating. She must have slept all afternoon, all evening and through most of the night. Yes, now she remembered. So who had brought her to her room? Whose hands had loosened those binding cords that had held her at the whipping post? Whose hands had eased her, naked and severely caned, into her bed?

Severely caned.

The words detonated in her brain like a couple of grams of semtex. Emily tightened her eyes – and her buttocks. She flinched. Her clenched cheeks, nestling into the cool sheets beneath, still stung after the burning kiss of the bamboo Ursula had used to punish her.

Emily shuddered and opened her eyes. Staring up into the silk canopy of her ornate bed, her grey eyes widened and adjusted to the half-light just before sunrise. A tiny movement up above caught her attention. Her eyes narrowed. Yes, there. Up in a fold in the silk of the overhanging canopy. A butterfly, fluttering with graceful frenzy. Butterfly. She remembered hearing on the radio how the young W B Yeats had written flutterby in error. They called it poetry then. Now it's dyslexia. She propped herself up on one elbow. The top sheet slithered down from her shoulders to her belly, sinuous and sensual as it rasped the breasts it revealed. The butterfly struggled against the silk in silent fury. A small white blur, its outer wings smudged orange. She decided to let the trembling captive free.

Emily stole out of her sumptuous bed and padded silently across the Chinese silk carpet to the window. Gently easing down the upper half of the sash frame a fraction, she stood back and watched. The sweetness of the early morning breeze rippled the velvet drapes. Up in the tented silk, the orange tip fluttered in the cool draught then zigzagged towards the fresh air at the opened window. It paused, hovering – hovering on the very brink of freedom.

Go on. Fly. Take your chance, Emily willed it. Freedom. But the orange tip flitted back into the shadows of the bedroom, alighted on the far wall and folded its wings together in silent surrender.

Emily stumbled back to her bed and sat down, her rounded cheeks dimpling the mattress, her golden hair curtaining her anxious eyes. Tear-spangled eyes. The orange tip had refused its freedom and remained. Here, in this house of the collector, everything beautiful remained trapped in captivity. Fine works of art. Butterflies. Her.

Emily moaned softly. The orange tip renounced its freedom, remaining within the walls of servitude. Had she too subconsciously chosen captivity? Was she in fact a stubborn-willing victim? Had she secretly longed to be stripped and striped? Had she really been forced to submit to the shameful lash? Or had she stumbled to her whipping post and embraced it with a sullen eagerness? Like the orange tip butterfly quivering in the shadows, had she chosen to remain?

Emily slept, face down on her bed. Outside, swallows squeaked and swooped as the first rays of the sun brought sparrows scuttling in the eaves. In her sleep, she dreamed. In her dreams, the stern hand that had gripped the whippy cane became a soothing, flattened palm. A palm that gently caressed her upturned bottom – a bottom that still burned beneath its crimson stripes.

Emily snuggled down into the stretched silk, squirming as she squashed her breasts deliciously beneath her. Her lips parted in a welcoming smile as, in her dreams, a delicately dominant fingertip traced each stripe across her upturned cheeks. Depressing the satin flesh of each soft buttock, the caressing fingertip stroked the crimson weals one by one. In her sleep, Emily grunted her assent and inched her bottom up submissively. The fingertip withdrew – only to be replaced by the touch of firm knuckles kneading her rubbery rump. Kneading her bamboo-striped cheeks with a soothing tenderness. In her dreams, Emily shuddered and sighed.

The fingertip swept down between her cheeks, skimming the velvet of her cleft and pausing to tap-tap at her anal whorl. Emily shivered as her belly imploded, sending sweet frissons rippling down to her innermost core. A fluttering troubled her stomach, as if the orange tip butterfly had become trapped inside her, raking the walls of her belly with its maddening wings. She awoke: her eyes wide with wonder. Twisting to look over her right shoulder, she glimpsed Susie perched on the edge of her bed. The maid gazed down, completely absorbed by the bare bottom below.

Their eyes met.

'Poor Emily,' Susie whispered, her flattened palm again soothing the surface of Emily's left buttock. 'Poor sore bottom.'

'What are you…' Emily began to ask, easing herself up and peeling her breasts away from the silk sheet.

'Sh,' Susie whispered. 'Let me kiss you better.'

Emily sank her nakedness back down onto the cool sheet, stretching her arms languorously out in surrender up at either side of her bolster and shyly inching her thighs apart. She held her breath as Susie's head bowed down, and squeezed her eyes tight as she felt the maid's warm lips kiss her punished cheeks. Susie's tongue flickered. Emily gasped and bit into the pillow, screaming softly.

'Sh,' the maid insisted, hissing the warning into the rounded buttock at her lips.

A liquid lapping filled the silence of the half-darkened bedroom. The liquid lapping of Susie's tongue busy at the bare bottom. Luxuriating in the tender aftercare, Emily snuggled down into her bed, offering her cane-striped buttocks up to the ministrations of the maid's wet mouth.

Soon the warm lips were kissing – kissing and gently sucking – the satin skin of each firm flesh-mound. Emily's breasts grew heavy, aching sweetly. Her nipples peaked, rasping the sheet beneath her soft warmth. She squirmed and spread her cheeks wide as Susie buried her face into the bare bottom before her, nuzzling into the dark cleft between the whipped cheeks with gentle ferocity.

Emily sighed, easing her bottom up as she signalled her impatience for more.

'I brought this,' Susie murmured, sitting up and unscrewing the top of a jar of face cream. Its fragrance filled the bedroom. 'It will soothe your stripes. Just keep still…'

Emily obeyed, happy to have her naked buttocks submit to even more delicious aftercare. Susie dug her fingertips into the jar. They emerged heavily anointed. Dimpling the dome of the left cheek down, she caressed the bare buttock with ever widening circles, skimming the shining skin with her creamed fingertips until they swept the outer curve of the fleshy cheek, and swept down along the inner curve, tracing the shadow of the velvety cleft. Emily squealed.

The maid's hand trembled and retreated, resting palm down into the crown of the ripe cheek. 'Sh,' Susie warned. 'If Ursula…'

Emily's buttocks tightened instantly at the sound of the name, but Susie giggled and gave the captive buttock a reassuring squeeze.

'It's all right,' she soothed. 'They don't know I'm here. I brought you some breakfast, but I'd better get back downstairs.'

'No, don't. Please don't go.'

'Just a bit more, then,' Susie relented, palming each cheek tenderly. 'Nice?'

Emily nodded into the pillow as she eased her thighs further apart and relaxed her buttocks so that once more the cleft opened invitingly.

Susie soothed both proffered cheeks until they glistened beneath the sheen of the healing balm.

'Wonderful,' Emily murmured, wriggling her rump.

After a further silence broken only by the soft sounds of skin caressing skin, Susie spoke.

'Did it… did it hurt?'

Emily burrowed down into the bolster and remained silent.

'Tell me,' the maid whispered. 'The cane, when Ursula whipped you. Was it dreadful?'

'Yes – no – I'm not sure,' Emily stammered.

'It did hurt, didn't it?'

'I don't want to talk about it.'

'I understand,' Susie replied, gently sinking her straightened index finger down between the creamed cheeks into Emily's pink anus. 'I hate the cane, and Ursula can be such a cruel chastiser. I hate it when it bites my bottom, but…'

'But?' Emily relaxed her cheeks, accepting the finger into her sphincter.

'I hate it when it's over,' Susie confessed, her tone suddenly frank, her words simple and sincere. 'The punishment – it leaves a hunger inside me. I miss it.'

Emily rose up from the pillow, twisting her face around to face the maid. 'Miss it?' Her bright eyes widened.

'You know what I mean, don't you,' Susie countered, driving her finger into Emily's rectal warmth. 'Don't you?'

Emily blinked and grunted softly, but she shook her head. 'No, I don't know what you're talking about.'

'Yes you do,' Susie persisted gently. 'Being tied, helpless, and having your bottom caned. Inching up on your toes and squirming as the quivering cane hovers over your bottom. The delicious dread. Being tied tightly, bound and helpless. The painful pleasure,' she added, pumping Emily rhythmically, 'the pleasurable pain.'

Again Emily shook her head, struggling to deny what she inwardly knew to be true. But it was truth she flinched from accepting or acknowledging. A truth she buried in denial.

Susie added a second straightened finger to the first and sank both deep into Emily's muscled warmth. The anal passage gripped them lovingly, longingly.

Susie closed her eyes and, as if in a trance, whispered excitedly. She repeated her words, mentioning once more the delicious dread of shivering before the next stroke, the next cruel cut of the cane. Of hating it – and yet wanting it. Hating and wanting. Hating what one secretly desired. The sweet paradox of masochistic delight. The dark desire to be disciplined…

'No, no, you're wrong,' Emily protested, grinding her hips and nudging her bottom against Susie's fist.

'Am I?' Susie scissored the two fingers open, stretching Emily's tight warmth and causing her happy victim to scream softly.

Just as the bedroom door burst open and Chloe strode in.

'So,' she snarled, 'this is where you are. I thought you were out feeding those peacocks. Breakfast is late. You'd better get down to the kitchen at once; Ursula's waiting for you, and she's got the strap ready.'

Susie scrambled up from the bed, hastily wiping her fingers against her thigh, and Chloe watched in silence as the frightened maid scuttled quickly from the bedroom. Emily, burrowing down hastily beneath her top sheet, attempted to hide her nakedness – and her blushing shame – from the raven-haired intruder.

'I've brought your bag, Emily, and your things. Seems you'll be staying here for a while.'

And your things.

Emily peeped up and saw Chloe gripping her dildo.

'This where you hid the letters, hmm?' Chloe raised the shaft, and Emily's shame and anger deepened, crimsoning her face. She looked away, but not quickly enough to avoid glimpsing the cruel grin on the lips of her tormentor; lips that fleeting kissed the tip of the dildo.

'And Ursula said you're not to have any outdoor clothes, and no socks or shoes. Just a vest and panties. Ursula's locked the rest of your stuff away.'

'But—'

'To stop you trying to escape. You wouldn't get very far barefoot, now would you?' Her tone changed to an authoritative bark. 'Let me see your bottom.'

In response, Emily drew her knees to her bosom and tugged the sheet up to her chin.

'Come along, face down, bottom up,' Chloe snapped waspishly. 'I want to see exactly what Ursula's cane did.'

Emily remained reluctant to submit her buttocks to the other's cruel gaze.

'Show me your bottom,' Chloe hissed. 'You've no choice, you know,' she continued, her voice a purr. 'You're not a guest here. Dr Stikannos made that perfectly clear. You're ours now.'

Emily knew that further resistance was futile. She was utterly helpless. She had become just another item in the collection. To be viewed, inspected and appreciated according to the whim of each of her captors.

'Thought you'd see sense,' Chloe crowed, sensing and savouring her power over the naked blonde.

Inching the sheet down and shrugging it from her shoulders as she twisted and turned, face down into her pillow, Emily presented her bare bottom for Chloe's intimate perusal.

Chloe, angling her elbows, cupped her raven hair up above her head and smoothed it into a ponytail as, chin jutting

99

and eyes sparkling, she gazed down imperiously upon the ravished buttocks below. After an intense silence she withdrew her hands from her hair – her ponytail collapsed, fanning out over her shoulders – and brought her palms to each breast. Squeezing them gently, she bunched her bosom up then thumbed each nipple beneath the tight stretch of her white cotton vest. Emily shuddered as she heard the dark-haired girl hissing her satisfaction in a sigh of carnal contentment.

'Ursula striped you well. Did it hurt?'

Emily refused to answer.

'I asked you a question and I demand an answer.'

Emily remained mute.

'You will have to learn to be obedient, bitch,' Chloe warned, raising and arching her right leg, flexing it at her supple knee, before planting her rubber-soled trainer down along the line of the cleft between Emily's cane-striped cheeks. Dominantly depressing her trainer into the shadowy cleft, she grunted softly as she trod the burgeoning buttocks below. The cleft yawned slightly, the bulging cheeks – flattened beneath the rubber sole – spread enticingly.

'Did it hurt? Did the bamboo burn as it bit?'

'Yes,' Emily confessed, her reply a muffled whisper as she crushed her mumbling lips into the pillow.

'And did you like it? Being bound so tightly and caned so searchingly?'

Squirming beneath the suggestive words and the cruel footwear, Emily buried her face deeper into the pillow.

'Hmm? Did you enjoy your punishment?' The rubber sole squashed dominantly, bullying the bare buttocks. Chloe reached down impatiently and clutched her victim's lustrous blonde hair. 'Answer me, bitch. Did you like receiving your stripes?'

Emily froze, unable to escape the cruel grip.

'Well?'

'No,' came the whispered, reluctant response.

'Little liar,' Chloe triumphed. 'I examined the post afterwards. When they'd gone and the gym was deserted. I saw the wet patch at the whipping post. Smelt it. Tasted it with my tongue…'

Emily moaned.

'The wet patch of soaked hessian you left behind after your punishment. The wet patch just where your belly crushed up against the whipping post. Can you not remember your hips jerking as the cane lashed down, forcing your pussy to kiss the frame?'

Chloe's foot suddenly slipped from Emily's cream-shiny rump, and Emily squealed as the raking sole skidded down the outer curve of the cheek Susie had soothed with the aftercare balm.

Chloe grunted as she knelt over her victim, straddling the bare bottom between her pinioning knee. 'I've got a little score to settle with you, blonde bitch,' she said menacingly.

Emily shivered, remembering Ursula's jealous green eyes; remembering the smothered screams she'd heard on the evening of her arrival; remembering Chloe's crop-striped buttocks glimpsed the next morning in the silence of the gym.

'No, please,' Emily whimpered, dreading the vicious tenderness she knew Chloe was capable of dispensing.

Reaching down to the side of the bed, Chloe snatched up Emily's bag and again fished out the dildo. Fingering it delicately, and licking its blunt snout with the tip of her tongue, she tossed it up and caught it, holding it dagger-like in her tightened fist.

Emily bucked in a desperate bid to dislodge her straddling tormentor, but Chloe rode her naked victim assuredly, taming and controlling Emily's writhing nakedness between her thighs.

'That's better,' Chloe purred as Emily slumped submissively, then she eased back onto her heels and aimed the dildo between Emily's tightened cheeks. The cruel snout nuzzled the shrivelled sphincter.

Chloe sensed the resistance. 'Open,' she commanded.

Emily squealed, waggling her rump to rid it of the dominant dildo at her anal whorl.

'Unclamp your thighs,' Chloe ordered, inching the tip of the dildo from the tight pink rosebud and swiftly raking it down along the cleft's velvet to the labial crease below. 'Come on, let me see pussy.'

'You can't, I'll tell Ursula,' Emily said defiantly, suddenly rallying. The cold tip of the dildo slid away from the warmth of her slit, and she sensed instantly that she had scored a direct hit.

'Little bitch, you wouldn't dare tell Ursula—'

'Tell Ursula what?' came the sharp demand from the opening door.

'N-nothing,' Chloe stammered. 'I-I was just telling her that she—'

'I will tell Emily all she needs to know,' Ursula broke in smoothly as she strode towards the bed. 'Go downstairs and be about your business.'

Chloe climbed sulkily from the bed, vainly trying to conceal the dildo in her clenched fist.

'Give me that.' The green eyes narrowed dangerously.

Slowly, her own eyes averted, her raven hair spilling down as she knelt and bowed her head submissively, Chloe surrendered the dildo to Ursula's outstretched hand.

'Head up. Look at me.

Emily heard the raven-haired girl's troubled moan.

'I see you have failed to learn from the lessons I taught you, Chloe dear,' Ursula said, sternly applying the dildo to Chloe's trembling lips. 'Perhaps I was not strict enough, hmm? Perhaps I shall have to be a little harsher with you, to make sure you learn your lessons well…

'Learn your lessons well!' she hissed, ruthlessly driving the dildo into Chloe's mouth.

From her bed, Emily heard Chloe whimpering as Ursula

bullied the kneeling girl, one hand plying the dildo while the other cupped, captured and squeezed Chloe's breasts.

'Go down to the gym,' Ursula eventually said. 'I will join you there presently. I have to teach you, Chloe dear, and you must learn.'

Chloe rose, staggering slightly, and silently left the bedroom.

'And as for you,' Ursula said, tap-tapping the tip of the dildo against her open palm as she turned towards the bed. 'Time you got to work.'

'Cataloguing?' Emily murmured, sitting on the edge of the bed and attempting to shield her naked bosom from Ursula's avid gaze.

'Get dressed.'

Emily scooped up the tiny white shorts and struggled into them, grunting softly as she dragged them up over her buttocks. Ursula echoed the grunt with her own as the material moulded Emily's cheeks, biting deeply into her cleft, and watched hungrily as her captive plucked the tight cotton from her pubic mound.

'Vest,' she instructed, thumbing the dildo firmly.

Emily buried her head into the cropped vest and wriggled it down over her shoulders. Its tight stretch squashed her braless breasts, squeezing them deliciously, deepening the dark valley of her cleavage. As she fingered the scalloped neckline, she touched the collar Dr Stikannos had placed around her throat; the glittering yoke of servitude. She blinked, her eyes brimming with alarm.

'Hard, honest work for a little thief,' Ursula murmured pensively. 'There's plenty to keep a spoiled brat like you busy in a mansion this size, girl. Scrubbing, polishing; even an art expert can appreciate the brushwork required to bring up the patina of a flagstone floor.' Emily's blush deepened. 'I'll see to it that you earn your keep, my girl. Follow me.'

Emily, still fingering the collar at her throat, turned towards the bedroom door as a slight movement – no more than a flicker in the corner of her eye – caused her to glance up at the ceiling. There, fluttering helplessly against the expanse of pale plaster, the orange-tip butterfly was struggling in its self-appointed doom. Head bowed, Emily followed Ursula through the door, her naked feet falling silently onto the carpet of Chinese silk.

For the next three long bleak days Emily's hands grew red and sore as she knelt to her tasks, scrubbing the endless maze of stone passageways that criss-crossed the rear of the mansion. Of Dr Stikannos she saw or heard nothing, and actually longed to hear the creak of his wheelchair or the smooth, modulated purr of his educated voice.

Every morning, after rising early, Ursula or the spiteful Chloe would dictate her duties for the day, providing buckets of hot soapy water and a scrubbing brush. And with the bucket and brush came plenty of strict supervision.

Kneeling, her sore knees bruised by the stone flags, time and its passage became unmeasured except for the shadows creeping before her as the late summer sun's rays pierced the mullion windows. Time. Would Emily still be there in the softer sunshine of autumn. Or, she panicked, peer out from her house of bondage to glimpse the greys and silvers of a winter landscape?

Helpless and increasingly hopeless, Emily scrubbed obediently, ever fearful of the quivering crop or cane her vigilant tormentors were eager to use on her upturned bottom.

Even Susie was a stranger, briefly appearing to serve frugal meals on a tray. Emily was no longer welcome at the communal kitchen table and was forbidden the dining room of Dr Stikannos. Susie brought scraps, or soup and bread and occasional pieces of stolen cheese or fruit, departing into the shadows as quickly and as anxiously as she had appeared.

Once, frantically signalling for silence, Susie risked

bringing Emily a teacup full of aromatic gin and tonic. Emily grinned, gulping it greedily, but Susie's frightened eyes had been brimming with mute eloquence. The maid had no doubt risked a whipping, Emily realised as she relished the stolen treat.

Ursula changed Emily's accommodation, moving her out of the sumptuous room with the silk carpet and canopied four-poster bed into a miserable little attic once occupied by servant girls. No more luxury. No more fridge full of delicious goodies. No more digital television or rejuvenating power-shower. Just a grim, iron-framed narrow bed with a lumpy mattress and two pauper's blankets. From the bare window, all Emily could see was the red brick of an abutting gable. Even the sweet birdsong that had greeted her each dawn now remained silent in this shadowed corner of the mansion.

Emily crawled into her bed, every limb aching. The iron frame groaned as she stretched out on the unwelcoming mattress. The room, darkened by the gable blocking out the sunset, was chilly. She pulled up the rough blankets. They grazed her nipples and scratched her shoulders as she dragged them up to her chin. Wriggling down in her irksome bed, she gazed around at her bleak quarters. Who had been the last to sleep here? A couple of land girls, billeted for the duration. Town girls, from shops and offices, their pale limbs darkening with a harvest tan. At night, breasts crushing, thighs melting into one another, they would twist and turn in ecstasy as they reaped darker pleasures. Emily could almost smell the chicken meal on the strong, slender hands of the dominant cupping and caressing the captive breasts of the quivering submissive. Land girls, denied the arms of men, seeking expression for their fierce lustful longings in each other's naked embrace.

Emily tossed and turned in her narrow bed. Her tired body ached for sleep but her imagination kindled brightly. Gazing up at the leprous walls of peeling paper and flaking paint, she pictured the room a hundred years before. A hundred years before, when the stables would echo to the clip-clop of horses across the cobblestones below; horses steaming and stamping after being unharnessed from the carriages that had brought the guests to dine. A hundred years before, when bright chandeliers would sparkle, illuminating the pride of the county arraigned beneath as they took their places around the table, eager for the roasts and fowls brought from the kitchens by scampering, uniformed maids.

Uniformed maids, their trim little bodies tightly attired in crisp white linen and gleaming black silks. Emily closed her eyes and tried to imagine the maid who had been quartered up in this attic room a hundred years before. A dark-eyed, pale-faced girl. Smuggling a stolen rib of succulent beef up in her apron to gnaw at hungrily in the flickering candlelight.

A rattle at the door. It opens without her say-so. Emily imagined the startled maid thrusting her stolen morsel under her pillow – too late. Harold, the sleek-haired footman spotted her greasy chin before she had the wit to wipe it clean. He closes the door behind him, unhurried and self-assured.

'Cook's in a fury, girl. Says there's been thieving this night. In a fury, she be, and means to tell the mistress.'

On the bed, naked beside her crumpled maid's uniform, the dark-eyed girl shivers as her nervous hands – plucking at her apron – confirm her guilt.

Harold nods, his eyes shrewd and gleaming. An oiled lock tumbles from his carefully combed hair. 'Course, shan't tell or say nothin' if you was to be kind to a fellow.' Already he was unbuttoned down to his tight waistcoat.

The girl on the bed shrank back, squirming in both fear and shame. Her eyes follow every flicker of his white fingers as they grapple with his white braces.

'Just between us,' he winks lasciviously. His fingertips

dabble at his balls. The sac swings gently beneath his nodding erection.

He takes her brutally, like a terrier at a rat. Squirming beneath him, the maid wriggles belly down into her bed, innocently believing herself to be denying him her fanny. He makes do with her bare bottom for his pleasure, thumbing her quivering cheeks apart. She curses him as he rides her, his powerful thighs scissoring her squashed cheeks after he has hammered home and emptied himself into her tight warmth.

Wiping his length dry on her starched apron, he dresses, carefully avoiding her tear-filled eyes.

'And what's all this then?' he barks, fishing out the half-eaten rib of beef.

'But you said—' she cries.

'And don't you go blubbin' to cook or mistress about any of this,' he warns, biting into the rib wolfishly and chewing hard. 'They'll be a whippin' you fierce enough for this, lass.' He held up the morsel, now bitten to the bone. He returned, like Judas before him, to betray her below stairs.

Below stairs. Emily pinched her nipples fiercely as she conjured up the scene. The rattle of the departing carriages, their tiny yellow lamps quite useless against the darkness of the gathering night.

Below stairs. Frightened whispering in the pantry and the still-room. Cook's with the mistress now, reporting the theft. There'll be a whipping before all gather for night prayers. A whipping. The servants are in a flurry. Livened men feel their cocks stiffening expectantly. Uniformed maids blush as their pussies melt and moisten. A whipping before night prayers.

Emily's fingertips arabesque across her flattened belly, then trickle down to her pubic fringe. Playfully, they part the feathery down curtaining her moist lips. Sternly they part them. A thumb traps and tames her clitoral thorn. A whipping before night prayers.

Below stairs. The male servants have been banished. Only the mistress, the housekeeper, cook and four maids are to witness the punishment. The little thief, shivering in her shame is forced, bare-bottomed, across the kitchen table. Her trembling hands grasp the black Bible. Into the dull, dark leather, her penitent lips mumble her contrition as cook marches to the far end of the table and grips the writhing maid's outstretched hands at each wrist.

'All yours, m'm,' cook whispers, her piggy eyes glinting in her fat red face. 'All yours.'

Mistress delivers a stinging rebuke to the little thief, and a solemn sermon to the circle of servants. And all the time, as her thin lips twitch to utter her sententious words on piety, probity and penance, her jewelled fingers feel the supple lash of the dog whip.

Emily masturbated furiously as she pictured the dog whip lashing the bare-bottomed maid, peaking and crying out as she imagined the mistress bending down to examine the striped cheeks – and catching the glint of the footman's semen, and the whiff of his seed. The dog whip cracked down furiously as, enraged, the mistress lashed the sinful flesh of the maid.

And then later, the master. Acquainted of the poor maid's fate, he slips from his dressing room at midnight, his footsteps silent on the carpeted landing. Opening the maid's bedroom door he enters, curious to see the mark of the dog whip upon her soft peaches. The master, in the moonlight, inching down the blankets and inching up her shift. The bared bottom in the moonlight. The master's proprietorial hand cupping and squeezing the punished flesh of his serving girl. His little whipped maid.

Emily felt her liquid flame between her clamped thighs as once more the ghosts from the past flooded her – flooded her brain and her pulsing slit.

The master.

Emily shuddered. She was no safer than that maid a

hundred years before. Like the maid, whose bottom belonged to her cruel mistress, Emily's flesh was Ursula's to punish as she pleased. And afterwards, could not the master take his pleasure too? Could not Dr Stikannos, at any moment, send for Emily and force her to be subject to his whim?

No, that was then – one hundred years before. In the moonlight the whipped maid would suffer her master's fingers at – then between – her weal-reddened buttocks. But that was then. Emily sighed; soon she would be fast asleep.

Emily, hot and sweaty after her orgasm, tossed fretfully on the brink of her elusive sleep. The master. The words insinuated themselves in her mind, gliding around her tired brain like the serpent around Eve's apple. The master. The cruel Victorian squire of her recent fantasy who held the whipped maid in his thrall. Emily opened her eyes and shivered. Dr Stikannos. Hadn't he held her, perused her intimately, dominated her nakedness as she slumped, bound and striped, at the whipping post?

She shivered again at the sudden memory of his blackened, twisted face glimpsed in the metal mask that had fallen down at her feet. Sitting up in her narrow bed, she hugged her knees to her bosom. The blanket slipped down, baring her shoulders and slender back to the night chill. In the gloom of the attic the image of his contorted features loomed large – threatening and potent with menace. In the humiliations and discomfort of her recent days of servitude, the image had receded, but now it grew before her frightened eyes.

She needed a shower, a hot sluice in a bright bathroom. Away from the tiny room crowded with reawakening fears. Emily knew that if she kept quiet, quiet and very careful, she could be showered and back in her bed without disturbing the sleeping household.

Out on the landing she tested the floorboards to avoid

any telltale squeaks. Inching along in the darkness, hugging her towelling robe to her nakedness, she pawed blindly along the plaster wall. Left, her mind-map told her feet when they touched soft carpeting. A forty watt bulb glimmered outside the room she knew to be the bathroom.

Inside, her robe folded cross a chair, Emily pulled the plastic shower curtain aside, stepped in and drew the curtain across. The sluicing waters were every bit as delicious as she had anticipated. Tilting her face up into the punishing stream she surrendered to it completely, letting it rinse away her dark imaginings for the moment. Deprived of shower gel to massage her breasts and scented soap to cream her belly and buttocks, she made do with the mean chunk of yellow carbolic Ursula had dispensed grudgingly on the morning Emily had woken up to her servitude. The hard cake of pungent soap yielded little lather and no sensual pleasure, but she worked it against her shining skin, gasping softly as its rough edge grazed her nipples and raked deeply into the cleft between her wet cheeks. Tormenting fears whirled away at her toes, carried off with the suds dripping from her nakedness. Emily forgot the menace of the face behind the metal mask – until, fingering her wet blonde hair from her face, her thumbs touched the collar at her neck. She shivered, despite the hot shower, as she fleetingly stroked her yoke of submission.

A sound. The bathroom door opening gently. Then closing firmly. Ursula on the prowl? Ready and eager to pounce and administer more cruel strokes? Emily froze; a glistening statue beneath the fierce, steaming cascade. Too late for her trembling fingers to twist the tap off. Footsteps padding their approach across the linoleum. A scraping noise. The intruder had nudged the chair Emily had draped her robe across. Her heart hammered. She closed her eyes tightly. Could it be Chloe? Cruel Chloe, whose predatory designs on her bare bottom had not diminished.

Emily opened her eyes. A silhouette loomed at the plastic

curtain. An upraised arm. An outstretched hand fingering then grasping the opaque screen. Emily, blinking away the blinding sluice, inched away, squashing the curves of her dripping buttocks against the wet white tiles. A soft rasp as the curtain drew back...

'Susie!' Emily gasped.

The maid giggled, then looked dismayed at Emily's frightened face. 'It's only me. I went to your room, then thought I'd find you here.'

They kissed lingeringly. Reunited after days apart under Ursula's constant vigilance and Chloe's jealous gaze. Urgent tongues parried and probed as Emily's fingers found the tap and twisted it.

'Up a bit late, aren't you?' Emily teased, mumbling her lips into Susie's.

'Mmm? Oh, Ursula had me humping till midnight.'

'Humping? What can she mean?' Emily interrogated her block of yellow carbolic.

Susie giggled. 'A Transit came down from London.'

'A delivery of champagne and caviar, we trust,' Emily whispered to her soap.

'No fear. Whatever it was, Ursula treated it like nuclear waste. Six boxes, and they were heavy.'

Emily, more interested in the maid's lips than the words coming from them, proved a dull audience, but Susie went on anyway. 'Stupid bloody things. Little rope handles like baby elephant ears to grip. Kept bumping against my poor titties.'

'Rope handles?' Emily's eyes narrowed.

Susie nodded. She described the packing cases in resentful detail, and the flurry of spanks she received when she almost, but not actually, let one slip from her fingers. 'More awkward than heavy,' she concluded, cupping and tenderly squeezing Emily's buttocks.

The glistening nude purred appreciatively as the dimpling fingers at her soft cheeks made her cleft ache sweetly. But

111

she did not respond. She was thinking fast. From Susie's description, and her own knowledge of auction rooms and art galleries, those crates almost certainly contained one thing. Paintings.

Susie made a soft mewing sound. The fingers at Emily's wet bottom became more urgent, more insistent, dragging the captive orbs of flesh wider apart and squeezing the satin skin with increasing boldness. Emily flinched and squealed.

'Sh,' Susie giggled, fluttering her fingertips along the exposed ribbon of Emily's velvet cleft. 'Shove up, I'm coming in.'

As the maid wriggled out of her clothes and stepped into the shower, twisting on the tap and deftly grappling Emily for the carbolic brick, Emily calculated rapidly. More rare art, she conceded, but with a dodgy provenance. And all for her to authenticate and catalogue for the impending clandestine sale.

'Was he there?' she asked. 'Dr Stikannos?'

'Hmm?' Susie replied absently, the yellow cake of soap now at her slit.

'Inspecting the goods,' persisted Emily, suddenly blushing at the irony of her own remark.

'What goods? Oh, the crates, you mean.'

'Yes. Did Dr Stikannos examine the contents of the packing cases?'

'Um, no.' Susie was concentrating hard on her clitoris with a corner of the soap, and Emily's fingers stole down and enclosed the slippery carbolic.

'He's asleep, not to be disturbed,' Susie murmured, inching her thighs apart. 'Oooh…' she thumbed her labia apart to greet the rasp of the soap cake. 'Ursula made a big fuss about it all.'

'Fuss?' Emily tried to repress her awakening curiosity; not from her brain – from her tone of voice.

'Made the Transit park miles away…'

'Miles?'

'Well,' Susie grinned suddenly, 'a hundred yards away. On the lawn by the lime trees.'

Emily nodded.

'No lights, no noise. Made me carry the crates around the back and down into the cellars on tiptoe.'

'The cellars? But aren't they cold and damp?'

'Course not,' Susie scoffed, her emotions making her voice husky, 'air-conditioned, thermostatically controlled heating for the wine. Especially the vintage port.'

Emily nudged the soap up against Susie's slit, ravishing the little pink clitoris mercilessly, and Susie sobbed with delight. 'So Ursula didn't want Dr Stikannos to be disturbed,' she murmured thoughtfully.

Steadying herself against the wet tiles with her outstretched hands, the maid merely nodded as she surrendered to her approaching climax. Emily's thumbtip replaced the soap, worrying the love-thorn furiously.

The girls were caught by Chloe as they tiptoed back to Susie's room, splendid in her seamless oyster silk brassiere and matching panties, who challenged them in the corridor outside Susie's bedroom door. The crop in her hand had quivered as it rose up in a grim salute of welcome.

'Out of your room, girl?' Chloe snarled, whisking the little loop of leather at the tip of her crop against Susie's left breast. The tormented nipple puckered to a peak against the hide. 'And out of bounds after midnight, bitch?' Chloe stroked the cruel leather loop down over Emily's blonde snatch, delicately but dominantly skimming the labia beneath her pubic fringe. 'Get inside, both of you. Ursula told me to pay your rooms a visit. Said it might be worth my while. There's a whole sachertorte missing from the pantry. Ursula noted its absence. There's a penalty to pay for theft, Susie. The bitch here can attest to that.'

Huddling together as they squeezed through the bedroom door, both girls moaned. Inside, Chloe pointed the crop

113

towards the unmade bed.

'Ursula gave me this,' she swished the crop down, thrumming the air with it twice, before grasping and flexing its suppleness. 'And,' she hissed triumphantly, 'full permission to use it.'

Naked and bending across Susie's rumpled bed, their soft thighs touching as they pressed against each other for comfort in their mutual sorrow, Emily and Susie squeezed their eyes and buttocks tightly.

Swish!

Chloe lashed the crop down, striping the upturned buttocks accurately, kissing the crown of all four cheeks with a vicious crimson weal.

Swish! *Swish*!

Savage double swipes that elicited shrieks from both the punished nudes and brought them up on their whitening toes.

Swish!

The fourth cruel cut cracked down across the defenceless reddening cheeks. Susie choked on a stifled sob.

'Stop that snivelling. You know the rules, and you chose to break them. Bed and lights out – just like boarding school,' Chloe whispered, licking the little loop of ox-blood leather as she lapsed into a private memory. 'Behave like a silly little schoolgirl and you'll have the Prefects to answer to, understand?'

Susie remained silent, apart from a smothered sob.

'Understand?'

Swish!

The stroke was for Susie's bare bottom and Susie's bare bottom alone. Chloe took a half step forward to administer the withering cut – a slice of such severity that it left the maid's crimsoned cheeks clenched tightly in anguish. 'Understand?' Chloe insisted, pressing Susie down with the crop at the nape of her neck and forcing the whipped maid face down into the duvet.

'Yes…' she murmured sorrowfully.

'Leave her—' Emily began.

Swish, *crack*! The stroke was aimed down across Emily's bottom, instantly silencing her protest.

'As for you, bitch. You get double.'

'No—'

'Silence. Double I said and double I meant. And,' Chloe mused, her tone silkily teasing, 'why should I strain myself, tiring my arm as I whip your bottoms, hmm? Here, you girl,' she barked, dominantly tapping Susie's bottom with her crop. 'Take this and give the bitch another half dozen.'

'B-but I…' Susie, rising and turning to face her tormentor, stammered her reluctance.

'Do it,' Chloe snarled. 'And make each stroke really sting.'

Trembling, Susie hesitated, then accepted the crop before turning to address Emily's upturned buttocks.

'Six,' hissed Chloe, kneeling at the edge of the bed and bringing her fingertips together at the dark coils beneath her silk-encased pussy. 'Six,' she repeated. 'And give them to her slowly. I'll count.'

'No, please,' Susie whimpered. 'It's not fair. We were only—'

'Disobeying strict orders to remain in your rooms after midnight,' Chloe broke in, a jealous note adding a shrillness to her wrath. 'One.'

Emily whimpered, and Susie plied the crop. The thin, leather-sheathed cane whistled down softly, singing a single note from the Song of Judas.

Swish!

A venomous whisper. Emily, buttocks jerking in response, squealed softly. Chloe, eyes shining, ravished her slit with her shining fingertips; fingertips already wet with the slick smear of her feral juices.

'Two.'

Again, feet planted further apart, arm raised, Susie obeyed

the cruel command. The white stitching along the length of the ox-blood leather became a sudden blur as the crop sliced down, biting into the proffered swell of Emily's buttocks devotedly. The whipped cheeks jiggled and bounced.

A frisson of exquisite anguish rippled down Emily's inner thighs, provoking Chloe's wet fingertips into a furious flurry at her weeping slit.

'Three.'

Susie moaned softly, but obeyed. The sheen of the crop's polished hide glinted with evil menace as it sliced down.

Crack!

Emily grunted as she pressed her thighs together and clenched her cheeks so fiercely her cleft became a thin crease between her blazing buttocks.

Kneeling at the edge of the bed, Chloe was now thumbing down her oyster silk panties, into a restricting band around her buttocks that bit into their bulging softness. The sound of her fingers at her slippery labial folds filled the bedroom with a haunting liquid lapping. In an attempt to defy the bite of the crop and the scald of its searing pain, as well as cruel Chloe's savage self-pleasuring, Emily flooded her brain with whirling thoughts: anything to crowd her crimson brain and drown out the silent screaming of her pain.

Crates. Crates of paintings hurried in at midnight. And what would emerge from this smuggled horde? The Vermeer all eyes in the art world were anxious to see once more? Or the Klimt which had vanished in Copenhagen sixteen years ago? But the heat and the pain at her buttocks broke through, as did the sounds of Chloe's masturbation.

'Four.'

Swish, *crack*!

Emily squealed and dug her elbows into the duvet. She must block out the agony that blistered her whipped cheeks.

Ann Corderey. Emily grimaced as she remembered the name in translation. Coeur de Leon. Lionheart. The gifted Frenchwoman was, no doubt, a direct if irregular descendant

116

of Richard the Lionheart bedding his way across France towards the Crusades. Ann Corderey, the Frenchwoman who had fashioned exotic furniture for Louis XV. Exotic? Erotic. Emily, desperate to escape the pain of the whistling crop, conjured up images of a delightfully fashioned fruitwood bed she had seen and admired in the Nantes collection. The fruitwood bed that had, she recalled, smooth holes bored into its frame to capture and contain the ankles of the French king's mistress. Emily imagined the naked courtesan writhing, her legs spread lewdly in their strict bondage as the ruler of all France was at his amorous sport. Ann Corderey. Was there an image of her for posterity? Perhaps Holbein had…

'Five.'

Nothing could prevent the penetration of the pain piercing Emily's mind. Not only did the slicing crop sear her bare buttocks, it blazed with crimson fury in her brain. She hissed, hating being thrashed for Chloe's perverse pleasure, hating being whipped so that the raven-haired tormentor could masturbate.

'Six.'

Emily had to bite deeply into the duvet to smother her scream as the crop lashed down once more across her upraised cheeks.

'Move,' Chloe grunted drunkenly, shuffling towards Emily's bending nakedness, her progress impeded by both her gathering climax and the tight oyster panties peeled down around her bunched cheeks. 'Out of my way,' she snarled, elbowing Susie aside.

Emily froze, rigid across her bed of pain and shame. Behind her Chloe inched closer, a heartbeat at a time, bringing her bra-encased breasts to bear down upon and crush into Emily's crop-striped bottom. The seamless oyster silk, burgeoning with the swell of Chloe's breasts, rasped against the crimson peach cheeks. As the fiercely erect nipples scored her flayed rump, Emily screamed and scrabbled at the duvet to escape such utter humiliation.

'Stay still, bitch,' Chloe snarled, her voice curdling with lust. Heaving her breasts in their silken bondage upwards, she thrust her hips forwards, kissing her wet slit against Emily's scorched buttocks. 'Perfectly still, bitch. I'm in total control. You are mine, at last. All mine.' She jerked her sex almost contemptuously into the buttocks she had yearned for; buttocks she had deeply desired to dominate.

Emily slumped down in abject submission, accidentally thrusting her buttocks back against Chloe's wet warmth. Chloe's raven hair spilled down to curtain her perspiring face as she shrieked her raw pleasure and rapidly raked her erect clitoris across Emily's scarlet wealed bottom. 'Mine, bitch, mine, bitch, mine,' she intoned in an unholy mantra, squealing and shuddering as she came, juicing the punished flesh as she rode the whipped buttocks with her splayed slit.

Susie, shivering in the shadows of the bedroom, stared wide-eyed and moaned, her soft note of anxious sorrow instantly drowned as Chloe tossed her head back to cry out her ecstasy and triumph.

Chapter Five

Two grey squirrels chased each other in and out of a neglected bed of bronze chrysanthemums. Through the open window Emily watched them, smiling despite her unhappiness. Sometimes, in London, she walked through Kensington Gardens to the top end of Gloucester Road, taking a cab on to Hans Crescent and her work at the gallery.

London. It was exactly eight days since she had taken the train that had started the journey. The journey that had brought her here. She remembered the thrillingly frightening bike ride, hugging Chloe's leather-clad warmth for dear life. Her first meeting with Dr Stikannos. Her first taste of punishment – so blisteringly raw. Other punishments, leading to the paradox of climax and orgasm as she writhed in the pleasurable pain. Writhed, her sex pulsing, the inner muscles tightening and spasming as her whipped buttocks blazed.

Eight long days – and longer nights.

Out in the bronze chrysanthemums, a peacock strutted up to investigate the playful squirrels. Emily grinned as she watched the splendidly plumaged bird mincing daintily on the lawn. The squirrels were deeply unimpressed, until the peacock shrieked its piercing, echoing cry. The scream scattered the squirrels, who scampered away to seek safety up an overhanging beech tree.

Emily returned to her duties. She was halfway through her appreciation of an early Poussin, fixing its date as sixteen thirty-three and confirming it as an untitled studio work depicting four nudes bathing. The delineation of their supple nakedness was exquisite, and yet it was an innocent piece, free from suggestive symbols or priapic emblems from rapacious mythology so beloved by the French Academicians. It had been executed, she wrote, before Poussin had become embroiled with learned colleagues – and fierce enemies – in the matter of Lydian, Dorian and Phrygian modes of neo-classical representation. A coy, platonic piece.

Bugger that. Emily chewed her pencil, her fingers growing clumsy and her throat tightening as she appraised and appreciated the four female nudes splashing in their secret pool fringed by nodding willows. Depositing her pencil and picking up her pen, she started to write a rough draft for the catalogue notes. Two minutes later, she concluded the piece with the suggestion that the bidding kicked in at a quarter of a million.

No. She read her notes and shook her head. Not good enough. Weeping willows. If they had been date palms, she could have given her torrid imagination full scope, introducing the sensuality of North Africa. Slave girls bathing before being brought, one by one throughout the heat of the dark night, to the damask couch of the Emir. But the weeping willows fixed the *mise en scène* firmly in France. In Poussin's Aix-en-Provence. She picked up her pen and scribbled.

Farmers' daughters, home from the heat of the livestock market. Flushed with strong wine, they had stripped and risked the icy waters. Moments later, just as they were scampering squealing up the bank, a cart would trundle by. Lusty young harvesters, dusty with toil in the barley fields, would plunge thigh high into the shivering reeds, driving the naked girls out like game before the assembled guns. Lusty young men, each one grasping and grappling with a slippery nude.

Emily put down her pen and grinned. Bidding, she had concluded, would commence at the reserve price of three and a half hundred thousand. Pleased with her effort, she scooped up and swept back her blonde mane. The weight of her collar brought her fingertips down to caress it. She squirmed, making her chair squeak in protest beneath her writhing buttocks. The movement made her gasp aloud, for it re-ignited the fire of the pale blue lines planted across her naked cheeks the night before by Chloe. Chloe, who had pounced, supple bamboo aquiver in her clenched fist, when Emily had tried to sneak half a cold chicken up to her miserable attic room. Chloe, who had ordered Emily to bend over, bare-buttocked, for the crisp caning that ensued. Chloe, who had gnawed the cold chicken as she swiped the cruel cane down.

Emily rose from her chair and sauntered across the room. Standing before the clouded glass of a full-length gilded Austrian cheval mirror, she swivelled, turning her face away from its reflection, presenting her pert rump to the dull sheen. Thumbing down her tight white shorts, she rose up on tiptoe and, glancing over her right shoulder into the glass, counted her cane stripes with a mixture of resentful pleasure and perverse pride.

Clenching and then unclenching her whipped cheeks, she became lost in the crimson delights of remembered pain.

'I trust you found the Poussin equally captivating,' the voice of Dr Stikannos said suavely.

Emily blushed, staggered and attempted to drag up her shorts.

'Bare bottoms are so delicious, I find,' he whispered.

She yanked at her shorts, wincing twice: once as the stretchy material revisited her striped cheeks; again when the severity of her sudden tug forced the cotton up into her cleft.

'Dr Stikannos,' she gasped. 'I've missed you.' Hell, she thought, blushing richly. What was she saying? Why did she say that? She clenched her fists, angry with her foolishness, blurting it out like some gushing ball-girl tongue-tied before the international female seed she adored. She stared at him – at the dark eyes behind the inscrutable metal mask. Was it true? Yes, damn it. And damn him. Where had he been for the past six days? She hadn't seen him since he had fitted her with—

'The collar,' he murmured, inching his wheelchair closer to the open window. 'How well it suits you, my dear. I am never mistaken. And how well you wear it. As you do those stripes across your bottom. Most becoming. Show me.'

Emily reddened, her fingers fluttering at her pubis. 'I've just completed my notes for the Poussin. Would you like to see—?'

'Your stripes, Emily. Show me your bottom.'

Emily buckled under a sudden surge of violent resentment. She hated him.

Yet she loved – yes, loved – being ordered to bare her whipped cheeks, she ruefully acknowledged, peeling down her shorts obediently and offering her caned buttocks for his perusal.

'Shorts further down, my girl. Below the knees.'

She waggled her bottom and jiggled her thighs. The shorts slipped further down, coming to rest at the shapely curve of her calves.

'Bend over, Emily.'

No, now he'd see her pussy, wet and welcoming. She hated him, but she squirmed deliciously as she caught the sound of his sharp intake of breath, as if he had just spotted a Renoir sketch among a folio of third-rate daubs.

'Beautiful,' he whispered, softly and simply, in full and frank appreciation. 'If there is anything more pleasing to the eye of a dominant than a bending girl's bare bottom it has to be a bending girl's recently punished bare bottom, my dear. Stand up now.'

A sudden devil stole into Emily's mind, and she waggled her bottom provocatively before pulling up her shorts.

'You flaunt yourself and tease me at great peril to yourself, my girl. Do not think that this wheelchair prevents me having you punished instantly. Instantly, do you understand? And to my complete and utter satisfaction.'

A wet bubble emerged from Emily's pouting labia. She clamped her thighs, but the bubble burst silently, wetting her shorts at the spot where the cotton kissed her pubis. The metal mask inclined a fraction, and she saw his dark eyes sparkle as they spotted her damp arousal.

'Do not take dangerous risks, Emily, unless you relish the painful consequences.'

Emily shivered, despite the heat of the late summer sunshine; shivered as she recognised the sobering truth of his words. Why? Why had she done that? What had prompted her moment of madness, her coquettish behaviour? She had stupidly felt a brief moment of false security, and had dared to taunt him.

'I-I'm sorry,' she mumbled.

He laughed easily. Silkily. The laughter of a master prepared, just this once, to indulge his penitent slave. But the dark eyes glistened unforgivingly behind the metal mask.

'I am, truly.'

'You certainly shall be, my dear, if for one moment I am given to think your misbehaviour anything other than the foolish mistakes of an untrained, ill-disciplined little novice.'

Emily squirmed. 'No please, it was very stupid of me—'

He held up a gloved hand for silence. 'Stupidity can and will be corrected, my dear girl. On that point be assured. Corrected with strict training and stern punishment. Discipline, Emily. Do I make my meaning perfectly clear?'

'Yes,' Emily responded shyly, averting her gaze.

He ordered her to look at him directly. She obeyed, the pulse at her throat plucking wildly.

'Perfectly clear, my girl?'

'Yes.'

'Yes…?'

There was a tense pause before she replied. 'Yes… master.'

Upstairs, in a spacious room converted by Victorian ingenuity into a sumptuous toilet over one hundred years before, Chloe gazed down through the coloured panes of a leaded window at the shimmering peacock strutting on the lawn below. The squirrels had returned, their impudent frisking mocking the proud bird's vanity. Pretending not to notice them, the splendid bird minced away to the laurel bushes with as much dignity as it could muster.

Her narrow window afforded only a narrow view of the garden below. Soon, the peacock had strutted out of view. Peering down, Chloe spotted Dr Stikannos propelling his wheelchair along the sanded path, and she stepped back instinctively as the sun flashed on his briefly raised metal mask. Dr Stikannos enjoyed his privacy. Insisted upon it most firmly. Anyone caught peeping, even accidentally, could earn their bare bottom several severe stripes.

Chloe sighed and turning, surveyed the room. Why, she wondered, had Ursula instructed her to be there, up in the remote part of the mansion? What could Ursula possibly want of Chloe in these unfrequented quarters, in a room with a toilet, a washbasin and a small castor-oil plant perched precariously on a polished mahogany round table. The brass and onyx fixtures winked back at her in the sunshine streaming through the coloured lights of the leaded glass, dappling her white vest and shorts with fragments of a kaleidoscopic rainbow. Violet, indigo and orange bathed her bosom while scarlet and gold danced playfully across her thighs. She gazed down at her own reflection in the highly polished cherrywood toilet seat, noting with pleasurable pride the cascade of her dark raven hair.

The small brass knob twisted silently and the door yawned wide, admitting Ursula carrying a four litre jug of iced water and, balanced against the swell of her bosom, a brown cardboard box. Chloe smiled, instantly stretching out her hands to take the jug.

'Leave that alone, please.'

In the silence that followed, broken only by the slight chinking of swirling ice cubes, Chloe paled. Ursula's tone had been brisk. Clinically brisk, and businesslike. Chloe edged back two paces until her lower thighs grazed the toilet seat, dimpling their soft flesh. Backing in against it so suddenly, she wavered and sat down, steadying herself with both hands gripping at the wooden rim.

Unhurriedly, and seemingly unconcernedly, Ursula busied herself quietly at the basin, depositing the jug of iced water onto the glass shelf above and carefully emptying the contents of her brown cardboard box into the gleaming white porcelain.

Straining to peep into the basin, Chloe could not quite see the objects Ursula had so carefully placed there. 'Is it a manicure?' she asked, her voice somewhat unsteady.

'You'll see.'

'Or is it a pedicure?' She scrunched her toes expectantly. But her wavering voice betrayed her mounting trepidation.

'I said, you'll see,' Ursula murmured, engrossed in her task. 'All in good time.'

'But Ursula, don't you think—?'

'Be quiet and slip out of those things for me,' the green-eyed woman said, raking her fingers through her cropped hair.

Chloe, recognising and knowing that tone, shivered. Rising from the polished cherrywood seat, she plucked nervously at the hem of her vest.

'Still dressed?' Ursula inquired, turning a few moments later and snapping on a pair of clear plastic gloves.

Chloe, her eyes wide with concern as they watched Ursula's fingers stretching into the tightness of the shining plastic, hastily tugged down her shorts and stepped out of them.

'Vest, if you please.'

Chloe's breasts rode up a fraction with the rippling cotton material as she peeled her vest up over her shoulders and bowed head. She struggled free, her bosom bounced gently, swinging loose and lovely in its new-found freedom. A pincered plastic-sheathed finger and thumb closed over the exposed nipple of her left breast, tweaking it painfully. Chloe gasped. Her nipple rose into an erect little bud of pleasurable pain, and Ursula pressed her plastic-gloved palm up against the captive flesh. The breast wobbled and submitted, and the prinked nipple kissed the clear plastic as it surrendered to its silent rasp.

'Sit down.'

Chloe inched back a fraction, her left breast still dominated by the fiercely controlling plastic glove, and perched her bottom above the toilet. With her peach cheeks poised above the polished cherrywood, she sank down, spreading her fleshy buttocks apart.

'Legs together.'

Chloe struggled to obey.

'Come along.'

'Can I ask—?'

'No. Just do as I tell you. Feet together.'

'Please, Ursula.'

'Closer. Touching.'

'But I—'

'That's better. Just obey me, understand?'

Buttocks clenched, her thighs pressed tightly, Chloe sat on the toilet seat. Down on the linoleum before her, her feet were clamped together. Bending, Ursula snapped black leather-linked restraining cuffs at her obedient victim's ankles, welding Chloe's shapely legs seamlessly from heel to thigh. The tiny silver chain binding the black leather cuffs glinted menacingly.

'Head up,' Ursula ordered, rising swiftly.

Chloe, lips trembling, eyes wide with fear, gazed up into the jealous green eyes staring dominantly down at her. Her fingers fluttered in timid defiance and her hands rose in a futile gesture as Ursula produced a gag and bound it across her victim's mouth. Above the soft wad, now efficiently and firmly taped over her sealed lips, the mute girl's nostrils flared, and the gagged girl's eyes spoke eloquently of her silent terror.

'So,' Ursula purred, perusing her handiwork, her nimble fingers checking the restrained heels and ankles once more. 'Enjoying your role as Emily's disciplinarian, were you, mmm?'

Chloe shook her head, violently denying the accusation.

'Oh yes, you were. Don't lie. I've been watching you, girl. Watching you very, very closely. You've been taking your duties a little too seriously, I'm afraid. Stand up.'

Chloe stumbled to her feet, staggering slightly. Ursula steadied the hobbled girl by planting a flattened palm at each of Chloe's breasts. Chloe whimpered. Ursula squeezed dominantly, her cruel hands busy at the warm, soft mounds.

'Turn around, and put your hands behind your back.'

Whimpering through her gag, Chloe submitted to Ursula, who briskly bound the proffered wrists, leaving the tied hands helpless above the swell of the soft buttocks.

'Turn.'

Their eyes met once more.

'Sit.'

The tight stretch of Chloe's cotton shorts kissed the polished cherrywood seat.

'I think it's time I purged you once and for all of this fascination you seem to have developed for Emily. For Emily's bottom.

'How fitting,' Ursula whispered, turning to the washbasin, 'that the purge I am about to dispense will be administered through *your* bottom.'

Chloe, her breasts wobbling, wriggled violently.

'Keep still,' her tormentor snapped. 'Yes,' Ursula continued, ignoring the grunts and whimpers from the bound and gagged girl in her thrall, 'a purge.'

Chloe heard soft sounds from the basin as Ursula carefully

uncurled a length of red rubber tubing. The supple hose seemed to spring into life in Ursula's fingers as she finally shook it out to its full length. Chloe watched, fascinated yet horrified, as Ursula grasped the tip of the tubing in one fist and lubricated it delicately from a gently squeezed tube of KY. The half-inch of anointed red rubber grew dark under the lubricant jelly, and sparkled as it caught the sunlight. Chloe moaned.

Turning, her right hand alighted on Chloe's throat. The plastic-sheathed fingers of the controlling hand felt Chloe's nervous swallow. Ursula smiled, then captured Chloe's chin.

'Up.' The plastic glove squeezed. It was a gesture of vicious tenderness. 'I want you across the seat.'

Despite the controlling glove pinioning her face, Chloe struggled to shake her head. Above the gag, her eyes pleaded mutely for mercy.

'Forgive you?' Ursula teased. 'Perhaps, after I've punished you. You've continued to show far too much interest in Emily, despite my warnings. I've witnessed you kissing her, kissing the bottom you have just whipped. Oh yes, don't deny it. I've got you taped, my girl. You'll thank me when it's all over, albeit tearfully, perhaps. I'm going to purge you of your dangerous desires. You have to be taught a lesson, Chloe, darling. A very painful lesson.' The dominant plastic-gloved hand tilted the captive face up into total submission. The jealous green eyes blazed. 'A lesson I trust you will learn and profit by. Down.'

Struggling, Chloe resisted, but Ursula's strong hands grappled adroitly, and Chloe was forced face and belly down across the cherrywood.

'Bottom up a fraction.'

Chloe dipped her tummy obediently and inched her hips up. Across the toilet seat, bare-bottomed, bound and utterly helpless, Chloe closed her eyes, and struggled to deny the vivid images conjured up by the soft sounds from the basin beside her. As the sunbeams warmed her naked cheeks, she shivered as she interpreted each slight noise: the soft murmur of the rubber tubing; the scrape of a plastic funnel; the crisp rustle of Ursula's gloves; the clink of ice cubes colliding in the swirling jug of water.

'There,' Ursula sighed contentedly.

Chloe squeezed her cheeks together and whimpered into the gag. She gasped, her gasp dissolving into a muffled grunt, as the tip of the lubricated rubber hose touched and worried her tight sphincter.

'Now stop being silly,' Ursula rasped. 'Open up at once.'

Grinding her breasts into the cherrywood, Chloe defied her tormentor, writhing onto her left hip and denying her bottom to the probing tube.

The severe slap echoed in the confined space as Ursula swiped her hand sharply across Chloe's rounded bottom. 'Back across the toilet seat at once,' she ordered. 'Now open your cheeks.'

A dominant, plastic-sheathed hand visited the spanked cheeks, splaying the flesh apart. Firm fingers depressed each swollen crown, dimpling the subjugated buttocks and spreading them painfully apart. The pink anal whorl winked and widened.

'Nnnngghhh,' Chloe choked, squealing.

Ursula made a soothing noise, as if whispering to a baby, as she plied the glistening rubber tube into the rosebud between the parted buttocks. 'Sh, sh, sh,' she soothed, smothering Chloe's stifled screams of protest. 'You know you've been wicked. Disobedient, disloyal and thoroughly wicked. This will cleanse you of your sins.' She pressed, and excruciating inches of the probing tube disappeared between the passive cheeks of the helpless girl.

'Clench.' Ursula smiled approvingly as, gazing down, she saw the tightening buttocks obeying her strict command. 'Do not let it slip out. If it does, I'll use it across your bare arse. Understand?'

The hose waggled as, across her seat of shame, Chloe

nodded, causing her bottom to quiver.

'I won't be a second.' Ursula flexed her gloved fingers, picked up the plastic funnel and insinuated it into the other end of the red rubber hose. Holding the funnel above the naked buttocks below, she gripped the heavy jug of iced water. 'Don't struggle or wriggle about, understand? Any spillage, girl, and you'll lick it up.'

Chloe grunted, sobbing, as the cold water trickled down from the funnel, slightly swelling the red rubber hose, and entered her rectal warmth. Ursula stopped pouring, depositing the jug and holding the funnel high. Chloe squealed, despite her gag, as the rush of icy water flooded her bowels, swelling her colon painfully.

'No, keep still. You can take more than that.'

A couple of inches above the point where the red rubber buried itself into the cleft between the naked buttocks, the bound hands spasmed in a reflex of submission and surrender. Ursula ignored the gesture and grasped the jug.

'Another half litre. You need a proper purge, my disloyal, treacherous little bitch. This should cool your ardour for Emily.'

Ursula dispensed a full litre. Chloe writhed in exquisite torment. Reaching down, the tormentor slowly tugged at the rubber hose, pulling it out from between the buttocks an inch at a time. It slid out with a loud liquid pop. Chloe stiffened her thighs, moulding her pliant cheeks into firm hillocks of taut flesh. Above her clenched cheeks her fingers scrabbled feverishly in their strict bondage.

Ursula slowly dragged the length of rubber tubing through her pincered finger and thumb, trapping the final inch of glistening hose and wiping it clean with a twist of toilet paper. Tossing the recoiled tubing back down into the porcelain basin, she straightened her index finger, dipping into then gently tracing the line of Chloe's creased cleft. 'Get up,' she said. 'But keep your bottom tightly clenched. I don't want you spilling a single drop. And for every drop you do, a tear must fall.'

Chloe moaned softly. Despite the agony of her swollen bowel, and the awkward humiliation of being bound at her ankles, she managed at last to struggle obediently to her unsteady feet.

'Stand aside.'

Chloe gazed down at the linoleum, avoiding Ursula's stern green eyes as the latter flipped up the toilet seat lid.

'Sit.'

Chloe, her eyes brimming with unshed tears, eased herself gently down.

'Now, my girl, prove to me that you can contain yourself. Can you, do you think? Can you contain your lust for Emily from now on, hmm? Prove to me that you can by containing that icy water in your bottom for the next four minutes. I hope you can. I truly hope you can.'

The delicious threat was there, explicit in her words. Chloe knew she had to keep her thighs clamped and her anus tightly sealed – or else.

'You've been very good,' Ursula remarked, brutally peeling away the tape from Chloe's lips. 'Darling,' she added, fingering out the wedged gag. 'That's ten, no, I make it twelve seconds already. Only three minutes fifty, no forty-seven, to go,' she murmured, ostentatiously consulting her watch.

At two heartbeats per second, Chloe had her own method of measuring the achingly slow passage of time. Helpless, her fingers now two agonised starfish above her tightened cheeks, Chloe almost buckled under the ache of tormented longing, and moaning almost drunkenly, she shuddered as the plastic-gloved hands visited her utterly defenceless breasts, palming and crushing them possessively.

'That's almost a minute, sweetheart. You see, you can contain yourself,' Ursula gushed with mock enthusiasm, and then her tone switched savagely as her palms began to become brutal at each breast. 'Make sure you continue to do so.'

Chloe squealed. The gloved palms crackled as the taut plastic of the cupping, mauling, dominating hands crinkled, and Ursula silenced the writhing girl's moans with a hungry kiss. Thumbing each nipple ruthlessly, the green-eyed tormentor ravaged the stubby peaks, while perched upon the toilet bowl, squirming her clenched bottom unashamedly, Chloe struggled to keep her thighs firmly clamped together.

Molten quicksilver of arousal juiced her labia, which yearned to peel apart and welcome the plastic-sheathed fingers at her breasts into the wet warmth within. Denied, the trickle became a tormenting scald. A shudder raked her bowels. Her belly tightened, and her eyes widened in alarm.

'Because if you can't contain yourself, Chloe dear, I'll have to punish you most severely.' Ursula tweaked then tugged the tormented nipples. Whitened toes scrabbled on the linoleum and Chloe's knees rose a fraction. Ursula, seeing and smelling the slick of arousal, nodded knowingly, then knuckled each breast, rhythmically dimpling the creamy pliant flesh with her plastic-coated fists. Chloe dropped her feet to drum the linoleum in an agony of ecstasy.

Ursula laughed at the response. 'Only another fifty-six seconds, my dearest, and you'll be home and dry.'

Chloe slumped and cried out in anguish as her sphincter spasmed, causing the icy sluice to pour loudly into the bowl below, and Ursula shook her head slowly as if in genuine sorrow. 'Bad girl. If you cannot even contain yourself for a couple of miserable minutes…'

'No, please Ursula, I'm sorry. Believe me, I'll never even look at Emily—' Ursula planted another dominant kiss on the upturned lips of her whining victim.

'How can I expect you,' she mumbled, lips to lips, 'to contain and control your heat for our little blonde art expert if you can't manage half a jug of cold water, hmm? I want you across the seat. At once, bitch.'

Chloe wriggled but remained stubbornly still. The cruel fingers suddenly back at her nipples had her up instantly, wobbling unsteadily on tethered feet. Her inner thighs shone with spillage. The wooden toilet lid snapped down loudly, and seconds later Chloe was once more breasts and belly down across the polished cherrywood.

Ursula's plastic-sheathed fingers snatched at another length of tissue from the white roll, crumpled it up within her clenched fist then raked it savagely down the dark shadow of Chloe's wet cleft. The girl jerked her buttocks in response as the tissue kissed her velvet, squealing as Ursula repeated the gesture with a second wadge of tissue.

'I promised you the rubber, didn't I?' she whispered.

Chloe, bumping her pubis into the cherrywood, refused to answer.

'Didn't I?' insisted Ursula.

Chloe responded with a sullen nod.

'Answer me properly, bitch.'

Chloe did so, begging for mercy, but was silenced by the harsh sound and bite of the doubled-up tubing whistling down and lashing her upturned cheeks. She shrieked as weals from the doubled hose reddened the smooth cream of her proffered buttocks.

Again the red rubber barked loudly, searing the whipped cheeks below. Chloe sobbed in distress, and eight strokes later Ursula tossed the lethal tubing aside and knelt down, her face a mere fraction from the seething flesh of the punished girl's bottom.

'I'm sorry, Ursula, I'm so sorry,' Chloe cried brokenly.

'You certainly will be, my darling,' Ursula whispered, her words smothered by the crimson cheeks at her lips. 'You most certainly will be.' Her lips parted, dragging deliciously against the whipped buttocks, and Chloe sighed, nestling her bottom up against Ursula's mouth.

'Naughty Chloe.' Ursula opened her mouth wide as if yawning, then closed it, biting deeply, and Chloe screamed.

'The peacocks do not seem to be comfortable with the heat this afternoon,' Dr Stikannos remarked, twisting his metal mask towards the window in response to yet another shrill shriek.

Emily, who did not think it was a peacock screaming, shuddered. Someone, Susie or Chloe, was receiving Ursula's intimate attentions, she decoded.

Dr Stikannos returned unconcernedly to the catalogue notes she had been working on, his wheelchair at the table she had just vacated, their moment of intimacy completely set aside – almost; from time to time, Emily absently stroking her left buttock with the curved palm of her hand.

'Now that is interesting,' he remarked, denying Emily the opportunity to detect approval or dismay by maintaining a strictly neutral tone.

'Interesting?' she was forced to ask, after an uncertain silence.

'Tiziano Vecellio.'

'Titian…'

'Yes, I know it's Titian,' he said impatiently, 'but will our prospective bidders and buyers? Will their erudition be equal to their fortunes? Hmm? And here, yes, you do it again. You list Raphael as—'

'Raffaello Sanzio. All the leading galleries are doing it now. Giving artists their full and proper titles.'

'There is a current affectation for doing so, to be sure, Emily. But once more I ask you, do dollar millionaires who prefer burgers to Beluga caviar know their—'

'Flemish Old Master from their Fiamingo? I think so. Besides, it will be an opportunity to educate them. Relieve them of their ignorance.'

'All I wish to relieve them of is their money. Let them call the artists by their household names.'

'But that's snobbery.' Emily was suddenly amazed at her own audacity.

'On your part, yes it probably is, my dear girl.'

Emily forgot her own amazement as she thrilled to his retort. He was conversing – bantering even – with her as an intellectual equal. Listening to her, anticipating her, engaging with her.

'If I came a quarter of the way across the globe to bid half a million for a Guercino…'

'The Squint,' she supplied, adding that a third of a million would secure one of the Squint's works.

'But you forget, my dear, that I am ignorant. I want the painting so I am prepared to pay the half million.'

'I see.'

'But not for anything by some artist correctly named.'

'Gian Fransesco Barbieri. You're probably right. Yes, I suppose you are right.'

'Do you think the galleries would attract vast crowds to view an acquired work of Masaccio?'

'If the billing had him down as Giovanni di Guidi. Okay, you win.'

'I always do.'

'They'll get what they're looking for,' Emily conceded. 'Titian it is.'

'I am pleased to hear you say so. We are not about to entertain the cognoscenti at auction, my dear Emily, but the rich. Please attribute all the works for sale to the artists as they are commonly known.'

Emily giggled. 'Commonly? Who's being a snob now?'

Did he smile behind his mask? She ached to know, but tipsy with the cut and thrust of banter between them, she failed to notice the stern tone return to his voice.

'Commonly,' she giggled.

'Generally,' he replied coldly.

A silence settled between them, and Emily's fingers fluttered nervously.

'If you say so…' she began, her voice uncertain and unsure.

'I do.'

More silence. As solid as the sunbeams. Another soft scream echoed eerily in the warm summer sunshine. Emily froze. This time she was absolutely convinced it was the wail of a punished female.

'The peacocks are restless. Perhaps it is time they had their wings clipped.'

Emily swayed at the irony of the remark, suddenly tumbling down into the crimson vortex of her servitude. She shot her hand down onto the desk to steady herself, and the metal mask flashed as Dr Stikannos glanced up.

'Please revise your attributions,' he rasped. 'Even I might overlook a Botticelli if some eager little cataloguer had attributed the work to… what was his real name? Remind me.'

Crushed, Emily blushed.

'Come along. You're the expert.'

'Alessandro Filipepi,' Emily muttered, hating him again. Even being able to answer his mocking question had brought her little comfort. The balance of power had shifted once more – against her. He had, in a few curt words, reasserted himself over her. They were, once more, and it felt as if it had always been so despite the fleeting moment of intellectual equity, master and slave.

Master and slave. Emily let the silent words haunt her spinning brain.

He broke into her unselfconscious silence. 'Are you sulking, Emily?' The wheelchair creaked as he pushed himself away from the table, signalling that the interview was over.

She blushed and shook her head vigorously, her blonde hair sweeping her shoulders.

'Answer me properly,' he ordered. 'Play the sulky schoolgirl with me, my dear, and you'll suffer a schoolgirl's spanked bottom.'

She looked at him, her eyes blinking. 'I will of course amend the attributions as you suggest.'

'As I insist, Emily. As I insist. See to it that you do so. Now carry on.'

He propelled himself towards the door, brusquely dismissing her offer of assistance. Returning to the desk, she sat down and picked up a pencil.

'Dear me, I almost forgot,' he announced, twisting his wheelchair around abruptly to face the room through the open door.

Emily looked up.

'You are no longer a schoolgirl, Emily, but a beautiful young woman journeying from innocence to experience. No, you are no longer a schoolgirl, but you still have many lessons to learn.' He raised a gloved fist, and from it, he released the coiled camel's penis.

The pencil snapped loudly in Emily's clenched fist.

'Come to my quarters at eight. I think you are ready to taste this.' He flicked his wrist. His gloved fist twisted. The supple lash whispered as it flickered out, searing the empty air. 'A taste of sweet sorrow.'

He snapped the camel's penis once again, causing Emily's belly to flutter, then implode.

'I think I shall be able to feed your growing appetite for the pleasures of pain, my girl.'

Her work finished, her curtains drawn against the dipping of the crimson sun behind the elms, her evening meal not touched, Emily lay naked on her narrow bed.

Behind closed eyes she pictured the camel's penis: that evil little length of supple flesh. Dark purple. Almost brown in colour. She shivered, hugging her breasts. What would it feel like? What would it feel like, biting into her bare bottom? Lashing down across her helpless cheeks? Her hands fell down to her thighs, clenching into small fists of anxious expectation, as she imagined the thin whistle of the lightning stroke. She whimpered, grinding her buttocks into the bed, her fingers spreading in alarm, as she imagined

137

the fierce kiss of the lash across her naked cheeks.

Her pussy prickled and moistened. No, it would be too painful for pleasure. It would not, she knew, be a sweet torment but a sharp sorrow. Dr Stikannos had said it himself, hadn't he? She was no longer a schoolgirl, desirous of discipline, eager to have her soft bottom spanked. She was trembling on the brink of stern adulthood, developing an appetite for a woman's pain. In her early womanhood, with keener desires and a deeper hunger to be filled.

Emily wriggled over onto her belly, squashing her naked breasts down into her bed. Her nipples thickened as she deliberately raked them against the prickle of her blanket.

The camel's penis.

It haunted her. Maddened her imagination. She discovered herself inching her bare bottom up as if to greet its cruel stroke with her submissive – yet eagerly impatient – buttocks.

Twisting over onto her back, and burying her bottom in the blanket in an effort to deny her dark desires, she thought about the history of the little whip. How many cruel hands had furled and unfurled it, dangling it deliciously before the sorrow-filled eyes of naked females about to be whipped, or who had just been whipped? How many cruel hands had oiled it lovingly, to keep the hide supple and the biting lash so sharp?

The camel's penis.

Fashioned to discipline rebellious female flesh. Plied to punish sultry slave girls in some distant seraglio. Some desert hell, Emily shuddered, where even the cries of the whipped fell mute beneath the vastness of the surrounding night, a night so dark that even the indifferent moon and canopy of spangling silver stars could not illumine the short span between the eyes of the whipper and the eyes of the whipped.

Emily's fingers stole down to her pubic mound, dappling at her golden nest delicately. The short whip last glimpsed in her master's gloved fist dominated her imagination. Its fearful fascination held her in absolute thrall. Its dark, disturbing history. Its evil note of venom when lashing down. Its potent promise of pain.

The door to her attic room yawned open and Ursula glided in.

'It's almost eight. Get up and come with me. Dr Stikannos wants to see you.'

Emily's hands cupped her pubis in a belated attempt at modesty.

'Hurry up... no,' she hissed, 'don't bother with those.' Emily had been tentatively been reaching for her vest and shorts. 'He'll see you as you are.'

Resigning herself to remaining naked and humiliated before Ursula, Emily propped herself up on her elbows.

'Get a move on.'

Emily slipped off the narrow bed, stretched briefly and walked towards the door. As she passed through it, under Ursula's stern gaze, strong hands pinned her bare bottom up against the peeling plaster wall. Emily struggled, but with one hand Ursula pinned her wrists together above her blonde head, and with the other she pinched Emily's pubic hair.

'Keep away from Chloe, understand?' The green eyes narrowed.

Emily twisted her face away but was unable to conceal a fleeting look of contempt.

'I'm warning you, bitch,' Ursula snarled, releasing the pubic fuzz and viciously knuckling Emily's pubis.

Despite her squirming nakedness, despite the cruel fist at her sex, Emily felt a wave of triumph surge up within her. It was a primal thrill, a primitive exultation. Ursula was jealous, and frightened. Frightened that her precious Chloe could be seduced by Emily's seductive allure. Even in her pain, Emily triumphed, reasoning that Ursula's bullying merely betrayed her insecurity. If the green-eyed tormentor was sure of her precious little Chloe, this would not be happening.

Emily carefully hid her triumph. Donning the mask of submission, she acquiesced. But secretly, as they walked down the passageway to the head of the stairs, Emily trod the threadbare carpet in delight. She was, she acknowledged, now stepping down to the plush red velvet carpet on the ground floor, naked and utterly at Ursula's mercy. But wasn't Ursula equally at Emily's mercy? At the mercy of her delightful charms – charms which constantly threatened to ensnare the fickle Chloe and her mercurial lust.

As they approached the end of a long corridor, Emily felt that she had at last broken the yoke of fear Ursula had burdened her with; rid herself of the harsh dominant's malign sovereignty.

They reached a double door. Ursula opened it, after knocking gently and waiting to be summoned inside.

'Here she is,' the woman announced, almost as if returning a wandering child to the tea tent at the vicarage garden party. But there was nothing in her following pronouncement that suggested cake stalls, tombola or grinning vicars exhorting their flock to spend. 'A pretty little slave willing to be trained to serve her master.'

Six years before, Emily had sat in the waiting room of her Baker Street dentist. She was early. The magazines had been dull and dated. As Emily sat, eyes closed, the sound of the drill broke into her thoughts. It forced itself into her imagination, reminding her disturbingly of a hornet trapped inside an inverted wine glass. Cold sweat prickled her palms. She knew that soon, she too would be receiving the hateful injection and then have to submit to the drill. In her rising anxiety she imagined herself fingering the wine glass. Accidentally tipping it over, she released the furious hornet which thanked her for its freedom by – in her feverish imaginings – lancing up to sting her face: just at the spot where a troublesome tooth had been aching.

In the Baker Street waiting room, Emily blinked her eyes wide open as she smothered a shriek of alarm. Dashing out in confusion and fear, she skittled down the steps outside into the driving rain, colliding with a crocodile of Japanese businessmen on a corporate jolly to the Planetarium.

As the double doors closed behind her, the memory of her fear in that dentist's waiting room returned. Emily recalled that to lull his nervous patients into tranquillity, the dentist had a tape of Delius playing softly in the background.

She blinked, shivering in her nakedness. Sitting in his wheelchair, his back turned towards her, Dr Stikannos was engrossed in conducting a piece of pleasantly soothing music. Emily's eyes stared with delicious dread as they followed the rise and fall of his leather-gloved hands. It was Delius. The same piece. On the desk, like a dentist's syringe or some other equally frightening piece of gleaming apparatus, the camel's penis awaited her naked flesh, coiled, oiled and ready for use. The room darkened all around her.

Chapter Six

'Light the candles,' he instructed as the dying bars of Delius faded into silence.

Emily stumbled into the darkened room, realising that he had dimmed the lights using the remote built into the armrest of his wheelchair.

'Use the matches and the taper by the telephone on my desk,' he answered her unspoken question.

Telephone. All she had to do was snatch up the receiver, jab three buttons and she'd be free. The blood sang in her ears as her fingers scrabbled stupidly with the box of matches. He'd be useless in that wheelchair. It could be done in seconds. Just one call, that's all it would take.

He was still sitting with his back towards her. The wheelchair creaked slightly. 'But you don't really want to make that call, do you, my dear?'

Emily looked up, guiltily, her face flushing in the darkness. Her right hand tightened around the matchbox, rattling it violently. Damn him, she thought. Damn him.

His glove hand rose, as if placating her. 'Yes, yes, I know. You are confused. What you are experiencing is perfectly normal for a slave about to undergo the delicious rigours of strict training. A sullen resentment. A reluctant willingness. A slow slide into utter submission,' he whispered in the darkness. 'Now light the candles.'

She struck a match, and with its orange flame lit the taper. Bringing the flickering taper to the dozen white candles arranged in their silver sconces in front of a huge oval mirror, she kindled twelve dancing yellow lights that suffused the darkness of the room with a lambent glimmer.

'Excellent,' he approved. He span the wheelchair round

towards his desk, judging the distance expertly. 'And now a glass of wine, perhaps, before...'

Emily's throat tightened. Before? Before what. She gripped the smoking taper in her fist. A curl of smoke rose up from its red wick, smarting her eyes with sudden tears. She brought the taper up to her lips, wetting them with her tongue, then wetting the smouldering tip of the taper between their moist shine.

'Wine,' he repeated.

On the desk, tightly furled, the camel's penis glistened in the dancing candlelight.

Wine before the whip? By carefully avoiding to directly mention her imminent suffering and sweet pain, Dr Stikannos had contrived to make it all the more dreadful. She blinked, placed the extinguished taper back down on the desk and reached for the uncorked bottle waiting patiently in its beaded ice bucket.

'No, no, dear girl,' he intervened gallantly, 'I may indeed be crippled but I still enjoy some of my former faculties, as you will no doubt shortly be able to confirm.' He chuckled darkly. 'Including the manners of a gentleman. The gentleman always pours.'

His dark gloved fist grasped the perspiring bottle and drew it out of the cooling bucket. From the dark green bottle came a stream of liquid gold. 'Try it, and tell me.'

Emily spoke quickly. 'It's a Moselle, isn't it?' she pronounced a shade anxiously, in her anxiety to please. She sniffed the bouquet deeply. 'Full bodied but not leggy and with a—'

'Drink,' he instructed softly. 'Tell me if you like it, my dear, not what it is or where it comes from. I want your response, not its provenance.'

He studied her closely, watching her white throat fleetingly constrict in the flickering candlelight. She found the wine to be delicious. She grinned, a wide, honest grin, and drank again. He nodded his approval at her undisguised pleasure.

She shivered with renewed delight as the chilled elixir seduced and mastered her delicate palate.

'Mmmm, delicious.'

'It's an Apostlewein. And yes, I find it quite delicious. A very pleasing wine. I was fortunate enough—'

'To acquire several cases,' Emily matched him, silently, word for word. Ever the collector, she mused to herself ruefully. An Apostlewein. Memory of fine wine sales kicked in. Surely not. She peeped at the label. Rudesheimer, a seventy-four. No rain that spring, and a frost-free Moselle growth. Yes, it came back to her. Four thousand pounds a bottle. A collector's item. She sipped guiltily, greedily. God, she'd just swallowed several hundred quid!

They finished their wine in a comfortable silence. Pouring another glass for her, Dr Stikannos saluted Emily in a silent toast. Across the room, the yellow candlelight danced gently before the huge oval mirror, the reflected glimmer making his metal mask eerily fluid as if still molten. Only his dark eyes remained fixed – fixed upon her breasts and the shadows between her clamped thighs. Emily placed her empty glass down upon the desk. He did not offer to replenish it a third time, but knuckled the bottle carefully aside. The wheelchair creaked.

Out in the grounds, where the azure of the dusk was rapidly darkening into the violet of the deepening summer night, an owl screeched as it swooped and taloned something warm and furry.

Inside the room, in a silence broken only by Emily's short sighs and gasps – and the shrill screech of an owl taking its kill – two leather-gloved hands were swooping down and clutching the warm pubic nest of the naked girl's delta. After relishing the rounded bosom above, the leathered fingertips were now busy at the pussy below. Her feral fragrance filled the air, a fragrance as delicate and as delicious as the bouquet of the Rudesheimer Apostlewein.

Emily swallowed and moaned softly as Dr Stikannos

144

spread her labia as a collector would spread the wings of a rare moth or butterfly. Then his fingertips firmly widened the wet inner lips, nudging insistently before probing gently. A finger, its full length. A second finger, alongside the first, stretching her tight warmth. God, her belly began to feel full.

The mask rose, his dark eyes fixed upon her collar. She interpreted his unspoken wish and brought her trembling fingers up to the symbol of her servitude. Inching her thighs wider to accommodate his fingers, she thumbed the spangled yoke at her throat. The metal mask glinted as he showed his approval with her passive complicity. Already she was exhibiting the appropriate behaviour of the eager, anxious slave; absolute obedience, passive submission. The metal mask lowered a fraction. Dr Stikannos was gazing directly into her fingered wetness. Rising up on tiptoe, Emily rode the phallus of fingers inside her, but her master showed no impatience, no signs of gathering haste. His actions were slow, deliberate and unhurried. The master was utterly in control.

Emily, untutored, became eager for the disciplined instruction and indoctrination into servitude to commence in earnest. Her cheeks ached for the fierce lash of the camel's penis. Her hot cleft throbbed between the quiver of her spasming buttocks.

'Be still,' he soothed, his whispered words oozing a velvet menace.

But the more Emily stared down into her widening pit of delicious depravity, the fiercer she desired to tumble headlong into it. Impatiently, the naked slave ground her hips and began to consciously contract her inner muscles. The metal mask rose up slowly, the dark eyes behind it carrying a glint of challenge as they met her blurred gaze. Emily whimpered as she felt his fingers beginning to withdraw. Obediently, in compliance with the silent instruction from his dark eyes, she loosened her tightening grip. His eyes closed, acknowledging her submission and return to passive surrender. The leathered fingers returned to fill her wet warmth, as if rewarding her obedience. Three of them. Emily choked down a scream of delight. Her cleft became a narrow crease as, buttocks tightening savagely, she suffered his thumb at her clitoral bud. Moments later, her knees seemed to sag and collapse in against each other.

'Good,' he observed. 'It's almost time. Time for you to taste the lash. Turn,' he ordered sharply. 'Turn around and give me your bottom.'

Emily whimpered as the leathered thumbtip ceased to torment her shiny little erect love-thorn, and shuddered unashamedly as the gloved fingers slid silently from her seething slit. Cheeks wobbling, she turned in the candlelight, presenting her bare bottom to him, as perfectly and as obediently, she hoped, as any novice slave learning the arts of pleasing her master.

He perused her bare buttocks for many minutes, sipping his wine twice to lubricate his dry throat. Emily basked and yet squirmed, hating yet loving being the naked object of his dominant, indifferent pleasure.

Then the moment came, suddenly, breaking into her trance brutally. He raked her cleft with his wet thumbtip – the thumbtip that had teased her clitoris. Emily squeezed her cheeks tightly together to contain the cruel probe. He grunted as her sphincter gripped; a low soft snarl of carnal arousal. Had she pleased him? Emily ached to speak, but knew that silence was imperative and that for the naked slave to speak to her master would break the spell that bound them.

Silence.

Despite her longing she knew it must be endured. But soon his whip would speak. A short, brutal crack. He would grunt again, his short delight drowned in her squeal of savage joy.

The whip. As Dr Stikannos prised her cheeks apart between his gloved fingers, Emily closed her eyes and imagined the furled camel's penis. Imagined it in his fisted glove, its oiled length glinting in the candlelight. Imagined the sudden flick – the short, sinister whistling thrum – and then the harsh crack. Imagined the unimaginable sear across her defenceless cheeks.

His hands were busy at her buttocks. His fingers firmly dimpled the soft swell of each imprisoned buttock, then slid away from their satin sheen. Emily opened her eyes, suddenly alert and alarmed. The tiny hairs on the nape of her neck rose, bristling with fearful expectation. His gloved hand pawed the surface of the desk softly, the fingertips inching towards the coiled whip. It was coming. Her sweet pain. It was time. Time for the searing lash.

'Bend. Bend over.'

She hesitated for a few seconds, then bowed before him.

'Further.'

Her blonde hair cascaded, fringing her eyes as she obeyed, raising her bare bottom in absolute submission.

'Feet a little wider apart.'

In the darkness, her tiny white toes scrabbled into the carpet.

'Now place your palms across your bottom, my dear,' he ordered firmly. 'No, not like that. One hand across each cheek. Fingertips almost touching.'

Slightly puzzled, Emily brought her hands across her straining buttocks. Her fingertips kissed across her cleft.

'Excellent.' There was a moment's silence. 'This,' he whispered, snapping the camel's penis sharply, 'is an anal whip.'

The vicious snap filled her mind with delicious dread. Emily shivered as he furled the whip back up into his gloved fist.

'It does not,' he continued, 'bite across the cheeks like a crop or bamboo cane. No, Emily, it is not destined or designed to whip you across you buttocks, but between them.'

She gasped, then moaned, swaying and clamping her thighs involuntarily together as the meaning of his words exploded softly deep inside her brain.

'Cheeks apart.'

She pressed her palms into the swell of each proffered globe, then spread her buttocks, revealing the dark line of her shadowed cleft.

'Wider.'

She pulled her captive flesh further apart, forcing her anal crater to pucker and pout.

'Excellent,' he murmured.

For a full half minute he examined and intimately inspected her submissive, surrendered flesh. Slowly, silently, he raised his right hand. Emily, sensing the slight movement, almost stumbled forward.

'Remain perfectly still.'

She froze instantly into rigid obedience.

'Good girl,' he purred, his soft voice caressing her consciousness, lulling her seductively into his mesmeric thrall.

A brief, eerie whistle. A savage crack. The camel's penis whipping down, searing her soft cleft.

Emily screamed as a crimson light imploded behind her eyes. Buckling helplessly at her knees, she writhed then collapsed face down before him, jerking her hips and hammering her clenched cheeks up into the empty air. A fierce scald blazed between them. She squeezed harder, vainly trying to extinguish the pain. The delicious heat quickly spread to her wet slit. Soon she was molten.

'In a moment you will taste the delights of discipline,' he murmured, kissing the camel's penis with reverence.

Emily ground her breasts into the carpet, and seconds later as she rasped her sticky labia into its silken weave, she started to come.

'Yes,' he hissed. 'The perfect little slave.'

Straining in his wheelchair, steadying himself at each

armrest, Dr Stikannos angled his left foot down and planted his polished shoe onto her trembling bottom. She squealed with delight at this delicate dominance, her first climax now gathering up and exploding into its successor. Her master relished her writhing nakedness, and trod firmly down into the flesh he had just punished.

'Suffer, my dear, suffer your sweet pain.'

Treading his naked, climaxing slave down, Dr Stikannos spasmed, tensed rigidly and then spurted, soaking himself massively as he emptied his seething sac. Beneath the controlling leather of his polished shoe, Emily writhed as she continued coming loudly.

Master and slave.

The whipper and the whipped: united in the paroxysm of their violent orgasm.

'Just one?'

'U-huh.'

'Really?' Susie propped herself up on one elbow. 'Can I see?'

'Nothing to see,' Emily whispered, reaching up to gather the minx in an embrace and bring her back down across her naked bosom.

'Just the one stroke?'

'Shush.'

Silence ensued as their breasts collided gently, nipples kissing.

'But I don't understand,' Susie murmured, peeling herself away slightly. 'Just the one.'

'You don't give up, do you?' Emily groaned. 'It isn't an ordinary whip. It doesn't lash horizontally.'

'I still don't see,' Susie replied, genuinely puzzled.

Emily whispered into the minx's ear. 'It goes down – vertically. Between your cheeks.'

'You mean,' Susie gasped, suddenly comprehending. 'Ooh,' she shivered, snuggling back into Emily's soft naked warmth. 'Is it very…?'

'Yes, it is – very. I started to come almost at once. I've never…'

'Where does old metal-face keep it, this whip that can make a girl come with just one stroke? I'd like a taste—'

'Don't. You wouldn't. Don't speak lightly of it; you don't understand.'

Emily pulled Susie's lovely face back down to her own, and their lips met. 'It's very special, and quite wonderful. Too special to make fun of, I promise you.'

Susie, impressed, lapsed into solemn silence. They lay together, kissing slowly, deeply, lingeringly.

When Susie did speak again her voice was small in the darkness. 'I heard you cry out. It scared me.'

'Where were you?' Emily asked, surprised.

'Out in the garden.'

'Bit risky.'

'I know, but I heard a fox barking in the spinney, so I went out to get the peacocks into their pen. A fox will take a peahen easily. I was just outside the window when I heard you. Scared the life out of me, it did. Peeped through the curtains but couldn't see much except the candles, but I could just make out a lot of grunting and groaning and I knew it was you in there with him. What the hell was going on?'

'I'll tell you all about it, one day. When I understand it myself.'

'Promise?'

'When, and if, you're ready,' Emily promised enigmatically.

'Was he sort of punishing you?'

'Sort of,' Emily conceded.

'But just one stroke? And…'

'And?'

'And you both came. I heard, you know.'

'I know. Yes, we both came. For the same, yet different,

reasons. I said I'll explain it all to you one day – perhaps.'

Satisfied, but avidly curious, Susie wriggled free and sat on the edge of Emily's narrow bed.

'Come back to me,' Emily whispered.

The minx returned to Emily's side. They lay, face to face, nose to nose, nipple to nipple, sex crushed to thigh. They lay on their sides, moulded together. Several minutes later, after a slow searching kiss, Emily pinned Susie face down into the mattress and mounted her, lowering her pussy down onto the younger girl's upturned rump. Gripping Susie's hair and pinning her face into the pillow, she sinuously rode the bare bottom beneath her, raking her wet slit repeatedly down across the trapped buttocks' soft satin swell.

Susie whimpered her delight into the white pillow, stiffening as she heard and felt the girl on top achieving a sweet climax.

'Me now,' the minx pleaded.

'You, now.'

Susie's pussy was already hot and wet, and Emily's fingers were quick to seek out and find its inner tightness. Susie whispered frantically, begging Emily to probe deeper, harder, faster, and soon Emily's efforts were rewarded with Susie's squealed orgasm.

They slept, fitfully, for a few hours. Then Susie woke up. She was peckish.

'You hungry?' she whispered.

Emily was difficult to wake, but Susie, determined to eat, eventually managed to stir the sleeping blonde.

'Be quiet,' Emily warned, rubbing the sleep from her grey eyes.

They stole downstairs and found all they needed in the larder. Licking her fingertips after the mayonnaise, Susie carefully halved, then quartered, the wholemeal bread sandwiches crammed to bursting point with moist turkey, lettuce and tomatoes.

'Sure Ursula won't notice?' Emily asked, after swallowing

a huge bite. She was anxious to spare the maid's bottom from the cane of the green-eyed tormentor. 'We've made a hell of a dent in that cold roast turkey.'

'It's okay,' Susie gulped. 'There's masses of everything. For the buyers.'

'Buyers?' Emily rescued a morsel of meat from her cleavage and wolfed it.

'For the sale. They're coming tomorrow. There's been lots brought in. Two extra van loads. The larder's bulging. Like some cake?'

Emily shook her head. Van loads. Her tired brain seized on the phrase – but why? Why did she find them so interesting? Then she remembered; remembered the van that had brought the packing cases; cases strictly supervised by Ursula as they were secretly consigned down into the air-conditioned cellar. Cases, Emily was convinced, that could only have contained paintings.

'Take me to the cellar,' she said suddenly, her tone as determined as her resolve.

'Can't,' Susie replied simply. 'Ursula's got the key,' she explained, shrugging apologetically. 'Started wearing it around her neck on a chain ever since those packing cases came the other night.'

'I would've loved a quick peep inside,' Emily confessed. 'But if…'

'A quick peep? You can have that if it's so important,' Susie grinned.

'You said Ursula's got the key.'

'Yep,' Susie nodded. 'Round her neck. It's there day and night, just like that collar thing you've been wearing. What is it, anyway?'

'Never mind. Tell you later.'

'Later? Like you're going to tell me about that anal whip that makes you come after just one stroke?' Susie's eyes sparkled.

'We'll see. Spare key, is there?'

'No, don't think so. But if you really want a quick look I can fix it. I've tumbled them and their funny little games.'

'Games?'

'They think I don't know about how they spy on everyone and everything that goes on this house. Come, I'll show you.'

Emily was still recovering from her initial shock. 'It's incredible!'

'Bit creepy. I'm extra careful now I know.'

'I bet you are. Is it everywhere? I mean, every room?'

'Yep, the whole works. Gym, gardens, the lot. Cameras covering every square foot.'

They were huddled together in front of the bank of monitors. Susie tweaked the joystick, panning down a dimly lit corridor on the second floor as she practised her tracking skills. 'The cameras are placed behind mirrors, inside smoke detectors, that sort of thing. Recognise this?

'But that's not fair,' Emily cried, gasping in dismay as the camera in her former luxurious bedroom suddenly kicked in, filling the screen above with the sumptuous four-poster.

'Bet there'll be one in the shower. Yep, told you.'

Emily flushed angrily as she remembered masturbating in the shower. Dr Stikannos and the green eyes of Ursula had no doubt witnessed it all.

Susie giggled. 'Let's turn the tables. Let's see what everyone's up to at this late hour.' Susie concentrated on the control panel. 'His nibs should be bye-byes by now. Wonder if he sleeps in his mask.'

Emily's heart skipped a beat. She squirmed uncomfortably at the thought of betraying her master; her master whom she was slowly but surely coming to love obeying. Obey, yes. Her servitude thrilled her. As did the sweet sharp sorrows of being disciplined. But love? Could a slave every really love her master? Fear, respect and serve, yes. But love?

'Oh, he goes to bed in it. Look.'

Startled out of her brief reverie, Emily glanced up. In view up on another monitor she saw Dr Stikannos. He was neither asleep nor abed. He was masked and sitting on the edge of his bed.

'I don't think we should be…' Emily murmured.

Susie giggled. 'He's probably getting out for a pee.'

Emily blushed, still uncomfortable at breaking the sovereign bonds that bound servant to master. She glanced up shyly at the screen. On it, naked though masked, Dr Stikannos was reaching up to grasp a metal bar suspended from the ceiling above. Emily watched, fascinated, as his leathered hands tightened around the dull steel. Straining, his biceps bulging, Dr Stikannos hauled himself slowly up onto his unsteady feet.

'Six to one the basket case doesn't make it,' Susie quipped.

Emily scowled, returning her rapt attention instantly to the screen.

'God, look at him. He's actually trying to walk.'

Emily only half heard Susie's running commentary. Her heart was beating wildly as she gazed up at the man who had, earlier that evening, plied an anal whip between her parted cheeks and caused her to come on the spot – right then and there at his feet. She sat enthralled before the screen. Dr Stikannos was struggling gamely, his torso well developed, as were his arms. But the legs were pale and poorly muscled, unequal to the task of supporting him. After gripping the metal bar for a few unsteady minutes he collapsed back down, defeated, onto his bed. Emily sighed as she watched his gloved fists clench in frustration.

'Tarzan's done for the night,' Susie remarked impishly, fiddling with the controls. 'Let's take a peek at what Ursula's got cooking for her darling little Chloe.'

'What about the cellar?' Emily reminded her. 'You promised.'

154

'Watched her cane Chloe's bare bum last night,' Susie giggled.

'You're terrible,' Emily laughed, despite herself. 'When did you discover this?'

'Complete accident. They left the door open, it was a hot afternoon, I was cleaning outside. Look, got them. There they are.'

Emily, still discomforted by the thought that her own nakedness – and intimate naughtiness – had filled the screen for the voyeuristic pleasure of others, looked up. In a medium close-up shot, she watched Ursula dominating a kneeling, tearstained Chloe.

'No sound,' Susie apologised. 'Or if there is I don't know how to make it work. But the pictures are clear enough. Look at her nipples.'

Emily did. Chloe's nipples were engorged, peaked and prinked with pain. Ursula was applying a strip of velvet across the eyes of the kneeling girl's upturned face. Now she was buckling a leather harness around Chloe's breasts, squeezing them and bunching the swollen flesh-mounds as she tightened the straps behind Chloe's back, fixing the leather harness like a bustier on the kneeling nude.

Emily swallowed, desperately trying to lubricate her dry mouth. Up on the screen, Ursula was screwing a silver dildo into a socket poised in the cleavage between Chloe's bound breasts.

'Oh, she's not going to, is she?' Susie squealed in disbelief.

Mesmerised, Emily could only nod in silence. They sat together, finding one another's hands and holding each other tightly as, up on the screen, the quivering dildo angled up, thrusting from the bosom and pointing like an accusing finger at Ursula's wet pussy – a wet pussy that inched ever closer to the waiting knout below.

'Bloody hell,' Susie whispered.

Ursula planted her slit onto the dildo, then inched herself down until her inner thighs captured and contained the outer curves of Chloe's breasts.

'Big close-up,' Susie gasped, springing up and twiddling frantically with the controls.

Up on the screen, Ursula's huge cheeks filled the glass, spasming and tightening as she clenched them, each paroxysm of her buttocks betraying yet another pelvic thrust, and with each pelvic thrust the dildo probed the dominant's tight, wet warmth.

Emily shuddered. She imagined the silver shaft, supported by the breasts of the kneeling girl, spearing Ursula sweetly. But unaccustomed to the dark delights of voyeurism, Emily felt slightly queasy about spying on the pair. Spying on Ursula at her savage games; the cat – feline and cruel. Spying on Chloe in her humiliation and shame; the mouse – quivering and helpless.

Emily cuddled Susie as they both watched Ursula ride the phallus, scream her silent climax open-mouthed into the all-seeing camera lens, then rapidly unscrew the silver dildo from its socket and force it with brutal tenderness into Chloe's mouth.

Susie caught Emily's hand and, separating her index finger from the rest, brought it up to her mouth, and Emily moaned as Susie sucked greedily. Up on the screen, the silver dildo probed the soft pink circle of Chloe's pursed lips. Ursula suddenly jerked her controlling hand up, withdrawing the dildo, and Emily withdrew her finger from Susie's warm wet mouth. On the screen, Ursula tipped the kneeling nude face down across the bed and, gripping the dildo like a dagger, stabbed the proffered buttocks with its glinting snout. They watched Chloe writhe as the smooth shaft probed between her cheeks. Emily wormed two fingers into Susie's cleft, seeking and quickly discovering the minx's sphincter.

Ursula was down on her knees now, the dildo gripped between her white teeth. Like a wolf at the helpless flesh of a lamb, she brought her mouth against Chloe's squirming cheeks, into which she had buried the brutal length. More tenderly, more lovingly, Emily scissored her fingers, stretching Susie's rectal warmth. As Chloe squealed silently under the dominance of Ursula, Susie mewed her sweet delight.

On the screen, Chloe and Ursula lay sprawled but separate in their bed. Sprawled, separate, unconnected in their sated sleep. Curled up and entwined before the screen, Emily cradled Susie as they both snuggled and slept, their hearts beating as one.

A shrill peahen calling for her customary breakfast of burnt toast woke them. Scrambling up in panic, Emily pointed to the monitor. On it, they saw Chloe getting dressed. She was alone in her bedroom. Naked, her white bra dangling from her left hand, she stood and stretched before a full-length mirror.

'Where's Ursula?' Susie whispered hoarsely.

Emily jabbed her finger down on the control buttons and tweaked the joystick frantically, desperate to discover the whereabouts of the green-eyed tormentor. A camera picked her up and tracked her as she prowled along a carpeted corridor – on the ground floor!

'She's coming this way,' Susie squeaked in horror.

They were trapped. Scuttling behind a pair of gunmetal grey filing cabinets, they cowered like kittens in a thunderstorm. Peeping out, they shrank instinctively as Ursula strode into the room.

'She's…' Susie whispered, but Emily placed her fingertip against Susie's lips, pressing firmly into their soft warmth in warning.

Ursula glanced up at the screen. She saw Chloe raising the empty cups of her white bra to the swell of her naked bosom, as the soft cups covered the thrusting breasts, as Chloe strained to snap the straps together at her back, causing her bosom to bulge in its cosseting bondage.

Emily and Susie huddled in alarm as they saw Ursula

flick her pleated mini-skirt up over her hips then quickly peel her taut white panties down. On the screen, Chloe was dangling a single nylon stocking from the fingertips of her right hand. In the bluish sheen of the mirror's surface, her dark pubic bush glistened.

Ursula's buttocks tightened into firm mounds as she strummed her labia apart. Up on the screen, Chloe had threaded her nylon stocking between her parted thighs and was now plying the stretched sheen ruthlessly into her wet heat, rasping the taut fabric against her clitoris. Tossing back her head in ecstasy and spilling her raven hair down in a tumble over her pale shoulders, the almost naked girl glimpsed in her bedroom before her mirror rapidly approached her climax.

Drinking in the scene through dreamy green eyes – and hungrily devouring every detail – Ursula shuffled towards the control panel, inching her parted thighs up to and then over the stubby joystick. The image of Chloe using her stocking at her slit slid jerkily off the screen as Ursula, up on tiptoe, filled her wet warmth and rode the joystick rhythmically, buttocks spasming and thighs quivering. With a loud cry she lowered and impaled herself, her cleft now a fierce crease between her clenched cheeks.

Emily and Susie, cowering behind the filing cabinets, smothered their gasps as Ursula, climaxing in time with the raven-haired nude on the monitor above, lurched forward and planted her fingertips down over the buttons before her. As her orgasm ravished her, she played the buttons of the control panel like a demented pianist, bringing eight of the monitors instantly into life. In a blaze of sudden exposure, every shadowed recess of the sprawling house revealed the creeping fingers of the early morning sunlight. But the screen showing Chloe writhing as she came snapped blank. Ursula growled lustily and eased herself up off the joystick. Emily saw the plastic knob glisten with Ursula's juices. Dragging up her panties so sharply they bit into her dark cleft, Ursula flipped down her pleated mini-skirt and, without looking back, strode out of the room.

Emily and Susie still held their breath, exhaling suddenly as the tense silence was broken once more by the shrill impatience of the hungry peahen calling for her toast.

Emily put down the page she had just plucked from the printer. The catalogue was completed, all eighteen paintings up for sale now carefully, and colourfully, given authentication and provenance.

Her mind returned to the contents of the cellar, and she wondered what had arrived under the cover and cloak of darkness to be hidden away by Ursula down there. A Renoir, perhaps? Her heart skipped a beat at the thought. Dr Stikannos had, like all collectors, a voracious appetite. Was the sale of the eighteen paintings being held to generate the millions required for the purchase of a major work of art? A Picasso? Her mouth dried. She felt thrilled and frightened.

Susie entered, smiling. She had brought coffee and moist orange and lemon cake. Not furtively, like recent treats, but quite openly, on a gleaming Georgian silver-chased tray.

'Doesn't Ursula mind?' she asked.

Susie smiled reassuringly. 'Things have changed.'

'What do you mean, changed?' Emily demanded, wolfing down the delicious cake.

'You'll see. Just finish your cake and coffee.'

A few minutes later Susie conducted Emily upstairs. They paused outside a door that, to Emily, seemed familiar.

'But this is the room I was in,' she said.

'Exactly,' Susie grinned. 'Dr Stikannos told Ursula you were to be given your room back. She was mad as hell but had to obey.'

They went in. Emily's feet trod the silk Chinese carpet once more as her eyes feasted on the sumptuous four-poster bed.

'I'd better be off,' Susie said. 'There's masses to do. Big

supper party tonight for the buyers.'

They kissed and Susie departed, leaving Emily to explore the exquisite room. She was delighted Dr Stikannos had reinstalled her, overruling jealous Ursula. Emily hugged herself in happy triumph; the master had rewarded his slave.

She examined the contents of the huge fridge. It was crammed with exotic treats. Belgian pralines and Russian caramels and Italian ice. Fresh flowers – heliotrope and tea roses – perfumed the room with the maddening scent of vanilla and attar.

Then she saw it. On the white bolster at the head of the bed, a small square of shiny silver glinting in the sunlight. Her name was neatly inscribed on a yellow tag in crabbed, black italics. An incisive hand, firm and sure. She prised the silver wrapping paper open then delicately fingered the softer tissue paper within apart.

She froze, the small portrait suddenly heavy in her trembling hands. It was a present from her master. A Holbein. God, a Holbein! Emily slumped down upon the bed, utterly stunned.

Ann Corderey, sometime favourite of the French Sun King, she read. It was perfect, framed simply but beautifully in a square of beaten gold, the miniature portrait of the French courtesan remained stubbornly dark, its chiaroscuro a heavy patina despite the bright summer sunshine flooding her room. Emily, her hands still trembling, gazed down at the pale, poignant face captured within the golden frame. Holbein had been honest. The eyes were darkly soulful but speckled with dancing lights of lust. The left eye was beautifully blemished with a provocative squint. The hair fell down in wanton abandon as if the sitter had just arisen from her bed of carnal sport. Yes, Emily acknowledged, thrilling to the Holbein, it was a truthful portrait, revealing Ann Corderey not as a mere academic footnote in French history but as a slightly stubborn – that tilt of the chin – deeply sensual woman.

Emily glanced down at the hands; the hands that had fashioned silver, gold and fruit wood into exquisite artefacts for her royal patron and master. The slender hands clutched a nosegay of saxifrage – the symbol of penance. The sinner's bloom.

A note plucked up from the discarded silver wrapping paper told Emily that Ann Corderey was more than a mistress to the French Sun King: she had been his slave. Dr Stikannos concluded the note by observing that the fierce bonds that bound the lovers had been forged in the pleasures of pain. Emily examined the dark-eyed Frenchwoman carefully, shivering as she suddenly discovered in them a willingness to be whipped.

She brought the Holbein up to her lips, slowly kissing the face of Ann Corderey. Heart of a Lion. Buttocks of a penitent. Suddenly conscious of the hidden camera in her room – he would be watching her, scrutinising her reactions to his wonderful gift – she slithered down from the soft bed, sinking her knees into the silk Chinese carpet.

Where was it? Where was the all-seeing lens? Intuitively, she sensed its presence behind a small light fixture up on the opposite wall. Yes, it would be able to scan the bed from there. Inching her buttocks towards the hidden lens, she bared her bottom and palmed her cheeks wide apart, signalling to her watching master her readiness, her eagerness, for the scalding kiss of his whip.

Chapter Seven

It was three o'clock. The sardonyx and gold long-case chimed the hour sweetly, its ting-tang Cambridge peal echoing around the sunlit room. Emily traced the orange, white and marbled gold casement of the Jacobean clock with her fingertip. Her tongue felt large in her dry mouth. Her pulse plucked wildly at her throat and temples.

Behind his desk, in his wheelchair, Dr Stikannos waited patiently for her answer.

As the Cambridge chimes faded and died, Emily turned, tentatively confident and hesitantly resolved. His mask glinted as he raised his head expectantly, his dark eyes staring directly into hers.

'I came here to thank you…'

He waved away her words with a gloved hand, and Emily sensed disappointment behind the gesture.

'No,' she added quickly. 'Not just with words. I've come to you.'

'As slave to master?'

'As slave to master,' she whispered. 'Now let me serve you.'

In silence, she trod the carpet towards the desk and stood behind his wheelchair, turned to the windows and slowly drew across the heavy velvet drapes. In the darkness of the banished sunlight, she returned to his wheelchair and gently propelled it away from the desk. Kneeling down before it, she slowly, tantalisingly, wriggled out of her clothes until she knelt naked and fresh before him. She heard him draw in his breath sharply as, reaching up, she took his gloved hands in hers.

'No,' he grunted, tugging them away.

'Please, let me,' she whispered, carefully retrieving his right hand.

'Why?' he demanded, his tone gently bewildered.

She kissed his hand briefly, rose, parted her thighs, then guided his leathered knuckles down to her slit. He squirmed in his wheelchair as she raked his glove into her wetness, and for long minutes, in absolute silence, she stroked her labia with his captive fist.

Then, slowly, with infinite care, she started to peel the glove away from the injured flesh within. The wheelchair rattled as he tried to withdraw his damaged hand from her, but Emily was gently insistent, and soon the glove was off.

Cradling his withered blackened flesh in her soft pink palm, she gazed down at it in the darkness. Bending lower, she tickled his hand with the tip of her tongue, then licked the damaged flesh, lapping at the crusted skin lingeringly and lovingly. Her grey eyes flickered up to meet his dark gaze as she repeatedly kissed his open palm, then sucked on each of his quivering fingertips.

'Why?' he pleaded softly, probing her mouth with two blackened fingers. 'Tell me. In the name of hell, why?'

The silk dressing gown at the base of his belly stirred.

'Shush,' she mumbled, her mouth full of his flesh. Keeping the two fingers trapped gently between her white teeth, and sucking on them, she slowly peeled away the leather glove from his other damaged hand.

'Be careful, little slave,' he grunted.

She nodded her solemn obedience, guiding his left hand, naked and reluctantly unclenched, to her pussy. When his fingertips were glistening with her dewy warmth, she drew them up to her right breast, positioning them against the ripe softness, and moaning as he tentatively squeezed.

'Harder,' she coaxed, groaning loudly as the master obeyed the slave. 'Harder,' she repeated, adding his right hand to her other breast.

Slowly, stiffly, he plied his fingers into her silky flesh,

squirming in his wheelchair as unaccustomed life flowed through his veins once more.

After a long silence his hands grew more confident, more supple, more dominant. Soon he was cupping and squeezing her with Sadean tenderness – viciously gentle.

Emily grasped his wrists lightly and, drawing the palms of his hands together as if for unholy prayer, guided them down once more to trap and tame them between her clamped thighs. She sighed as her fig split wide, oozing its hot trickle onto his imprisoned flesh, and thrilled to his snarl as his throat tightened in response.

The clock chimed the half-hour. Ting, tang… Ting, tang…

'And now your mask.'

'No,' he barked. Was there a note of fear there? Of fear, in the master's voice? It was a vibrant, quivering retort.

'Please,' she whispered. 'Allow me to heal.'

'Heal?' he countered sharply.

'Sexual healing,' she murmured, clamping her thighs tightly to trap and contain his hands as she gently reached out to his mask. Despite her uncertainty, it came away surprisingly easily, but although fleetingly familiar with his twisted features, the blackened flesh of his face still came as a brutal shock.

She managed to smother her gasp of dismay – just.

Had his dark eyes caught the flicker of revulsion in hers? Emily began to breathe rapidly.

'Satisfied?' he challenged. 'Still prepared to heal me, eh?' His tone was twisted with a sad satisfaction, a perverted triumph.

'Always willing to serve,' Emily replied softly, bending down and burying his hideous face in the warm cushion of her satin-skinned breasts.

His dry lips sought and found her left nipple, captured it and sucked savagely. Cradling his head, she gently smothered her bosom against his upturned face, teasing and delighting him. She saw, with satisfaction and feminine pride, the stretch of his yearning erection stiff beneath the rise of his silk dressing gown.

'Witch,' he mumbled, humble now at the swell of her breasts.

'Witch doctor,' she rallied lightly, burying his face deep in her sweet-smelling cleavage. Easing back a fraction, moments later, she dragged the warm weight of her breasts slowly down across his face, finding his mouth once more. Using her right peaked nipple like a lipstick across the line of his dry upper lip, she maddened him until his white teeth flashed hungrily, and she tapped his nose as she would a frisking puppy.

'Kiss,' she invited, offering her nipple to his pursed lips, and he obeyed instantly. 'Suck,' she instructed.

For long minutes he suckled feverishly, and she anointed his trapped, crippled fingers between her thighs.

Ting, tang... Ting, tang... Ting, tang... The soft Cambridge chimes delicately broke the spell.

'The mask,' she asked gently, easing his face away from her soft breasts and gazing down upon it. 'Why? Tell me, why do you wear it?'

His black eyes glinted, signalling a flash of impatience with the naïve stupidity of her question. Emily caught the glint of contempt and responded in silence by stroking the ravished flesh of his cheekbones with her caressing fingertips. He shook his face, withdrawing abruptly, but Emily persisted, drawing him back to her and burying his face once more into her warm flesh, continuing to stroke his flesh lovingly.

Lovingly, as only a true slave can.

'Why?' she whispered.

'Not for myself,' he replied, mouthing the words into her silky bosom. 'It's not mere vanity; it's to spare the feelings of those few who must look upon me. To spare their feelings. To relieve the awkwardness.'

She had, for the first time in their intense relationship,

prompted him into something approaching fluency, and she sensed the simple candour in his words. Emily remained silent; a silence she calculated he would feel obliged to fill with more revelations. Telling her what she longed to know, but dared not ask to discover. And it worked. She had gambled psychologically – and won.

He took a deep breath and sighed, and she thrilled to his warmth at her nipples. 'The mask is a curiosity. But people can remain curious yet continue to do business. Their concentration is not impeded. The mask becomes a mere distraction, unlike the damaged face behind it. They wonder, of course, and speculate. But soon the mask becomes no more than the gloves. But without the mask, and the gloves, people would shy away.'

'And you can observe them closely without their realising it,' Emily added.

'Little witch,' he grunted into her flesh. 'But, I do wear it for others, not for myself.'

Emily touched his face, motioning that she understood. It was a gesture for him to continue.

He bit both of her nipples, mouthing them softly then holding them between his teeth before kissing them tenderly.

'And now I suppose you want to know how it happened?'

Emily continued to cradle him to her bosom, and said nothing.

'Well?' he growled softly, his lips busy at her nipples. 'Don't you?'

She remained silent, and as if punishing her he sucked hard at her nipple, already a swollen peak of purple pain. But she managed to smother her groan.

'Eve,' he hissed, shuddering. 'Her curiosity, her desire for knowledge. You are truly the daughter of Eve. Look at all the misery one woman's wanton curiosity and disobedience unleashed. The apple,' he whispered, mouthing her left breast, a note of rising excitement thickening his voice. 'The apple. Plucked by her from the forbidden tree. Tempted, she did eat.' He bit her breast softly, taking much of the ripe flesh into his mouth. 'She did eat. Bruising the fruit. Fruit from the Tree of Knowledge. That is why,' he whispered into her ripe warmth, 'woman is designed and destined by nature to be apple-buttocked. Ripe and firm. And, like the apple, doomed to be reddened. Woman is apple-buttocked. It is her fate, her eternal punishment, and she must forever endure to have those buttocks beaten for her original sin of disobedience. Bruised fruit.'

His voice, rising as if in a mesmeric incantation, fell quiet. Absolute silence reigned.

'Dodgy theology,' she whispered, and he laughed despite himself, all the tension of the past moments draining from him as he tossed his head back and roared. She thrilled to his storm of happiness. Holding him, they laughed together.

'It was a fire,' he said suddenly, returning his face almost shyly to her breasts and whispering his secrets into their silken warmth.

She hugged him tightly, squeezing the confession from his dry lips.

'Switzerland, five years ago. I was back in the hotel after a successful private sale. I was there with only two staff. One was down in the garage, tinkering with the car. Hans, my butler, was down in the kitchens. It was late. Hans was greasing the palm of the chef for a late-night supper. I had suggested sea bass in a sorrel sauce and wild strawberries in a champagne sorbet.'

Emily was fascinated by the sudden wealth of detail. She realised that this was the first time since the incident he had spoken of it so openly, so freely. Probably the first time he had faced it. Faced the dreadful horror of it all. She held him tight.

'The bells rang and the lights flickered and went out. I took the lift down from the penthouse suite. Everything was calm and orderly, except for the bells. I got out at the seventh

167

floor and ran back up the service stairs.'

Hesitant to break the silence, Emily simply squeezed him to her breasts, prompting him to explain.

'To get a picture.' His voice was trembling now. 'A picture I was particularly fond of. Not the most expensive, but the most beautiful in my collection.'

Emily's mind rounded up the usual suspects. Van Gogh, Picasso, Pissaro.

'I was not prepared to sacrifice it,' he affirmed. 'I retrieved the painting but was caught up in the confusion of the smoke-filled darkness when descending the service stairs. I met a wall of flames. I ran through them and struggled to the ground floor, where I collapsed, and awoke in an ambulance. You can guess the rest.'

Emily placed her fingertips at his lips. He had, she sensed, said enough. Enough to stir very disturbing memories. Too much, perhaps. Bending lower she kissed his face, peeling her lips away from time to time to lick his charred flesh.

Suddenly she stepped back, her heart beating wildly. No, it couldn't be. She was insane to even think it – but she had to know.

His hands, wet from her weeping slit, fell down by the wheels of his chair. He gazed up at her, his dark eyes scanning her quizzically.

'It was the Holbein, wasn't it?' she gasped, unable to check the question as it tumbled out. 'You ran back into certain danger to rescue Holbein's miniature of Ann Corderey.' Emily spoke these words not as a question but as a statement – of which she was sure and certain.

His face, distorted though it was, managed to register his amazement. 'Little witch,' he grinned, his blackened face contorting. 'Yes, it was the Holbein.'

Overwhelmed, Emily grappled across him, crushing her bare breasts into him as she reached for the desk. There, her groping hand found and snatched up the furled camel penis. Taking a step back, she thrust the coiled hide into his right

168

hand then turned, bending, thighs apart – offering her naked bottom. 'Whip me,' she begged.

His ungloved finger swept down and touched her intimately. He repeatedly fingered the moist velvet of her cleft until she was quivering and moaning. The anal whip barked aloud, twice. Emily screamed, twice: collapsing onto the carpet and sobbing with dread delight. The wheelchair creaked as he sank down on his knees behind her, his thighs colliding gently into hers. She felt the urgency of his erection glancing the plump swell of her naked buttocks, and the cool kiss of his silk dressing gown at the seethe between her cheeks.

He tongued her hot cleft hungrily. She shrieked as his ravished face pressed into her buttocks, and shrieked again as his firm tongue quenched the fire kindled there by the lash of the anal whip. With a grunt of satisfaction he entered her, his ruined black hands gripping the whiteness of her breasts, spearing her between her soft cheeks with his brutal length of engorged flesh.

Though his seed was hot, it soothed her as it trickled from her tight little sphincter to glisten in her whipped cleft.

They dozed, curled up closely together on the Moldavian carpet in the darkness. Fitfully, in her troubled dreams, she reached back and clutched at his silk dressing gown, as if abed and pawing for the duvet to cover her nakedness. He pressed the length of his body to her softness, happily accommodating the roundness of her bottom just below his hard belly. She was dimly aware of his renewed erection thrusting up between her slightly parted thighs. Sleepily, unselfconsciously, she trapped and squeezed it, submissively triumphant, obediently dominant.

The sardonyx and gold long-case Jacobean clock ticked off the slow seconds until the filigree hands touched the hour. The Cambridge chimes ting-tanged five times, and they awoke, deep into the summer afternoon.

For a full four minutes Emily remained passive in his fiercely possessive embrace, happy to feel the warmth of his breath on the nape of her neck, happier to have his thickened length nuzzling her wet heat.

But had the spell been broken – that special spell binding slave to master? Were they now merely lovers? She hoped not. She wanted to be his slave, wanted to serve him, obey him, suffer his slightest whim gladly. Bare her bottom – and her mind – to his will. Emily realised that she wanted – needed – things to remain as they had been.

Neither spoke as they lay awake, listening to one another breathing. Both knew the other to be awake. At last, buckling under the suspense, Emily could bear it no longer.

'Master?' she whispered.

'I am here,' he murmured sternly, squeezing her dominantly.

A rush of happy relief swept over her. Scrambling free from his possessive clutches, she playfully pinned him down onto the Moldavian carpet and straddled him.

'Have a care, girl. Do not for one mistaken moment think that—'

'I won't,' she interrupted, shushing him with a quick kiss. 'Nothing has changed. It has only got better – much, much better. I am yours, totally. You must know that. Yours to do with as you please. To pleasure, to punish. To pleasure with pain, master.'

Slapping her bare bottom, he grunted, satisfied.

Wriggling her spanked cheeks, she begged to be allowed to serve him again. 'Please, let me,' she begged, still straddling him and thrilling to the slow trickle from her weeping pussy as it soaked his wiry chest hairs.

Straining up his head, he nodded his permission.

She shuffled forward, repositioning her buttocks down onto the wet patch left by her sex on his chest and inching her pussy towards his chin.

'What—?' he started, but she silenced him, squatting

down on his mouth, burying his face beneath her bottom. She sensed his damaged hands pounding the soft carpet then felt them as they flew to her buttocks, gripping and stretching each cheek apart savagely. Rising in a spasm of discomfort, she lowered her glistening slit onto his upturned face. Thrusting her hips and taloned buttocks, she raked her wet heat down across his eyes.

'I will heal you,' she whispered, rhythmically grinding herself on his face. Helpless beneath her, he released her buttocks and spread his arms out and, to her unutterable delight, passively submitted to her ministrations. The slave mastering her master. The words burned deep inside her brain.

'I am in your thrall, master,' she whimpered, brutally ravishing his trapped face.

'In my thrall,' he echoed, unable to stir.

'I'm completely under your sovereign spell,' she moaned, dominating his smothered lips with her juicy slit.

'Completely,' he managed to splutter.

'You own me, every naked inch of me,' she murmured, riding him ruthlessly.

'Every naked inch,' he gasped, drowning under her succulent flesh.

She spasmed, rolling her hips and smearing him with her feral juices, leaving the charred flesh of his helpless face glistening.

To serve. The word seared her brain.

To submit and surrender. Those words triggered another implosion deep below her belly. She started to come. Astride him though she was, riding him between her thighs, she knew he was her true master and she his true slave. The delicious paradox of briefly dominating him quickened her orgasm, squatting on his upturned face, she came long and loud, anointing his twisted features with her scalding slick.

His tongue flickered out, long and hard, lapping hungrily at her clitoris. His teeth gently nipped at the erect little love-thorn. Ravished by his mouth, Emily collapsed beneath the sweet savagery of a second orgasm, writhing anew across his upturned features.

'Dr Stikannos,' Ursula rasped, her voice directed to him, her green eyes burning into Emily's nakedness.

Rolling apart, they blinked into the light from the open door. Reaching into the darkness, Ursula's fingers snapped down the switch, and neon strips above flickered into life.

'Dr Stikannos,' she repeated impatiently, her harsh tone streaked with brittle jealousy.

'What?' he demanded, snatching up his mask and covering his face. 'What is it?'

'Your guests – the buyers for the sale. Contact has been made. All have arrived safely and are scheduled to leave Gatwick in the helicopters you laid on. I thought—'

'I do not pay you to think,' he broke in curtly. 'And there is no need for me to meet and greet them personally on their arrival. See to it yourself, if you think you can manage it.'

'But of course.'

'Then go. Leave us.'

'As you wish,' Ursula whispered softly, reaching out to switch off the lights, and her green eyes glared down at Emily as her hand whitened on the door handle.

'No, just try, I'm sure they're stronger than you think.'

'My physio said—'

'Physios deal with muscles and sinews. I'm talking about strength of will. Walk.'

Dr Stikannos grunted softly as he propped himself up over his desk. He planted his hands down onto its polished surface, arms stretched and shivering. He shook his head. 'It's no good. Bring my chair here.'

'Please try.'

His palms skidded, causing him to lurch drunkenly, and Emily gave a small cry of alarm.

172

'I've felt their strength, remember,' she whispered. 'I know you can do it. Walk.'

There was challenge in the tone of the slave as she spoke to her master. His mask flashed as he tossed his head back. 'And do you know better than those who have tried – tried and failed to help me?'

'No, not better. Different, that's all.'

Placated by her genuine humility and sincere wish to help, he straightened himself up, wobbling slightly, then clapped his hands together. Emily winced, both hands instantly covering her eyes.

'What about this?' he demanded, tapping the metal mask with a single blackened fingertip.

Emily peeped at him through her parted fingers then dropped her hands to her thighs. 'One thing at a time. Walk for me. We'll get a routine going in the gym; bring in the very best. Trust me. Remedial therapy is at the cutting edge these days. You'll be out of that chair in nine, no, six months.'

'Perhaps,' he replied grimly. 'Every long journey must begin with a single step. For you, little one, I will take five. Position the chair there.'

Emily obeyed his instruction, wheeling the chair to the appointed spot and snapping on its brakes. 'Careful,' she gasped, her eyes wide with concern as he took one, a second, and then a third faltering step. 'That's wonderful,' she encouraged.

Staggering uncertainly, his dark eyes fierce slits of concentration, he walked jerkily towards the chair. Five, six, seven paces. He paused, ignored the wheelchair and continued, taking the four extra paces necessary to reach her welcoming embrace.

'You did it, you did it,' she squealed excitedly, hugging him.

'The mask,' he laughed gently, 'remains.'

'I understand,' she murmured.

'And the gloves.'

'No, keep your hands in the fresh air. I'll dress them with tea tree oil every evening. It will speed their recovery.'

'Endocrinologists, the best in their field, have warned me otherwise, little one,' he whispered into her blonde mane. 'These hands will remain exactly as you see them until they come with me to my grave.'

'Ungloved. Masked if you must be, but ungloved.

'If you wish it,' he relented, grudging her the words as if reluctant to speak them, and was rewarded with a strong kiss on his lips, to which he responded vigorously.

Emily slid slowly and sinuously down against his body, licking, kissing and gently biting at the pale flesh revealed through his parted dressing gown. Kneeling, she peeled the curtain of silk apart and buried her face into his groin.

He grunted softly. 'Is this to be my reward for taking those few small steps?' he bantered. 'Or for taking off my gloves?' He gripped the blonde hair at his belly with his crippled fingers.

Emily, her wet mouth full with his cock, slurped an indistinct reply.

'Bitch. I saw you, seducing him. Just can't keep your sticky little fingers to yourself, can you?'

Emily, dozing on her bed in the crimson glow of a clouded sunset, sprang up in alarm.

'Tie her hands to the bedposts. Use stockings and tie her tightly.'

Before Emily could wriggle off her bed and escape, Chloe had pounced. Pinning her writhing, naked victim down, she drove her knee into Emily's soft rump, rendering her helpless. Stretching each captive arm out to the waiting posts at the head of the four-poster, she tied both wrists to the wood, using stockings that burned into the whitened flesh.

'We don't want anyone prying into this strictly private little matter,' Ursula remarked, dragging a small stool towards her then hooking it with her right foot and positioning it against the far wall.

Over her shoulder, biting into the gag Chloe had just bound around her mouth, Emily saw Ursula mount the stool and wedge a hand-towel into the small light fitting, blocking the lens of the hidden camera.

'Did you gag her tightly?' Ursula hissed.

Chloe edged right up against the bed and spanked her hand down harshly, instantly reddening the swell of Emily's proffered cheeks. The punished nude's squeal was muted by the efficient gag, rendering her shrill response softer than a turtledove's sibilant moan in a shivering elder at dawn.

'Excellent,' Ursula grunted, approaching the bed, her cane aquiver. She lowered the bamboo, nursing the left buttock with its inquisitive tip, then pressed it down firmly, dominating the bare flesh. 'The sale goes ahead tomorrow evening. The following day, you must depart.'

Because she was jealous, Emily thought, taking some small comfort in her ability to rattle her green-eyed tormentor.

'I want you out of here in forty-eight hours, understand?' The cane pressed down firmly, dimpling the soft buttocks. 'This is what you'll suffer if you defy me. Hold her head down,' she thundered.

Chloe, her eyes shining with sadistic glee, pounced obediently, eager to participate in the naked blonde's impending pain. She pinned Emily face down into the white pillow.

On the opposite side Ursula's thighs collided with the edge of the bed as she positioned herself for the punishment. Her green eyes narrowed as she raised the yellow bamboo above the trembling buttocks below.

Swish!

A thin red weal appeared where the cane kissed the swell of the domed cheeks. Emily stiffened and cried in loud silence into her smothering gag.

Swish!

The second cruel cut swiped down. Emily's whipped buttocks clenched in agony, then loosened to rid themselves of the burning pain. Chloe's grip on her victim's neck tightened.

Swish!

The third crisp stroke across pliant flesh was planted just below the previous stripes, biting viciously into the swelling curves of the helpless cheeks just above the invisible crease where they melted into thighs. Emily's fingers splayed out in mute anguish in their bondage at the bedposts and she flounced her golden mane in an agonised reflex, despite Chloe's controlling grip.

'Hold her,' Ursula warned, tap-tapping Emily's blonde hair dominantly with the tip of her hovering cane.

Swish!

The bamboo glinted as it lashed down, adding a fresh pink stripe to the three already paling into bluish badges of pain.

Swish!

Ursula chuckled as Emily bucked beneath the onslaught. Dropping the cane to the carpet she bent over the punished rump and knuckled the scolded cheeks savagely. Perusing the ravishes of the cane, she intimately inspected the punished buttocks, parting the reddened cheeks briefly to glimpse down into the dark cleft within. 'Take off her gag. Let's see what the bitch has to say for herself now.'

Chloe's cruel fingers loosened the gag and Emily spat it out, gulping for air. Tears spangled her wide eyes.

'Forty-eight hours, understand?' Ursula had retrieved the yellow cane and, gripping it firmly, pressed it down into the flesh she had just striped.

'I'm not going anywhere,' Emily hissed, writhing in her bondage. She squeezed her punished cheeks tightly. Despite the heat in her buttocks, they shivered beneath the caress of the cane tracing the swell of her rounded curves. 'Dr Stikannos—'

'Is out of bounds to you from now on,' Ursula snapped. 'Out of bounds, do you hear?' The cane twitched menacingly above the quivering cheeks. 'You've no more business with him. Is that perfectly clear?'

'I'll let him decide that,' Emily retorted bravely.

Swish! *Swish*!

Emily screamed as the cane lashed down, whipping her defenceless cheeks savagely. Between her sobs she managed to blurt out – before she realised what she was saying – that Dr Stikannos might be interested to see the contents of the cellar. 'I think he should be told.'

Swish! *Swish*! *Swish*!

Emily howled, wriggling and writhing as her buttocks blazed beneath the slicing bamboo.

'What do you mean about the cellar?' Ursula demanded, almost losing control. The cane remained silent and still. That had rattled green eyes. Gathering her thoughts rapidly, Emily decided to tough it out.

'I know and you know what's in the cellar, but he doesn't... yet,' she said, her voice strained.

'Are you so sure he doesn't know?' Ursula sneered, unable to conceal the slight doubt in her voice.

'You've more or less told me so yourself.' She was playing blind now – bluffing. What the hell *was* down in the cellar? The cane remained inert across her buttocks. She was bluffing, but winning. She had stopped Ursula dead in her tracks.

Gripping her bamboo wand firmly, Ursula raised it aloft. Emily flinched, squeezing her striped cheeks tightly.

Swish! *Swish*!

Two searing strokes that bit – and burned. Emily blinked, recoiling at the whiff of feral arousal from Chloe's wet heat mere inches away. Ursula snarled, struggling between alarm and anger.

'She knows nothing,' Chloe said softly, flexing her fingers in Emily's blonde hair.

The cane tip flickered up, alert and potent. 'Meaning?' Ursula demanded.

'If she really knew anything, she would have told him already,' Chloe reasoned.

Ursula's pale face creased into a triumphant grin. She nodded her agreement. 'Gag her, quickly. Gag the bitch. And as a reward for your sharp thinking, you may remain here, remain here with her and enjoy her until I return.'

Chloe crouched possessively over Emily's nakedness. Already the strong fingers that had just gagged the captive were stroking the defenceless buttocks, a questing thumb raking the deep cleft between them.

'Where are you going?' Chloe asked, but the chatter of approaching helicopters skimming the distant beech trees answered her question.

It was worthy of the Ritz, but more decadent, more intimate. Five types of vintage champagne accompanied nine international dishes on tables draped with crisp white linen and boasting Cantonese, Tunisian and cordon bleu delicacies. Dr Stikannos, masked but ungloved, presided over the supper from his wheelchair, receiving his millionaires like the pontiff at a papal audience.

Mikhov, the Russian entrepreneur, a sharply suited, shaven-headed, bull-built gangster who ran a huge private medical insurance group at a loss – profiting enormously from a bigger protection racket conducted with AK-47 finesse. Mikhov thumbed through the catalogue, constantly demanding the exact exchange rate between the dollar and the Swiss franc. He drank sparingly from a tumbler of frosted glass barely wet with vodka, but ate heartily and indiscriminately. He spoke a staccato English with an unsettling Birmingham accent: the short bursts of long vowels as harsh as the machine guns that held much of Moscow in their grip.

Eduardo, the titled Portuguese effete, monocled and

dapper in white evening dress, as wily as a Jesuit and as ruthless as a cobra. Publicity shy, he moved invisibly from Lahore to Lucerne like a shadow, his Midas touch turning gold into untraceable currencies on every shady deal. He drank freely, remained silent and was drawn like a ghostly white moth to the flame by some Da Vinci studies of the young male nude.

Ayani, the Lebanese businesswoman providing hotel entertainment throughout the Middle East. Girls; dark-skinned Arab girls for the media moguls in Tel Aviv; dark-haired Jewish girls for the Sultanate princes. Big money. Her red lips chewed noisily as she devoured lightly minted halal lamb. Her kohl dark eyes scanned the catalogue notes carefully.

Two Hong Kong twins swathed in heavy silks. Twittering and giggling as they fluttered around Dr Stikannos, refusing choice Cantonese fare and opting for the salmon mousse.

The super-rich, gathering and circling like sharks before another kill. Originals of their species and survivors, being the richest. Darwin would have been proud of them.

Ursula, silently efficient and attentively adroit, circulated inscrutably, ever at their side to refresh an empty glass or replenish a depleted plate. Steering them towards, then away from, the wheelchair of Dr Stikannos. Nobody noticed her brief absence.

Up in her room, tied to the bedposts, Emily squealed into her gag. Chloe was riding her again, straddling her whipped cheeks and trapping her buttocks between her pinioning thighs. Riding her naked punished bottom relentlessly, easing up to rake her hot slit down repeatedly against the swell of the passive buttocks beneath. Chloe, coming again, pounding her pubis into Emily's caned cheeks.

The door opened, and Ursula strode in. 'Enjoying yourself?'

Chloe blushed, but was unable to conceal the spasms of

179

her orgasm. Writhing against Emily's bottom, she ground her wet heat into the crimson buttocks.

'Go and shower. I may need you later.'

Chloe slithered from the bed, her inner thighs glistening, and scampered from the bedroom.

'I've decided that you should sing for your supper, bitch. Some of our guests downstairs will require a little amusement. Some diverting entertainment.' Ursula's tone darkened. 'It'll keep them occupied before the sale, and you busy. Too busy, in fact, to allow you to see Dr Stikannos before your departure.'

Bending down and gripping Emily's buttocks – still slippery from Chloe's two orgasms – Ursula spread the soft cheeks apart until the dark cleft yawned. 'Listen to me, bitch. You have tasted my cane, briefly. Should you wish to feast on pain, one single attempt to communicate with Dr Stikannos will bring you, sobbing, to the banquet of bamboo.'

Emily shuddered.

Sliding unobserved back into the small assembly of vast wealth, Ursula mingled with unobtrusive charm. She approached the Russian, speaking softly into his ear. He nodded, the shaven pate glinting with sweat. But the Portuguese nobleman shook his head, withdrawing slightly from her whispered words, his monocle popped from his startled eye. The Hong Kong twins giggled and leaned more closely to cloak their misunderstanding. Ursula repeated her offer – more giggling, which the green eyes took as a polite refusal. When approached, the Lebanese blinked like a lizard and nodded, her red lips pursing appreciatively at Ursula's invitation.

Emily twisted around as the door to her room opened, and writhed in shame at her nakedness as Ursula ushered in Mikhov, the thuggish, dark-suited bully, and Ayani, an olive-skinned beauty with dark eyes accustomed to seeing suffering – in others.

Ursula closed the door gently. Introductions were minimal. They viewed the naked blonde bound to the bedposts as they would a Persian carpet or a bowl of cut and polished jade.

'As I promised,' Ursula drawled, palming and smoothing Emily's proffered cheeks, 'a little entertainment for your diversion. It is important that you both relax, each in your own way, before the stress of the sale tomorrow evening. So,' she bantered, dragging her straightened index fingertip down the length of Emily's velvet cleft, 'who will take her first? Hmm? How shall we decide?'

Mikhov seemed eager – Ayani even more so. Ursula recognised her dilemma.

'Who can guess correctly, is she a natural blonde?' Ursula purred, deftly delving her fingers down to conceal any stray wisps of pubic hair

'I doubt it,' Ayani murmured. 'I know so many, many girls. I know their wiles, the tricks they use.'

'And I say da,' the Russian grunted brutally. 'Me, I think yes, she is blonde. How do you say it, the nature's blonde?'

'Natural,' Ursula replied suavely. 'Then let us see. Whichever of you is right takes her for the night. The loser may have the afternoon, for a sexual siesta.'

Bending, her ripe breasts bulging as they strained at her crisp blouse, Ursula slipped her palm under Emily's belly. The bound nude's hips rose a fraction. Ursula twisted her wrist. Emily squeaked into the gag, clenching her buttocks as Ursula withdrew her hand, the pincered fingertips of which clutched at the golden pubic curl she had just tweaked from Emily's blonde bush.

'Take her,' she whispered, holding the glinting coil up before Mikhov's greedy eyes. 'She is yours to do with as you please.'

Chapter Eight

Out in the darkness of a wet night, the moon struggled to shine through the boiling clouds. On the edge of the estate dripping elms stretched upwards, almost seeming to touch the swollen-bellied clouds that had just drenched them.

A vixen, drawn along by the delicious promise of peacocks, trotted through the yew hedge and, skirting the gleaming laurels, trod the rain-spangled lawns on dainty feet. Hungry for succulent flesh, she sniffed inquisitively, her little fangs bared. Pausing by a stone sundial she raised her head and sniffed the damp air. The white stone – salvaged from the shattered pulpit of St Wulfric's after Cromwell's New Model Army had ransacked all beneath the flint, fifteenth century tower – bore maddening traces of peacock. The vixen barked.

Inside the mansion, locked behind the door of the Russian's darkened room, Emily opened her eyes. It must be, she calculated, just a little after midnight. The rope that bound her breast burned her nipples. She wriggled, the cruel blaze spread to encompass the crushed swell of her bosom. The rope between her thighs bit softly, deeply, raking her wet seethe. Mikhov was insatiable, his silent assistant deaf to her pleading. Emily tried the waxed ropes again with a slight wriggle, only managing to tighten them more fiercely. Even the slightest movement drove them deeper into her bound flesh. She grunted, so fierce was the silken rope burning into the cleft between her cheeks.

Emily heard the vixen bark. Heard the sharp yapping of the little fox out in the rain-drenched night – and yearned to share her freedom.

Her curiosity satisfied, but her appetite unsated, the vixen abandoned the sundial and trotted down along a moss carpeted brick path sunken with age back into the dark, wet loam. Passing by the untroubled surface of a pool, she shied from her glimpsed reflection as the black mirror briefly caught the emerging moon above. The vixen wrinkled her nose at the swarm of midges drawn to the limpid waters. Man's hand was everywhere, bringing nature sternly to heel with strict husbandry. Ignoring the tidied beds of scented stock, and the neat rows of aromatic geraniums, the vixen shouldered her way through pale lilac syringas, glowing silver or darkling black in the cold moonlight.

Suspended from the light steel framework – a geometry for pain – Emily swung face down, her heels tied to her wrists, her breasts spilling freely. Upturned, her bare bottom bulged within the broad leather straps that bound and squeezed her cheeks. Spinning slowly down from her sex, a spindle of silvery arousal lengthened as it stretched under its own slight weight. Crouching, Mikhov studied it through narrowed eyes. With a soft, silent movement, he caught the quicksilver spillage in his outstretched palm, imprisoning it instantly in his clenched fist. Emily grunted as the fist rose up to knuckle-kiss her slippery labia. Jerking in her bondage, she turned in her own momentum: spinning slowly, turning north, then north-east, east, then slowly back to north. Just like the little golden cockerel glittering in the moonlight atop St Wulfric's flint tower, some miles away on the edge of the estate beyond the shivering beech trees.

The vixen despised those scents from flowers tamed and tended to by human hand. No, for her the sharper scents from wilder blooms – weeds growing rampant and unchecked in the neglected, uncut sedge – held all her pleasure. Her little eyes glinted as she snuffed up the astringent, feral perfumes from smokewort, lover's loss, sorrel, and the faintly urine-like whiff from the pinkish yellow vetch.

Emily sniffed cautiously. She wrinkled her nose at the glutinous pomade. Mikhov's oily-haired assistant was very close. Bending down over her helplessness, he wiped her cleft with a cotton wool swab. The soft wad was soaked in surgical spirit. It stung, adding fresh tears of pain to those brought already to her eyes by shame. She swallowed her dry-mouthed scream of protest as a dry swab visited her pussy, prising the outer labia apart and tickling her inner wetness. She could not deny it, her ankles being spread a metre apart directly above her head as she hung inverted in the harness of her dreadful bondage.

The swab from her anus was brought to the nose of the Russian, who sniffed. The swab dipped into her slit was brought to the lips and tongue of the Russian, who kissed and then licked its feral softness. Emily jerked in her restraints as she saw the two swabs being popped into a little silver dish which was then reverentially sealed with a lid by the silent assistant. Mikhov, sweating freely now, clapped his hands approvingly. Emily saw the opaque rubber gloves collide, the fat fingers gleaming in the single yellow light rigged up on the ceiling above.

The vixen stood stock still, quivering. She bowed her head down, bringing her nose to a rain-drenched spray of untamed saxifrage. Yapping shrilly, she saluted the whiff of cruelty exuded by the midnight bloom of sorrow: the penitential blossom.

The bark of the distant vixen faded. Had Emily been dreaming? Had she really heard a little fox yapping, or had her mind been playing tricks on her as she drifted from disorientation into a brief but troubled sleep?

She yearned, ached, to wriggle free from the tight embrace

184

of the rubber corselette into which her nakedness had been roughly squeezed and over which the zip had slid so tightly when fastened. She hated it; its clinging heaviness, its haunting yet deliciously disturbing smell. She would wear it in proud submission for another master. Yes, Emily's secret flesh juiced at the thought of wearing the rubber for Dr Stikannos. But not for these brutes. The silky soft rubber burned as it stretched across her bulging buttocks. The stretch moulded them, clinging firmly to the curves that flowed down to her cleft. Deep within, her anal crater puckered to kiss the black skin. At the base of her belly, Emily sensed the fierce scald of it shiny at her slit. At her breasts the rubber cupped and punished her swelling breasts. She writhed as her nipples suffered the torments of the supple bondage.

Her arms were tied tightly at her wrists above her head. Her feet were bound and buckled at her ankles, welding her thighs and knees together. Mikhov, gloved and plastic-gowned, supervised the degradation intimately, his erection proud and hard behind the apron of green leather. Emily, glimpsing the bulge, shuddered. The cock was huge. She almost fainted at the terror of it stretching her rectal warmth. Kneeling down suddenly, the oily-haired silent assistant, obedient to his master's whim, gently lifted the apron and slowly thumbed the wet snout of the purple glans.

The pain soaked through her stretched limbs. Shutting out the grunts from the sweating Russian thug, Emily was forced to recall how it had begun.

'Wrists,' Mikhov had barked.

Silver studded cuffs were weighed in the open palms of his silent assistant then snapped harshly into place. Compared to their cruel bite, the bejewelled collar that had been attached around her throat by Dr Stikannos felt like a filigree necklace. The cuffs were brutal. Helpless and immobile, utterly unable to resist as she hung in her bondage, Emily had suffered Mikhov's sour breath warm at her breasts then whispering in the curls of her pubic nest.

'Ankles,' the shaven-headed Russian commanded.

Supple leather, latticed with a fine steel lace, instantly clamped each ankle. The sickening pomade of the assistant's oiled hair rose up to her nostrils as, above the efficiently ruthless bondage imprisoning each helpless foot, Emily stiffened as she felt Mikhov's nose probing deep between her tightened buttocks.

More helpless than a mouse quivering between the paws of a cat, Emily had suffered the burning ropes, then the clinging, suffocating rubber, followed by the strict embrace of supple leather. Supple leather, with its harsh tang of haunting hide. Dead hide that had once been living flesh itself. Hide flayed from a skinned beast. Emily's mind juggled these fragmented thoughts as her brain retreated from her pain and humiliation. True, neither crop or cane had lashed her breasts or bare bottom, but still she burned with shame in her strict bondage as the Russian, helped at each intimate step by the silent assistant, subjected her to increasingly perverse degradations.

More helpless than a mouse. Trapped and quivering. Shivering in her bondage. Three blind mice. The absurd rhyme echoed in her brain. Blind mice. Blind. The horror of it. A blindfold. Gagged, yes – that at least would leave her deaf to her own screams and curses.

But blindfolded? Mikhov, she realised as she peeped anxiously at her tormentors, unlike other bondage-dominants, had elected to leave her gaze unobstructed: unobstructed to brim full with tears of sorrow, a sorrow he drank in with his own glinting stare.

The waxed cords, when first produced from the black velvet bag, bore the faint odour of – what? Emily found the smell elusive. Petrol. It came to her suddenly. Yes, petrol. She concentrated on the fact as she shrank from their kiss. The cords were thin, shiny and devilish at her flesh. Criss-crossing her bound breasts, they had bitten deeply into her bulging bosom. Lashed around her buttocks and lower thighs, then threaded viciously between her tamed cheeks, the waxed cord had buried itself deeply into her scalded cleft. And yet Mikhov had grunted his displeasure. The oily-haired assistant, like some dark acolyte serving an unholy priest, fluttered his hands in anxious agreement. The waxed cord was gently loosened, knotted and replaced between her bound buttocks. One knot strategically worrying her anal whorl. Emily had writhed as Mikhov chuckled. A second knot, fashioned by the oily-haired assistant, along the threaded cord between her aching thighs, bullied and bruised her trapped clitoral bud. That was when she had screamed. That was, she remembered through the dull pain, when they finally gagged her, with industrial strength tape, dark and sticky.

She heard a strip of it being torn away from the large roll with a searing rip, and panicked as it sealed her lips painfully. So painfully, she dared not swallow.

After the burn of the waxed cords, keener than a bamboo stroke against her soft flesh, a full hour and a half of the rubber.

The rubber. She hated the intimacy of the firm, stretchy rubber that became a second skin from her throat down to her thighs.

The overwhelming totality of the rubber. Almost impudent, with a careful negligence, thumbing and flattening her nipples as it cupped and crushed her breasts. It hugged her as closely as a finely meshed body stocking yet ruled her trapped softness with a rod of iron. At her bottom it splayed her cheeks painfully apart, squeezing each buttock dominantly and causing her widened cleft to seethe.

Emily hated her own Judas juices for flowing so freely from her wet heat, lubricating the latex at her labia. Hated her body's betrayal. Hated it almost as violently as she hated watching Mikhov sniffing the wet rubber when his assistant had peeled it away from her slit.

Had she fainted? She was not sure. All she knew was that after the rubber had been peeled away and carefully sniffed and licked, there had been the leather.

The leather. The harsh hide that burned as it bound. Its animal tang. To have been whipped with it would have been easier to bear, better to endure. As supple as a snake, it caressed her curves as it bound her within its coiled clutches. The leather – a pelt flayed from a beast. Flayed. Oh God, would the silent assistant produce a whip? Tied, trussed and completely helpless, was she to be whipped before dawn? Whipped, with the supple hide of a dead beast. Dead skin across the living flesh of her soft buttocks. Emily suddenly remembered the sweetness of her suffering under the dark spell of Dr Stikannos. The master who had cracked the anal whip, causing her to come instantly in a paroxysm of fierce joy. The anal whip, fashioned from the preserved penis of a bull camel. Dr Stikannos. She started to come. It began in her head as she whispered his name, raged down through her belly like a bush fire and erupted at her slit, soaking the leather. The leather, soon to be inspected, sniffed and licked by Mikhov.

Emily lost all sense of time. She couldn't even remember the day, or the date. Suspended from the light metal structure that caged her, she span around utterly helpless in her burning bondage.

From time to time the silent assistant checked her, his cold hands at her thigh or bottom, staying her twisting body long enough to swab her cleft and sex again. She saw the glint of his silver tweezers as they dipped to ply the swab between her cheeks with a single stroke. Then the heron's bill of glittering silver brought the tiny bundle of cotton wool back. A single delicate gesture, dipping again, once, to dab at her sphincter. She groaned as her buttocks tensed: quivering as the cotton swab kissed her wet, pink rosebud.

Out in the beech woods the vixen bayed at the moon. Lonely in her freedom, she sensed her isolation. Something vital missing from her midnight world. The pinkish yellow vetch had enflamed her, the wet thyme had made her dizzy. The scent from the moonlit brambles had maddened her, quickening her pulse. The saxifrage had awoken her craving. For what? Nose up, she gazed through the brooding canopy of the crowded beeches – and barked at the moon.

Trotting into a thicket, the lonely vixen, uncertain of what it was she pined for, approached a larch. The pale silvery bark glowed in the dappled moonlight. Squatting, the vixen emptied her bladder, her swishing tail skimming the rustle of last autumn's forgotten leaves.

Mikhov nodded, wiping the sweat from his wrinkled brow with the back of his rubber-gloved hand. The glove skidded across his perspiring forehead, just as his victims skidded in their own blood seconds after the AK-47's staccato blaze.

The oily-haired assistant, dutifully deferential, set to work. Emily wondered in silence as, now stretched down on her back, she watched her arms being threaded under her knees and her wrists being brought down to her ankles. Her fingers, folded over her toes, were taped tightly. The position stretched her anus and drew her outer labia apart. The silent assistant inserted a rod between her splayed ankles, fixing them apart and rendering her feet immobile. Naked, except for the leather brassiere squeezing her tightly bound bosom, Emily lay trussed and passive in her indecent shame.

She was helpless, and open. Open to their eyes. Open to their probing fingers. Open and vulnerable, for whatever those in control of her decided was to be her doom. The thought took hold in her brain like a flame at dry kindling. Leaping up, the flames of her imagination illumined the darkest corners of her desires. Anything was possible now – even things she could not put into forbidden words. A river of dry heat coursed down from her belly to scald her pubic mound. Between the stretch of her spread cheeks her sphincter widened a fraction into a glistening little oval of reluctant anticipation: puckering up as if to kiss that which was about to torment it.

In her passive helplessness, Emily's face burned as she acknowledged her masochistic yearnings. Flushed by the shame of her sudden self-knowledge, she craved the whip and the cane. Craved the searing lash that would purge her and punish her for entertaining such carnal longings. The kiss of the lash that would drive out the demons of her dark desires.

Something smooth and small touched her secret flesh between her parted thighs. Emily glanced down, frustrated by the leather brassiere at her swollen bosom she could not see the small glass phial in the silent assistant's fist being pressed against her pee-hole. The controlling hand twisted the glass tube a half turn. Emily squealed, almost drowning in the indignity, but her muscles betrayed her and, denying the surge of relief, she let go. She groaned into the gag as she felt her warm urine flooding out, filling the glass tube until it overflowed, scalding her inner thighs and the cheeks of her bottom.

The dildo was a sudden shock. Carved from a wild boar's ivory tusk, it was long and finely tapered. Mikhov kissed it reverentially, feverishly, before passing it across into the open palms of his silent assistant.

Emily froze in the extra bondage of her fear; a fearful dread that rendered her more helpless than the bonds that burned into her wrists and ankles.

Gripping the dildo like a dagger, the oily-haired assistant approached. He nuzzled the knout at her glistening labia, stroking them firmly until they peeled apart in sullen acceptance. Emily screamed, choking into her gag. Having aroused and enflamed the slippery outer labia, the knout of the dildo pressed between her inner, darker flesh, teasing and deliciously tormenting their satin sheen.

The silent assistant withdrew his hand as he stood up dominantly above her helpless nakedness in its bondage. Out of her line of vision, the dildo was presented to Mikhov. Emily heard the slurp of his mouth at the smooth phallus, then heard his dark chuckle. Why? What next? Where next?

A soft click. Her eyes blinked and watered under the intense blaze of a powerful arc lamp that flooded her in its fierce white light. She saw their dark silhouettes bending to peer at her anus, flinching as a gloved fingertip stretched her sphincter open. Juiced and puckering, Emily knew it would be winking wetly in the blaze of merciless white light. No, she screamed silently, remembering the boar's tusk. No, not there, please not there.

Her prayer was unanswered – it was to be there.

Slowly, almost tenderly, the dildo probed her anus. Guiding it in between her cheeks, the assistant occasionally twisted the shaft a half circle, ravishing the muscled warmth of her tight rectum. The dildo entered her completely, filling her painfully, driven deep between her buttocks. The silent assistant left the phallus in place for long minutes, during which they attached a tiny silver crocodile clip to each outer labial fold, and to her clitoral bud. Emily came, writhing, three times in violent succession, Mikhov at her slit with a lint pad to soak up her juices. As she came she gripped the smooth length of the dildo in her anal passage, rhythmically squeezing the ivory between contracting muscular spasms. More fresh dry lint visited her brutally exposed pussy, returning to Mikhov's nose and lips sodden with her wet heat. He savoured her juices as he would Beluga caviar.

As Emily hugged the dildo unashamedly, unrepentantly, she tumbled down the dizzy slopes of yet another orgasmic climax. Her eyes were stinging with her own perspiration. Blinking through them, she glimpsed the Russian gazing down at her, nodding decisively. What, Emily suddenly panicked, had Mikhov just resolved to do? What was the dark decision he had just reached?

The brilliant arc light was switched off. Emily sank her head back down in the darkness, sighing softly with relief. Her eyes ached from its intense glare. Almost at once, crisp flashes exploded in the darkness around her, dazzling and partially stunning her. It was like being caught up in a silent thunderstorm.

Her brain decoded the flashing lights. They were photographing her as she writhed in her strict bondage, helpless in her stern restraints. Mikhov with an SLR, whirring and snapping frenziedly. The silent assistant stalking her with 35mm shots; each take accompanied by an explosion of eerie blue-white light. She could deny them nothing. Utterly exposed, they photographed their greedy fill. Every inch of her ripe breasts, the shadowy cleavage, the soft curves in the snug confines of the straining leather bra, the shimmering outline of her nipples. From the side. Down from above. So intensely, Emily felt as if the lens of each camera was a finger probing her. Her body was mapped and recorded intimately, thoroughly, as it remained tied and tamed by the rubber and the ropes.

Several close-ups, lingering shots of her sorrowful eyes, were taken. Shots that captured the fear and alarm in the wide pools above the band of tape stretched across her silenced mouth. They put their cameras down carefully and roughly repositioned her in the harness and metal frame. The blood sang in her ears as she hung from her bound ankles. They picked up their cameras. More intimate shots: shots of her inverted body, vulnerable in the harness. Suspended, displayed, upside down, spindling and twisting before their cameras.

Then came the series of more contrived, more artistic poses: of Emily, belly down, buttocks proffered, each wrist and ankle stretched out to the four metal posts. Of Emily, crab-like, dangling from the creaking metal frame above. Swaying gently, her wet pussy gleaming in their flashlights.

By the time the photo-shoot was over Emily burned with

indignation, feeling ravished as if the protruding lens had actually entered into her wet warmth.

The silent assistant arranged her, tightly sheathed in a rubber one-piece, in a submissive, kneeling pose. She recoiled from his inquisitive fingertips dappling just below her cleft, then gasped as he deftly unzipped the rubber, revealing her tightly bunched cheeks and her rosebud anal whorl deep between their bulging flesh. Mikhov's SLR nosed closer, closer still until Emily felt the cold lens kiss her shrivelled sphincter as he snapped his fill.

The ultimate humiliation remained. On her back, thighs spread wide apart. Her pussy exposed, the small clips removed from her clitoris and labial lips, replaced by strips of clear tape that held her wet flesh down in strict bondage. Emily writhed, knowing that the tape fully exposed the gleam of her pouting slit to them. Both cameras ran riot, devouring the image of her bound in absolute submission and surrender. Emily saw the green leather apron at the Russian's groin swell and peak as his stiff erection raked the soft hide.

And yet he had not, as yet, mastered her completely. He had toyed with her, bound and roped her fiercely, exposed her cruelly, inspected her intimately and, in photographing her so thoroughly, subjected her naked helplessness to extremes of humiliation. But he had yet, she realised, to pierce and penetrate her. Pierce and penetrate her, she shuddered, with his painfully engorged shaft.

As they carefully replaced their cameras back into the expensive leather cases, Emily wriggled and writhed. Now, she was convinced, the Russian would enjoy her in her utter helplessness. The bulge behind the green apron could be denied no longer. She tested the leather cuff at her straining wrists and ankles, grunting as the hide instantly tightened and burned. Escape was unthinkable. Even the slightest movement was becoming impossible.

To her surprise, the silent assistant bent down across her,

his fingers busy at her restraints. Emily caught once again the rank pomade of his oiled hair as he leaned over her to release her wrist from the bite of its leather cuff.

She was ordered to stand, the bra removed, and positioned shivering with fearful anticipation, naked and gagged, beside a low bare bed. Surreptitiously, Emily's freed fingers crept up to touch the bejewelled collar – her true token of servitude. Yes, she realised, she was willing to serve her true master, in absolute obedience.

But not these two bastards – not the Moscow thug and his mute henchman. Rapacious bullies without finesse. No, her sweet servitude, she thought as she fingered the sparkling collar, was dedicated to one master and one master only. She tightened her buttocks as she whispered his name softly – Dr Stikannos.

She watched in mounting dread as a red rubber sheet was carefully unfolded and spread across the base of the bed. The assistant had donned clear plastic gloves now, and Emily continued to stare in horror as he sprinkled snow-white talc on the dull red rubber surface, then smooth it into a sheen beneath his gloved palms.

A gleaming finger beckoned her down to the taut stretch of red rubber, then gestured for her to mount. Reluctantly, Emily obeyed, smothering a gasp as her soft buttocks kissed the talcumed sheet. The gloved hand, index finger erect, twisted slowly until the fingertip jabbed downwards, inviting Emily to do the same. Wriggling face down, squashing her breasts and rasping her thickening nipples into the rubber sheet stretched beneath her, she froze as a velvet blindfold greeted her eyes, smothering their startled gaze.

All was done in silence. No words were spoken, but she heard soft grunts. She knew that as she lay face down, buttocks upturned, the assistant was preparing his aproned master, preparing Mikhov for her nakedness. Her head became dull and stupid, her brain refusing to work. Her thoughts began to congeal with fear. Would there be the use of a whip before the Russian mounted her, straddling her and taking her brutally from behind?

Straining in the suffocation of her blindfold and gag, Emily willed her tired, terrified brain to decode the soft sounds around her. The whisper of the apron being peeled away? Had, she wondered, his fierce erection jerked up in triumph, suddenly unrestrained and unleashed. A carnal grunt, then more soft rustling. What the hell was happening? Her imagination ran riot, instantly fearing the touch of his glistening glans at her lips or, she shuddered, nuzzling between her soft buttocks.

Mikhov. She was now his mere plaything, a toy for an adult child. She imagined him, sweating, his eyes screwed up in pre-release agony as he masturbated – or was being masturbated by the silent assistant. The apron, peeled away and furled up at his feet. Mikhov, fisting his erection, or having it teased into savage stiffness, prior to mounting her and spearing her bottom.

She frowned as she felt the first coin.

The second flat round disc of metal – gold, her skin told her – fell upon the first. They clinked. She knew from the sound that they were coins. Krugerrands, most probably. A third coin, bouncing off the softness of her left buttock. A fourth… then three more. A sudden shower of them, chinking as they fell with the fat pitter-pat of heavy summer rain. God, she was not being drenched in his hot semen but showered with gold krugerrands.

Mikhov was grunting thickly now.

Wriggling, Emily raked her face down into the rubber sheet, managing to dislodge the band of velvet from her left eye. Twisting cautiously, spilling as she did so a small fortune nestling in the dimple of her spine, she risked a peep over her shoulder. She saw the assistant, the green apron draped over his face, kneeling alongside his master, a gleaming gloved hand pumping Mikhov's erection. The Russian, teetering tipsily with lust, stared down at the coins he was showering upon Emily's nakedness, his sweating face contorted as his approaching climax threatened to explode.

Emily blinked just as it did. He came massively, his thick squirt of warm silver soaking the gold of the krugerrands. She bucked in her attempt to evade the ejaculation. The heavy coins, lubricated with his seed, slithered across her slippery flesh. Cursing as he came, Mikhov emptied his sac over the naked girl beneath him, relishing her shame and writhing humiliation as, grinding her breasts into the rubber sheet beneath her, her quivering rump sparkled with his quicksilver. A single krugerrand lodged between her heaving cheeks, the milled edge wedged firmly into her cleft. Brushing aside the apron-blindfolded assistant, Mikhov stretched down, plucked the winking coin from her buttocks and neatly balanced its flat weight on the tip of his wet-nosed cock. Emily, glimpsing most of this through her left eye, shivered and sobbed aloud.

Emily drowned slowly in a crimson sea; a crimson, spinning ocean in which black lights blazed brightly and the sinuous weeds glowed gold. Her breathing, like that of a drowning girl, became shallow and rapid as she trembled, panicking, on the very edge of consciousness. Her body felt heavy with exhaustion, like a swimmer running out of strength against a current. She was being sucked down into an abyss of misery and shame, a deep chasm lined with the haunting tang of talcumed red rubber. But she knew she had only partially passed out, and was already emerging back up to the surface of wakefulness. Smells tormented her, haunted and confused her. The pomade of the silent assistant. The rank semen squirted by the Russian on her skin. The cloying rubber into which her face was crushed. The delicious dread hinted at by the waxed cords and the leather harness perfumed the room of her degradation and shame like the rotten attar of blighted blooms in a frost-stricken garden.

Flexing her painful wrists, she remembered everything: pain sharps the mind, she thought, rolling over onto her side and falling into a sleep-troubled dream. But her agony stalked her into the brief escape into unconsciousness, stalked her with the terrible truth her brain could not deny: never in her life had she imagined or experienced such utter helplessness, such total surrender and such absolute submission.

Her brief sleep was broken into abruptly. Flickering her eyes open as she felt gloved fingers prising her semen-sticky buttocks apart. Emily saw three krugerrands on the red rubber before her. She was puzzled, then her face crimsoned as she remembered. The fingers at her cheeks grew stern. Emily grunted as her cleft ached, ached as it yawned between her brutally stretched cheeks. The green leather apron that had shielded the Russian's erection was draped over her head and tied tightly. Emily felt slightly sick as she sniffed the rank scent of semen and pomade – not unlike saxifrage when overblown and run to seed.

The hands that tied the apron tied it viciously, the green leather filled her mouth and nostrils, almost suffocating her. Struggling wildly, she flinched as she felt fresh hot seed spilling down upon her bare bottom. Clamping her cheeks together, she trapped the trickle of wet warmth at her cleft. Then she squealed in protest as gloved knuckles dimpled her wet cheeks. It was Mikhov. She sensed his weight. Mihkov, kneading his seed into the satin flesh of her upturned buttocks. She twisted and jerked, desperately trying to avoid this fresh outrage, but the imprisoning hands of the Russian's assistant instantly at her shoulders pinned her down effectively. Effectively, as brutally efficient in their task as the brute knuckles of the dominant Mikhov at her helpless cheeks.

Ursula, closely followed by an inquisitive Chloe whose eyes widened in wonder as they glimpsed Emily naked and face down on the rubber sheet, entered.

Mikhov motioned his silent assistant aside and turned, unselfconscious in his naked and erect state, to greet them. Grasping Ursula's right hand in both of his, he bowed his shaven head down and kissed her fingertips.

From her bed, still smothered in the green leather apron, Emily strained to listen.

'She is all you promised. I must have her. I will begin with ten, no twelve thousand.'

'Yes, yes,' Ursula hushed him quickly. 'Tomorrow. Wait until then.'

That was all Emily was able to overhear. Just a few hurried words spoken excitedly. They made little sense to her at the time.

In the bathroom at the end of the corridor, Emily, naked except for the jewelled collar at her throat, shivered under the less than tepid shower. Chloe was being cruel, switching the raw cold tap on from time to time with a vicious twist of her hand, relishing Emily's shrieks as she suffered the icy drenching.

'Stop that,' Ursula snarled. 'Just sponge and scrub the bitch. I want her fresh for the Lebanese.'

Chloe nodded obediently, set the shower back onto warm and rolled up her sleeves. Ordering Emily to face the white tiles, hands spread up above her wet blonde mane, Chloe squeezed aromatic gel onto her open palm and commenced to cream the nude's back, buttocks and thighs until the passive flesh foamed. Emily grunted as a big yellow sponge was dragged down her spine, then sighed as a corner of it was deftly twisted inwards to rake the cleft between her shiny cheeks. Emily's fingers splayed up against the wet tiles as Chloe plied the sponge vigorously, angling it at the dripping pussy.

'Stop playing with her,' Ursula warned, clapping her hands sharply together as she strode towards the shower. 'I warned you.'

Chloe, savagely deploying a loofah between Emily's sensitive inner thighs, squeaked in alarm as she sprang back from the shower.

'Give me that,' Ursula snapped, her green eyes flashing dangerously.

Chloe surrendered the blunt-nosed loofah.

'Not that, the nailbrush,' Ursula hissed impatiently. 'Now watch, I'm going to teach you how to scrub a bitch thoroughly clean.'

Emily whimpered and tightened her checks. *Smack!* Ursula's red handprint deepened to a crimson shade of pain across the swell of the wet, spanked bottom.

'Spread them,' Ursula snarled, and timorously, the drenched girl obeyed.

Ursula thumbed the bristles of the nailbrush, then rammed it down over her fingers like a knuckle-duster. 'Watch and learn,' she murmured, fleetingly kissing the upturned bristles.

Chloe, kneeling down, looked up eagerly, her eyes brimming with adoration as they watched the green-eyed dominant addressing the bare-bottomed girl spread-eagled against the tiles of the shower wall.

'Wider, cheeks out further, bitch,' Ursula demanded, spanking the shiny cheeks harshly, adding a second red palm-print across the first. 'Give me your bottom.'

Emily squealed in response, instantly dipping her spine and crushing her breasts against the tiles as she obediently offered her buttocks in total submission.

'I told you to get those cheeks wider apart. I've a strap here to help you if you need it.'

Terrified, Emily squeezed her eyes tightly shut as her cheeks parted and her shadowy cleft yawned. The hours with Mikhov had drained her spirit. She was like a broken doll under Ursula's cruel command.

'That's better,' the woman grunted, stepping in under the

shower to trap and control Emily's left leg between her clamped thighs. 'Let's make sure your bottom's nice and clean for your next spell of servitude and submission, shall we?'

The nailbrush glistened briefly as, bristles turned up into the sparkling shower, Ursula soaked it thoroughly, then vanished down between the pliant flesh of the bulging cheeks as Ursula buried its bristles down into the dark cleft. Emily wailed pitifully. Skimming the sensitive ribbon of velvet deep between Emily's cheeks, Ursula rasped the bristles viciously. Emily, her second outburst drowned in her broken sobs, finger-clawed the wet tiles up above her wet blonde hair, that plastered her eyes. Down in the swirling foam, ankle deep, her writhing feet danced mute arabesques of anguish.

'Now turn around. No, keep your hands up, bitch,' Ursula warned.

Emily, quivering against the wet tiles, her peaked nipples crushed fiercely into their glaze, refused to stir, stubbornly proffering her bottom to her tormentor.

Spank! *Spank*! *Spank*! The freshly punished wet cheeks crimsoned instantly under the sudden onslaught of firm palm down across naked flesh.

'I told you to turn around.'

Whimpering softly as she clenched her spanked cheeks, Emily reluctantly obeyed, her hands drawn down across her belly to shield her blonde pubic nest.

'Hands back up above your head.'

Despite the brusque order, Emily's interlocked fingers remained curved protectively at her pubis.

'Chloe,' Ursula called.

The raven-haired girl jumped up at once to do the bidding of her stern mistress.

'Take her hands,' Ursula nodded imperiously.

Disregarding the drumming shower at her shoulders and breasts, Chloe stepped in beside Emily, pinning the wriggling blonde's wrists up against the tiles. Pinioned and helpless, her feet skidding frantically beneath her in the swirling suds, Emily struggled in vain to evade the threat of the bristles hovering an inch from her delta.

Half an inch. Her throat tightened.

A quarter of an inch. Her pulse pounded.

A whisker away… her heart hammered wildly.

'Completely forgotten all about the cellar, haven't we?' Ursula purred, pressing the bristles home.

Broken, bowed and bending, Emily nodded, shaking the wet slick of blonde hair from her eyes.

'Sure?' Ursula insisted, dominantly applying the bristles into the vulnerable labial lips.

Emily squealed.

'Better make absolutely certain,' Ursula pronounced judiciously, suddenly twisting her wrist upwards so that the bristles caught and ravished the pink clitoris after searing the pouting lips.

Chloe, giggling in sadistic glee, pinned both the captive wrists against the tiles with her left hand, dropping her right hand to capture, cup and squeeze Emily's breasts.

Up on her scrabbling toes, their victim gasped then moaned. Up between her seething thighs, the nailbrush whispered softly as it burned into her wet heat, snagging painfully on stray wisps of golden pubic fuzz.

She opened her eyes, awakening slowly after sleeping heavily for – how many hours? Emily could not tell. And there was no clock in the room to help her. She was back in her bleak attic cell. Grim and spartan, it held an even more bleak promise to the waking girl: she no longer enjoyed the protection of Dr Stikannos. She was completely at the mercy of Ursula now, utterly helpless in her green-eyed thrall.

It was eleven minutes past two. She discovered the time after Chloe and Ursula had frog-marched her briskly downstairs to the opulent lair of the kohl-eyed Lebanese.

Sitting on a silver and gold divan, her heavy buttocks dimpling the damask cushions beneath their swell, Ayani carefully ate diced melon, black grapes and coffee ice cream from a quartz dish. Her long tongue licked and then lapped the curved back of a golden spoon.

'As I promised, yours for the rest of the afternoon,' Ursula announced, forcing Emily down onto her knees before the divan. 'Use her as you wish.'

Emily, naked, briefly fingering her studded collar nervously, averted her gaze down to the carpet. Ayani too was naked. Her dark bush of oily, matted curls glinted. The labia were dark purple, almost as dark as the grapes in the quartz dish.

The Lebanese continued to eat in silence after Ursula and Chloe had departed. Leaning forward, she guided a dripping spoonful of coffee ice cream down to Emily's lips. Emily shook her head slightly, refusing. The spoon remained at her lips, and tiny globules of ice cream splashed down onto Emily's left nipple. The pink bud rose, stiffened with the sudden cold. Emily flinched, her breasts quivering. Ayani snarled softly, her carnal grunt softened by the melon juice lubricating her throat.

'Eat,' the Lebanese ordered.

Emily shook her head again, gently refusing to be subjected to further degradation.

'I have a cane,' Ayani whispered, spreading her thighs apart and revealing her bright pink slit. 'It is a specimen of the rare, pale bambusa. Some call it the Borneo White. A little over a metre in length. The women of the forest where it thrives fear it. They even tremble when the dry hot winds blow through the forest. Because,' Ayani paused, slowly sucking on her spoon before continuing, 'when the hot wind blows, the bambusa canes shiver and sing. The canes sing a song of sorrow. A song as sorrowful as the shrill squeals of a bare-bottomed girl being whipped.'

Emily shivered, clenching her soft cheeks in a reflex of

alarm.

'I shall make you sing, girl. I shall open those stubborn lips of yours and listen to your shrill squealing.'

'No, please, I'm sorry,' Emily gushed. 'Please don't.'

Ayani sucked hard on the golden spoon. 'Now let me see,' she murmured, ignoring the kneeling blonde, 'where did I put that cane?'

Chapter Nine

Face down in the damask cushion of the divan – still warm from the weight of Ayani's bottom – Emily tugged in vain at the silk cord binding her wrists above her upturned buttocks.

Legs astride, her bottom poised above Emily's bowed head, her kohl-dark eyes gazing down dominantly upon the kneeling blonde's proffered cheeks, Ayani gripped the pale length of whippy bambusa. Tapping the soft swell of the left cheek imperiously, the dominatrix signalled her desire for Emily to raise her bottom a fraction higher. As Emily strained anxiously to obey her lips pressed into the damask, smothering but not quite silencing her pitiful whimpering.

Just as Ayani had promised, the pale bambusa whistled a thin, eerie note as it lashed down, eliciting a sorrowful sob from Emily's parted lips. The first and second strokes were administered vertically downwards, the first across her left buttock, the second searing the right. Both bequeathed venomous crimson weals that bisected exactly each plump cheek. Emily jerked twice in response to the stripes, grinding her pubis into the divan and wailing aloud. Stepping over the kneeling blonde to stand alongside, facing the punished rump, Ayani gripped and flexed her cane.

Two more strokes followed in rapid succession. *Swish, swipe! Swish, swipe!*

Emily squealed then bit into the damask cushion to smother her anguish. Above her lashed buttocks, as the fresh horizontal stripes deepened from pink to mauve, her bound hands writhed.

Ayani dragged the tip of her whippy cane down from the nape of her kneeling victim's neck to the dimple where

Emily's cheeks swelled at the base of her spine. Emily writhed. The tip of the pale bambusa traced the line of the cleft before dominantly tap-tapping the wet plum at its base. Emily jerked and moaned. The tip of the cane rose, hovering above the striped cheeks below, its pale shade of pain darkening with the soak of the blonde's juices.

Swish, crack!

Ayani swept the whippy wood inwards, and slightly upwards, to bite into the straining buttocks' fleshy curves. Emily howled, jiggling her cheeks frantically. Another stroke – an evil cut – cracked across the unprotected cheeks, setting the crimson-wealed domes ablaze as they danced in agony. Emily bit into the cushion, savaging it like a terrier with a rat, and ripped it open. White stuffing caused a sudden snowstorm. Ayani taloned the kneeling girl's blonde mane dominantly, jerking Emily's head up. A ribbon of torn crimson damask fluttered from Emily's clenched white teeth.

'Now you must truly suffer,' the Lebanese whispered, dragging her naked victim up from the divan and levelling her glinting cane in against Emily's painfully peaked nipples. 'Truly suffer.'

Emily flinched as the smooth wood toyed with her engorged buds. Ayani plied her cane adroitly, rasping it then rolling it firmly over the tiny peaks. Emily shrank back, sinking her caned cheeks down onto her ankles, squirming and pleading, but Ayani controlled her victim expertly, managing to bring a fresh hot bubble to the kneeling girl's labia.

Swish!

The bubble burst, its hot scald on Emily's clamped thighs nothing to the fierce burn across her caned breasts. With less venom but more vicious tenderness than the strokes across the bare buttocks, Ayani lashed Emily's breasts four more times. Caned, the nipples seethed. Ayani wrestled the blonde over onto her back. Her hands bound, her sobs ignored by her cruel chastiser, Emily lay helpless beneath the menace of the quivering cane.

Ayani knelt in front of the whipped nude, the onyx dish in her left hand, the golden spoon in her right. Digging the dull gold into the coffee ice cream, the Lebanese smeared Emily's caned breasts with the burning cold confection. Seconds later, Emily felt the fierce red lips sucking at her nipples, then the warmth of a strong leathery tongue lapping away all traces of the coffee ice cream from her bosom. After the scald of the cruel bambusa, her breasts had suffered the shock of the ice cream's burning chill. Trapped, ashamed and utterly helpless, Emily experienced the deepest humiliation yet: unbidden as it was unwelcome, her orgasm welled up and spilled over. Bound and subjugated, Emily started to come.

The nostrils above the thick red lips narrowed as Ayani sniffed. The lips creased into an ugly smile.

Tossing her blonde mane back, Emily cried out softly as she orgasmed uncontrollably, her feral juice perfuming the air with the raw musk of her wet heat.

The kohl-black eyes gazed down, amused. Ayani, shouldering her cane, rose up, turned Emily face down into the ripped crimson cushion and lashed her buttocks twice. Two crisp withering slices of cane across soft flesh. Emily, cheeks clenched and screaming softly, clamped her shiny inner thighs tightly together in a desperate attempt to control and contain the threat of a second climax. The cruel bambusa had ignited a fiercer heat at her satin skin that coursed down her cleft like molten lava, licking at the crease of her slit with invisible flames.

Two fingertips dipped into the sticky heat between Emily's cheeks. 'Too hot for you, girl?' the goading voice drawled.

Emily wept gently into the shredded damask.

'You'll have the ice cream after all, I think. And welcome it. Be grateful for it, and for my mercy.' Ayani tossed her cane aside, grasped the onyx dish once more and skilfully spooned a generous lump of coffee ice cream down between the whipped cheeks. The blonde squealed – and squealed again as the ice cream trickled down between the squeezed cheeks into her sensitive slit.

Her squeals froze into silence. All was silent except for the wet sounds of a thick tongue licking and lapping as Ayani buried her face into Emily's buttocks and tongued vigorously.

Sitting on the carpet, its rich weave prickling her pussy, Emily hugged her knees against her breasts and gazed down at the black, leather-bound book. As thick as the Bible, it bore the title *The Book of Sin* in gold lettering. Ayani, naked on the divan, stretched out luxuriously, her thighs wide apart, her left foot resting lightly on the carpet.

'Read to me. I like the sound of your voice, although I have only, as yet, heard it proclaim your sorrow and your pain.'

Emily shivered as she thumbed the pages nervously.

'But it is a sweet voice. The true voice of a beautiful English rose. Educated. Yes, I will like it, I am sure. Read to me, girl. Read to me from the fifth chapter. The Sin of Female Lust.'

Emily fumbled as she turned the pages rapidly, and came upon the chapter Ayani had demanded. From the corner of her eye, Emily saw the sprawling Lebanese select two black rubber thimbles from a silver tray by the divan and press them carefully down onto the tip of each of her straightened index fingers.

'Attend to your task,' Ayani snapped, flexing her fingers, then bringing the two rubber tips to her nipples.

With the stripes of the pale bambusa still as crimson in her mind as they were across her caned cheeks, Emily needed no further bidding. She concentrated on the text before her. Fingers trembling as they held the black leather binding, she drew in a deep breath and read:

'Of all the Sins recorded within these pages, that which is most pernicious and which merits punishments most severe is the Sin of Female Lust. In her hot lust, womankind is like the tigress. Like the tigress, lustful womankind must be striped, and caged. Wise men record that this Sin of Female Lust is occasioned boldly and bodily three times during a wanton's lifetime – in the virginity of her early flowering; in the excesses of her wifely bloom and later, in the full fruiting of early widowhood. At each stage, transgression is likely, and must be uncovered and atoned for with all expediency. No thought will be given at this moment to the excesses of the harlot and the whore: their sinfulness is of a special nature and the punishments prescribed for such sinners must be reserved for a later chapter…'

On the divan, Ayani closed her eyes into a kohl-dark smudge and rubbed the dimpled thimbles sternly into her peaked nipples. The stubby reddening flesh submitted to the black rubber obediently as Ayani's thick lips parted for a silent snarl. At the base of her white belly, within the luxuriant dark bush, her outer labia juiced.

'In her maidenhood, the curiosity of a young wench will goad her venal appetite and draw her hands down to her forbidden flesh. The bolder among these young wantons will use their fingertips cunningly at parts no maiden should acquaint herself with so immodestly. Down at her Gate of Eden, there is enfolded within her Eve's Rose a tiny thorn of Love. This must not be touched. If the wanton girl is discovered doing so, punishment must come swift and hard. For it is late at night, or before the dawn breaks, when these sins will be committed. Those who are charged with the guardianship of young virgins must be vigilant. To discover the occasion of sinfulness, elder females should listen at the midnight hour and again before the sun arises; listen at the door of the virgin's chamber; listen for her moan for she will moan at her sin like the turtledove; listen for her soft cries of sweet sorrow. Further measures must be taken to determine if sin has taken place. The linen from the bed must be examined by the light of tapers before the stains of lustful pleasure dry. The elder female tasked with the strict observance of the young virgin's continence should examine the fingertips, smelling them carefully for traces of the Devil's Scent.

Punishment of the sinful young virgin must be harsh. Let not her youthfulness spare her stern measures. An aunt or other elder from the family is the most fitting to dispense the chastisement. A birch twig bundle – no less than eight supple rods – lightly applied to the palms of the sinner will bring forth tears of penitence and promises of purity from the lips of the punished. When the sin is repeated, the birch twigs must be applied harshly to the naked buttocks. It is held to be most instructive for the punished girl if she be made to gaze upon her stripes in a looking glass. Constrained to behold her whipped cheeks as they burn, she will see her pain through tear-filled eyes: sudden will be her contrition and solemn her vow to desist in her wickedness.'

On the divan, the stubby nipples strained up in scarlet anger beneath the ravishing rubber thimbles. Emily risked a quick glimpse at Ayani's sex. It was slippery with arousal, the outer, darker lips already peeled apart. The inner pinkness glistened. Ayani grunted as she dragged her rubber-coated fingertips down across her belly and dappled them at the fringe of the dark bush below.

'To deal with the discontent of the young wife, her kinswomen must remain alert to the signs of her sinful lust. If her eye wanders to the manservant in attendance at table, be sure that she will use him for more intimate attention. Discharge all menservants from the household and be sure and certain of this singular truth: the higher her station, the lower the lustful young wife will stoop for her lewd sport. Watch her closely about the household and keep keen vigilance, for even the blameless candle and the innocent long-handled spoon may be pressed into service by her to do the Devil's Deeds. Here are signs to look for about her person; bruising at the lips will betray fierce sucking and kissing; a robe in disarray will tell if her fingers have been busy at her bosom or at another privy place. Kinswomen, be vigilant. The honour of the family is in thrall. Spy upon her craftily as she bathes. Remember: her Path of Sodom will be inflamed if the wanton has used forbidden objects at her hot flesh…'

The rubber thimbles were now soaked and silvered with Ayani's juice as she ravished her exposed flesh. Between her rigid, splayed thighs, her strong white fingers strummed into a blur. Grunting softly, the Lebanese masturbated openly as Emily, head bowed, continued to read aloud from *The Book of Sin*.

'The rose blighted by an early frost before summer has run its hot course is like the young wife in her lust. Punishment of the transgressor must be applied mercilessly. The rod of sorrow must stripe her, repeatedly, across the softness of her thighs before barking aloud when visiting her bared buttocks. Let the whipping be leisurely and protracted. Let the punishers pause to take small cakes and wine. The mother-in-law, sister-in-law and elder cousins, all acting as one to protect the family honour, must remain deaf to the penitent's pleading as they ply the wand of woe. And remember this as you lash her hard: promises of repentance drawn forth by the switch and the crop are all too soon broken. All there is for you to do is to break her dark will. When a young wife turns wanton, stripe her hard.'

Grinding her buttocks into the ripped damask, Ayani lolled her head and surrendered to the vicious climax imploding between her wet thighs. Emily, peeping up from her page, saw the vein pulsing at Ayani's neck. Shrieking softly, the Lebanese twisted in her delicious torment, her left hand suddenly spread out.

'Early widowhood is a bitter harvest. But beware. The young widow is ripe for the worm of lust. Seek out her sin and punish her, lest the contagion spread. The young widow, when caught with the parson, the doctor or young married men at her pleasures, must be dragged by the women of the village to a privy place for punishment. She must taste both sorrow and shame so tie her hands high up above her head and let her hair fall freely down like the pilgrim in sackcloth and ashes. Strip her naked of her widow's weeds and let every hand present pick up and ply the whip. Spare her not, and sting her sinful flesh severely. But—'

A renewed gasp from the divan brought Emily's eyes up from *The Book of Sin* to gaze directly on the seething, thimble-tormented slit. Cursing in a tongue unknown to Emily, the nude writhing on the stained damask screeched a second orgasm.

'But,' Emily repeated, her voice quickening and rising an octave as she resumed her reading, 'be sure that this punishment itself does not bring unsuspected pleasures to the sinner. Be cautious as you stripe her buttocks, for so depraved is she who in her widowhood turns to lewdness and lust, that the very stripes of pain bring a dark pleasure to her wanton flesh. It is well observed by wise ones that a young widow, bound and naked for her stripes, can become pleasured by her pain. Indeed, so wanton are these wicked wretches, they do seek the sugared sorrow of the whip's keen kiss…'

Ayani screamed, a brutal salute to raw pleasure. Emily paused, uncertain if to continue. Upon the page, her fingers trembled.

'Bring it to me,' the Lebanese gasped, writhing. 'Bring the book to me.'

Emily remained kneeling before the divan, uncertain what to do.

'Place it at my flesh,' Ayani hissed.

Emily scrambled towards the divan, the heavy book gripped in her left hand. The powerful aroma of Ayani's hot slit drenched the air. On the damask silk – now damson dark where juices stained the torn crimson – the naked buttocks jerked in their sweet paroxysms.

'The book,' Ayani screamed.

Emily snapped the volume shut, turned its weight around in her trembling hand then guided the thick spine in against the splayed labia before her. A carnal moan greeted her efforts, followed by the wet rubber thimbles scrabbling at her lips. Suddenly tasting the tang, Emily flinched from the slippery dimples tormenting her mouth.

'Use it,' Ayani cursed, 'use it.'

Emily raked the leather-bound spine against Ayani's wet heat. Pressing hard against the pink flesh, she ravished it savagely with the stern binding of black leather. Another shrill scream split the air as the naked Lebanese on her divan came violently, her thimbled fingertips punishing Emily's lips as the orgasm squeezed her within its fist of vicious velvet. Emily almost choked as the frantic rubber fingertips probed and filled her mouth: filled her mouth and stretched its warmth with spasms of Ayani's orgasmic fury.

'Shave me. I want you to kneel obediently before me like a little slave girl and shave me as smooth as a swan's egg. But,' Ayani, recovered from her climax, warned, 'be careful with the razor. Be very, very, careful. My whip awaits.'

Trembling, and recoiling from the indignity of fresh humiliation, Emily knelt in obedience before the naked woman. Where was Dr Stikannos? Why was he not protecting her? Protecting and reclaiming her for himself?

Emily bitterly resented his betrayal. She had, for him, torn aside the final veil of all doubts, all misgivings, baring her body and mind to him in utter submission and sweet servitude. Where was the master now?

'My whip awaits,' Ayani whispered, her slightly slurred vowels breaking into Emily's thoughts.

Emily picked up the tiny brush and silver dish that held the shiver of foam. Dipping the brush into the dish she twisted it, loading the dark bristles with the aromatic froth. Taking a deep breath, she guided the whitened bristles up into the dark pubic nest. It was a superb bush, the oily curls deeply thick and densely matted. Emily worked assiduously with the brush, worrying the dark nest until it was thoroughly foamed. Foamed, and waiting for the razor. Emily swallowed nervously.

'Be quick about your business,' Ayani rasped, clenching her buttocks tightly as the razor glinted in the rays of the setting sun.

The flash of burning orange on the silver blade's edge made Emily blink; blink away all resentful thoughts of her master's betrayal. She knew she had to concentrate, and concentrate very hard. One slip – just one small slip. If the razor so much as grazed the flesh of the naked Lebanese dominatrix, her bare buttocks would suffer beneath the waiting whip.

She applied the razor tentatively. A narrow band of bald flesh appeared in the wake of the skimming blade. She dipped it and rinsed it clean, then revisited the dense mass of foamed curls. A second, delicate downward stroke. A barely audible whisper as the blade caressed the pubic bush, rustling softly as it left a second narrow band behind it. Emily breathed out slowly but her fingers shook a little. She steadied her hand then brought the thin steel back to kiss the curls.

Her eyes widened a fraction. The perspiration beading her temples gathered at the corners of her eyes, stinging harshly. She blinked twice, managing merely to scald herself with her own sweat. A brief wipe of the back of her left hand brought some slight relief, and an immediate snarl from the cruel Lebanese.

'My whip aches for your buttocks, girl. The leather is longing to lash.'

Emily mumbled her apology and busied herself with renewed alacrity, prising the stretched flesh beneath the fingertips of her left hand while plying the tiny razor accurately.

Some minutes later the pubic delta was shaven close and clean. Emily had even pinched up the fat labial lips and skimmed the razor across their purplish flesh to remove the stray pubic wisp.

'Not one single hair must remain.' That was all Ayani said. Not in praise for the delicate task completed but in a promise of pain if Emily's efforts were found wanting. Emily fingered the surface of the shaved pubis tenderly. As her fingertip skimmed the clitoral hood, her heart skipped two distinct beats. Two minute hairs remained unshaven.

She froze. It was such a dangerous task. Without using foam, she teased each individual pubic hair up and nicked them clean away with the dry blade.

Ayani, using a small mirror, pronounced herself satisfied. As Emily accepted the mirror from the dominant's hands, she saw that the small oval of glass had become clouded with Ayani's feral heat. To her surprise the Lebanese turned, presenting her heavy buttocks. As Ayani shuffled and spread her legs apart, the cheeks wobbled gently. Strong fingers swiftly appeared at each, depressing deeply into the fleshy mounds before drawing the buttocks apart. Emily gazed directly into the yawn of the dark cleft.

'Tidy me up in there, then oil me.'

Emily gulped.

'Not the razor,' Ayani barked as she heard Emily's fingers returning to the silver dish. 'Tweezers.'

There were several little dark coils along the dark valley of the exposed cleft. Emily plied the tweezers as gently as possible, flinching as Ayani grunted at the removal of each plucked coil.

'Oil me,' came the crisp command as the tweezers rattled in the silver dish.

Emily reached down for the white jar of attar. She unscrewed the top and dipped her nose to sniff at the rich unguent. It had a haunting, cloying sweetness. Anointing her fingertip with a thick smear, she extended her straightened finger and guided it into Ayani's sphincter.

The anal ring opened to receive her glistening finger's length and tightened responsively as Emily probed. But the oiled finger met with the tight warmth of muscled resistance. Emily withdrew a fraction, then twisting her hand, probed deeper. Ayani grunted. Suddenly, and to her burning shame, Emily realised that her greased finger was being gripped by the anal muscles and sucked into their tight warmth. Gasping her dismay aloud she jerked her hand away, and the Lebanese hissed her frustration.

'How dare you?' she demanded, her voice shrill with outrage. 'For that, my little slave, you will suffer. Depend upon it. You will most certainly suffer. Not now,' she whispered, crushing her naked breasts fiercely with her knuckled fists, 'no, not now. Later, when my whip kisses your bare bottom, repeatedly. Kisses you passionately but entirely without affection.'

Emily's beating heart betrayed her calm silence as she knelt penitently before the naked dominatrix. Knelt penitently, her face mere inches from the heavy cheeks before her.

'You will learn to obey, girl, however painful the lesson must be. Get up.'

As Emily rose unsteadily her face pressed into the swollen cheeks. Steadying herself, a flattened palm at Ayani's left hip and right thigh, Emily crushed her face into the soft bottom, digging her nose deep into the dark cleft. The cheeks spread. In her surprise, Emily gasped, and her opened lips accidentally kissed the anal whorl.

'A little late for that, girl,' the Lebanese grunted contentedly, mistaking Emily's accidental kiss for true and abject submission. 'Go to that drawer. No, the second drawer down,' Ayani commanded, snapping her fingers and pointing impatiently as Emily hovered by a walnut cabinet.

The drawer slid out obediently. Inside, Emily saw the leather harness which was not unlike a pony's martingale.

'That goes on your head, and the dildo,' she continued suavely, 'goes between your teeth.'

Emily weighed the soft leather head-harness on her open palm. The dry hide prickled her damp skin. She folded her thumbtip down onto the dull leather. As her flesh touched the hide, her labial lips peeled gently apart. Leather. The pelt of penance. The skin of submission. Leather across the buttocks, or binding the submissive's wrists and ankles. Yes, that she knew; knew intimately, and understood.

But a tight leather harness strapped around her head, criss-crossing her face. Her belly grew heavy with delicious dread. Ayani, she realised, was relegating her to the level of the dumb beast. Long leading reins trailed down from the harness held in her levelled hand. Emily flinched back from the annoying tap-tap of the traces against her knees. No, she decided, tossing the harness down, not that.

'No?' Ayani queried, her tone deceptively light. 'Do you know,' she added nonchalantly as she glanced down at the curled hide on the carpet, 'what will happen to you if you do not have that harness in place before I have stopped counting ten? Do you, girl?'

The polite tone held all the velvet menace of a raised whip. Emily, panicking, knelt down and struggled to don the head-halter.

'*Cinq*, *six*, *sept*…' Ayani counted, slowly and deliberately, as if enumerating the separate cane strokes across a birched bottom.

'No, please…' Emily squealed, desperately trying to wriggle into her restraint. Elbows angled, breasts bouncing, she made a final bid to beat the count.

'*Huit, neuf, dix…*'

Panting, Emily peered above the bulge of her cheeks. The leather bit softly down against each temple. Another strap trapped her nose. Her chin ached under the stricture of tightly tied hide. She gulped and tried to work her jaws, but the harness was cruelly restrictive. Despite her bitter resentment and shame, Emily's sex grew slippery with perverse pleasure.

'The dildo,' Ayani prompted.

Emily picked up the black length of ribbed, wickedly curved plastic and, raising the blunt base up to her lips, inserted it into her mouth.

'Bite,' the Lebanese instructed curtly. 'Bite it and keep it firmly between your teeth.' Ayani planted her feet wider apart and waggled her bulging buttocks imperiously. 'Kneel,' she barked, jabbing her thumb down behind the ripe swell of her bare buttocks. 'Kneel and pleasure me.'

Stumbling clumsily in her faintly jingling harness, just escaping tripping over the trailing traces, Emily approached the naked dominatrix and knelt before the splendid cheeks. The ponderous dildo, protruding from Emily's clenched teeth, nodded as she knelt.

Gathering up the leading traces with difficulty, Emily placed the looped leather lengths into the impatient hands at Ayani's hips. She shivered as the Lebanese gripped them firmly and jerked her fists forward, pulling Emily's face closer to the ripe cheeks.

'Commence.'

Guiding the tip of the black dildo towards the dark wet sphincter, then nuzzling the knout into the anal whorl, Emily closed her eyes and sought escape in sweeter memories. Memories of school sports days, when coltish girls in pleated skirts, proudly aware and shyly ashamed of their sixth form bosoms, skittled inelegantly along the shaven sward for the fifty metre egg-and-spoon dash. Jaws aching deliciously as they held the heavy spoon. Eyes watering as they concentrated to keep the egg in place. Hips swaying, buttocks joggling as they scampered towards the fluttering tape. At the finishing line, bronze-thighed and superb in a candy-striped blazer, the amazonian Head of House. With the promise of a cuddle in the showers for the fleet of foot and a sharp spanking in the dorm for the slowcoach.

'Concentrate,' Ayani hissed savagely, breaking into Emily's daydream.

Emily blinked. The dildo had slipped out, raking the curve of the left cheek's satin swell. Realigning the phallus she speared it between the buttocks, burying its black sheen deeply. Emily shuffled closer until her nipples kissed and then her breasts crushed into Ayani's thighs. A sharp tug at the reins brought her half an inch from the buttocks before her, and drove the dildo deeper between the swollen cheeks. A second short tug brought Emily's face against the cool, pliant flesh. The buttocks were like pillows of velvet with a stretched satin surface. Supple and rubbery, massively soft and sensual. Emily's nipples stiffened fiercely.

'Pump.'

Emily nodded, as if in a mute show of obedience, causing the ribbed dildo to probe deeper into the tight warmth. At her nostrils, the feral heat from the parted cleft tormented the kneeling blonde.

Ayani grunted her satisfaction but tugged once again at both reins. Emily's teeth gripped as her face was brutally buried into the bare buttocks' warmth. The jerk drove all eight inches of the dildo ruthlessly home. The Lebanese howled then, up on whitening tiptoes, gently tugged at each rein, rolling her victim's face across the curves of her buttocks. As Emily's face was dragged into the soft left cheek, then into the velvet of the right cheek's curve, the dildo twisted and barrelled inside the rectal warmth. Ayani screamed, dropped the traces and hammered her heavy rump into Emily's helpless face. Spluttering and gasping for air, Emily tried to edge her face away from the smothering buttocks but the Lebanese gripped the leading reins, keeping the squashed face trapped and completely under control.

'Harder,' Ayani demanded. 'Harder and faster.'

Struggling to breathe, Emily fought stubbornly against the stern embrace of the leather head-harness.

'Finish me,' the Lebanese snarled.

Biting hard into the acrid black plastic shaft, Emily butted the buttocks frenziedly. Hot juice from the climaxing nude seeped down, silvering Emily's nipples as her breasts squeezed through Ayani's splayed thighs from behind. With a final shrill scream of dark delight, the Lebanese buckled beneath the violence of her anal orgasm.

It was almost dusk. Out in the grounds, treading the lengthening evening shadows, the peacocks paraded elegantly back towards the terrace. The Lebanese had bathed, languidly, attended to obediently by Emily who towelled and intimately talcumed the olive-skinned dominatrix.

Aching for a shower to ease her tired limbs – and the oblivion of sleep to soothe her troubled mind – Emily slipped silently into a trance-like state in which shadows proved to have substance and time slowly congealed.

She remained naked. Every inch of her body now thrilled with the dull ache of exhaustion. Deep inside the blaze of her alert brain, Emily's resentment seethed. Used and abused, she had visited the very depths of humiliation, depravity and submission. No sweet surrender to a beloved master – no. For Emily, it had been a bitter submission to the hateful dominatrix. Powerless to resist and repeatedly whipped and punished, she had been forced to pander to Ayani's merest whim.

The naked Lebanese sat in a high-backed chair by the French window. The tall glass pane flashed red fire as it reflected the last of the sunset. Ayani smoked a cheroot. A thin serpent of silvery-blue smoke snaked up to the ceiling. The tip of the cheroot glowed orange as Ayani drew on it between her thick red lips. From time to time, almost absently, the Lebanese sipped aromatic mocha coffee.

The coffee cup chinked as Ayani returned it to its waiting saucer. The brittle sound exploded in Emily's keen brain like a grenade. Snapped out of her drifting lapse towards wakeful sleep, she blinked and tried hard to focus – focus on and make sense of the nightmare she was enduring.

With Dr Stikannos it had been quite different; the gradual duel of minds. His increasing knowledge of her true nature, her reluctant willingness to obey. The dance, gentle and potent with significant gestures. His seduction of her body, wooing it with the pleasure-pain it craved. Ensnaring her nakedness with sweet torments. Making her come, instantly, as she bowed down bare-bottomed before him to shiver and squeal under the lash of the camel's penis. A secret, private, intimate servitude. Darkly delicious; disturbingly delightful.

But in the hands of the brutal Mikhov and the dominant, kohl-eyed Ayani, Emily had been their mere toy: broken on the wheel of their keen lust and caught like a butterfly in the mesh of their depravities. Kneeling, naked, on the carpet in the gathering shadows, she felt empty. Almost empty, except for the puddle of fear as heavy as cold mercury weighing in her belly. When, her fear asked, would it end?

The coffee cup settled into its saucer for a final time. Emily tensed. Ayani stubbed the half-smoked cheroot out. It was over now, surely. She would be given her freedom now. The insatiable Lebanese could not possibly need her any more tonight.

'You are exactly what I have been looking for,' Ayani said, brushing a speck of grey cheroot ash from her bronzed, naked thigh.

Emily raised her head but remained silent. This was it. This was the moment when her nightmare ended.

'Ursula was right,' the Lebanese reflected.

Ursula. Emily's pulse quickened at the sound of the name. It had been Ursula who delivered her into the ropes and bondage of the Russian. It had been Ursula who had presented Emily, as a blonde and tempting tit-bit, to tickle the jaded appetite of the vicious Lebanese.

'Of course,' Ayani murmured, rising from her high-backed chair and slowly treading the carpet to where Emily knelt, 'you are still young. Young and very naïve. Naïve and as yet unripe in the arts of the flesh. But, like the espalier tree tied and stretched out tightly, trainable. Teachable. Yes, teachable: obedient and responsive to the whip.'

Remembering the whip, and her squealing responses to it, Emily shuddered.

'That is what I prize most highly in a girl. Not a mastery of the crimson pleasures, but the readiness to learn them, a readiness to learn. On your back.'

Puzzling the meaning of Ayani's words, Emily was taken by surprise. Ayani's concluding words were spoken harshly in sharp command.

'Teachable,' Ayani purred, 'and responsive to the whip. Do I have to make my meaning painfully clear?'

Emily sank back down onto the carpet. Legs together or apart? What gross indignity awaited her. Was the kohl-eyed monster about to bind her loins with a leather girdle, insert a dildo into the socket at her pubic mound and ride Emily as a man would? Were her breasts and belly to be lingeringly lashed with a cruel cat o'nine? Emily writhed in dread.

'Face up. No, look directly up at the ceiling.'

Emily did, and saw the Lebanese, legs straddled apart, descending slowly, her wet fig open and glistening.

'No,' Emily squealed, trying but not succeeding in her attempt to roll aside.

Ayani stamped gently down, pinioning both of Emily's

wrists beneath her sure and certain tread. The blonde watched in horror as the shaven delta approached her face inch by inch. Emily cried in feeble protest as the Lebanese sank down, kneeling astride and then onto the pale face below. Emily screamed, and continued screaming, as feral lips, dark and swollen, smothered her own.

'Tongue me.'

Timidly, Emily licked, running the tip of her quivering tongue across the salty flesh filling her mouth.

'Deeper, girl. Deeper and harder and all of your tongue. Do it.'

The soft buttocks started to joggle, the undulating cheeks smothering the trapped face beneath. Emily spluttered and gasped, her lips and tongue shrivelling from the perfumed oil she had anointed Ayani's secret parts with not an hour since. Gasping for air, Emily accidentally caught and nipped the rubbery outer labia between her teeth. Ayani screamed, then knees burning into the carpet, pounded her buttocks down into Emily's glistening face.

'Tongue only, girl, or you'll taste my whip!' screeched the woman.

Emily thrust her thick muscle directly up into the wet heat. Ayani groaned, slumping forward onto her hands for support before raking her juiced crease up and along Emily's face.

'Like a fresh little virgin every time,' the Lebanese grunted, cursing obscenely as she came.

The sale was being conducted in the west wing, a late eighteenth-century addition. The walls were of double brick and stone, giving the room muffled acoustics. If the vixen was barking outside beyond the laurels, none of those assembled in the large room heard her. Mint green silk lined the walls, further softening all sounds. Ultra modern spotlights encircled the huge chandelier that seemed to float between the ceiling and the silk carpet below. The music was Iberian, an incongruous selection of Albéniz salon pieces. The Portuguese nobleman scowled into his quivering catalogue.

Dr Stikannos presided over the sale in a grand manner. Eighteen pictures had been carefully arrayed and displayed, under discreet and flattering illumination, along the length of the far wall. The bidders sat apart, like dogs in a backyard before a scrap, assessing each other's strength. They sat in Adam chairs that did not squeak as heavy buttocks twisted on the cream, white and gold upholstery.

Emily, naked, gagged and bound at the wrists, had been brought into the large room along with a small Matisse by Ursula, an hour earlier. The Matisse had been carefully mounted by Ursula and Chloe for all to see. Emily had been secreted behind an eighteenth-century folding screen, from which she peeped in silence as the sale got underway.

The bidding was brisk but, at first, confused. The Hong Kong twins twittered and bid against each other, causing Dr Stikannos to abandon the bidding and start anew. The metal mask glinted ominously as his dark eyes quelled their giggling. In atonement, they raised the bid by a thumping twelve thousand – to a quarter of a million – and snapped up the exquisite Beauvois *mermaid*, the mural plaster in the gold frame as fragile as it had been when painted eight hundred years before.

Mikhov became excited – greedy and excited. He bought three in a row. Like a pig in an orchard, Emily thought as she watched his screwed up eyes, shitting on the apples he could not manage to eat. The Russian did not want art, he simply wanted more.

With a sly self-effacement, like a fox asleep with the hounds, the Portuguese announced his intention to bid with a dry cough. It turned all heads. He coughed again, as if apologetically. He beat them all to the lubricious Klimt sketch of *Lilith*, sensual symbol of rampant female lust. The heads of those assembled twisted around, amazed, and contented with his surprise victory, the Portuguese retired behind his raised catalogue.

Ursula and Chloe fawned on the assembled millionaires, refreshing their champagne glasses and collecting the cheques as Dr Stikannos readied himself for the next item on the catalogue. Reading crisply through Emily's careful annotations regarding provenance and authenticity, his voice softened to a sibilant purr as he repeated aloud her more salacious context notes.

Emily's heart thumped. The Orozco had not attracted much response earlier on at the final viewing, but now, heads rising from her catalogue notes, the prospective buyers viewed the depiction of the kneeling capitalist at the buttocks of the whore with keen interest. Emily blushed gently as she heard Dr Stikannos draw attention to the top hat, and explained the wet rind of the orange. It was bid for eagerly by all assembled and went to the Portuguese nobleman well over the expected price. Emily's fingers spread out excitedly above her bare bottom as, childlike, she calculated her cut.

It was the Overbeck next: the haunting images of sadistic pleasures and masochistic pain. Emily's pussy prickled as she remembered her first encounter with the painting, and how she had been forced to describe it, in frank detail, to Dr Stikannos. How his dark eyes had studied her as her eyes studied the disturbing images on the canvas.

'And five.'

'Twenty-three thousand.'

'Twenty-four.'

The bids rattled out. Gazing through the screen at the depiction of the flagellant nuns – and their bound, whipped victims – Emily recalled her most recent, painful experiences under the lash. Shivering, she clamped her thighs to quench the seethe at her slit.

Ayani bought the Overbeck, bidding a full million.

Chloe escorted the Portuguese nobleman to the supper table along the corridor beyond the impressive double doors. Dr Stikannos, rubbing his gloved hands with pleasure at the success of the private sale, allowed the Hong Kong twins to propel his chair towards the waiting meal.

Behind her screen, gagged and bound, Emily shivered. With the lights of the elegant chandelier dimmed and the large room almost deserted, a chill visited her nakedness. The air-conditioning, switched on to its lowest setting to preserve the arrayed fortune of paintings, brought goose-pimples to her pale thighs.

Ursula had remained, and was talking in a soft tone with Mikhov and Ayani. The Russian and the Lebanese had emerged as financial, egotistical duellists during the auction. Matching dollar for dollar, vanity for vanity, they had emerged from the dogfight honours even. Emily peered at them, sensing that even now rivalry hung in the air between them.

Ursula turned on a spotlight. It punched a pool of white light onto the silk carpet. Turning to the screen behind which Emily shivered, she clapped her hands twice.

'Step out into the light, girl, where we can see you properly.'

Emily, startled by the summons, felt the cold fingers of dread squeezing at her belly. Why had they remained instead of joining Dr Stikannos at the supper table? What did they want with her, now that the sale was concluded and their departure imminent?

'Are you coming out here, girl, or must I come and make you?'

Slowly, blushing in her nakedness and shame, Emily stole out from behind the folding screen and stepped beneath the fierce spotlight. The bluish-white beam bathed her nudity, lapping into every soft curve and secret shadow of her body. It gave her breasts a deliciously inviting cleavage. With her arms tied at the wrists behind her back, Emily's breasts thrust

225

forward, accentuating their ripeness. She bowed her head, longing to cover her pubic thatch with modestly protective cupped hands: hands that remained bound and helpless above her bare bottom.

'Exquisite,' the Lebanese hissed, leaning forward to stroke Emily's belly and outer thigh.

The Russian, not to be outdone, patted Emily's soft bottom and fingered the ropes at her wrists as he grunted his delight.

'You have both had the chance to sample the goods,' Ursula announced.

Mikhov and Ayani nodded.

'As I promised,' Ursula continued, deftly steering Emily back into the spotlight her naked feet had strayed away from, 'the girl is for sale.'

Emily squealed into her gag, and above it her eyes widened in fear. Oh God, no. She staggered almost drunkenly under the blaze of the spotlight. She was to be auctioned off to the highest bidder – sold into servitude to either the brutal Russian or the vicious Lebanese. Sold off into the misery of domination, humiliation and pain – pain for another's perverted pleasure.

'Cash only,' Ursula announced briskly. 'No credit or cheques.'

'Currency?' Ayani queried.

'US dollars,' Mikhov broke in anxiously. 'Good? Yes?'

Ursula nodded matter-of-factly. 'Good, yes.'

Half-remembered, less than half-understood words and phrases came back to Emily, suddenly making sense. The Russian's remarks after the session of bondage and humiliation. Emily had thought his mention of bidding referred to the paintings. And Ayani's words – about Emily being green and unripe but trainable and teachable – filled Emily with foreboding. Trained and taught to do what? And at whose bidding?

If she went to Moscow she would suffer the cruel indignities of rope and leather, rubber and chains. If Ayani bid the highest, Emily would be smuggled into the darkest corners of a Beirut brothel to be painfully prepared for a life of pleasure – others' pleasure.

She shivered and struggled to fight down the panic rising inside her. The preliminaries had been settled. Already the bidding was underway. Ayani had just said that she might have to write out a cheque.

'Cash only,' Ursula replied firmly. 'Mikhov? The bid stands at eighteen thousand.'

Sensing a weak link in the rival bidder's armour, the Russian grinned. If Ayani had mentioned cheques, her dollar funds must be limited.

'Twenty-three,' he grunted, smelling victory.

Ayani's eyes flickered. The kohl-dark lids barely moved – no more than a cobra in a troubled dream. 'Twenty-five.'

The Russian winced as if biting onto a bad tooth. He remained silent. Sweat prickled his sallow face. He wiped his palms against his thighs.

'Remember,' Ursula whispered, cupping and squeezing Emily's breasts and offering their silky flesh to the Russian's excited gaze. 'Remember how the leather strap bound these breasts and made them bulge. Remember how you emptied your hot seed over them…'

'Twenty-eight,' Mikhov groaned.

'Twenty-eight?' Ursula murmured, gently caressing Emily's upturned wrists. 'Think of the waxed cords binding these wrists so sweetly and,' she swiftly dropped her palms against the swell of the buttocks below, 'those waxed cords burning as they bite deeply into this bottom.'

'Thirty,' he gasped, forgetting he was bidding against himself.

Ursula turned in silence to the Lebanese. Ayani gazed longingly at Emily's squirming nakedness.

'The bid is against you. At thirty thousand.'

Ayani shrugged helplessly. She had the desire, but not, perhaps, the dollars.

'Consider,' Ursula whispered, bending Emily down to present the blonde's bare bottom to the kohl-dark eyes. 'Whipped into obedience and fully trained to serve, you will be able to command a very high price for her usage in your seraglio. All the pleasure of training her to your strict standards and,' Ursula continued seductively, 'at least a thousand a night.' Parting Emily's cheeks, she allowed Ayani a brief but enticing glimpse of Emily's exposed pink anal rosebud.

Mikhov struggled with his money-belt and started to peel off one thousand dollar bills. Fourteen... Sixteen... They fluttered down to tickle Emily's toes. Twenty-six... Thirty...

'Thirty thousand dollars, cash,' Ursula remarked. 'Ayani?'

'I cannot match that bid.'

Mikhov clapped his hands in delight.

'In dollar bills. But,' Ayani hissed, standing up and delving her right hand down into her skirt, 'I bid twenty thousand dollars, and this.'

Her fingers withdrew, their tips shiny from her pussy. Delicately poised between the first finger and the thumb was a pearl. 'I keep it there at all times. A pearl is international currency. This one is worth – the girl.'

In silence, Ursula weighed the bid. Twenty thousand dollars in cash and the slippery pearl. She nodded. 'Sold.' Slapping Emily harshly across the bottom instead of banging the gavel, Ursula closed the bidding.

'But...' the Russian spluttered, dropping down onto his knees and showering the thousand dollar bills up into the air. 'I want... I must have—'

'She is mine,' hissed Ayani.

Despite the blinding spotlight, the room seemed to be growing very dark for Emily. Dark, and spinning around her. Shrill bells seemed to be ringing as, sinking down on sagging knees, she fainted at the feet of her new owner, mistress and ruthless dominatrix.

'She'll be fine,' Ursula remarked, prodding Emily's naked

bottom with her toe. 'Fit enough for the helicopter tomorrow morning.'

The Lebanese nodded, gazing down with savage tenderness at her new possession.

'Absolutely fine,' Ursula murmured, popping the wet pearl into her mouth and sucking hard.

Chapter Ten

The peacocks screamed from the terrace, hungrily demanding their early morning toast. Susie, busy at the Aga – so much to do with so many exotic palates to pamper and please – rescued the tray of buttered trout fillets browning in the slow oven. On the Aga's dull red plates, two large silver kettles steamed.

The shrill call from the peacocks for toast broke into Susie's train of thought. Distracted, she dropped the blue tea towel between the steaming kettles and turned to slice the bread and feed the toaster.

Dr Stikannos lay propped up against four white pillows. Naked, his gloved hands covered his curled penis. The metal mask glinted in the early morning sunrise as he twisted onto one elbow and gazed up into Ursula's green eyes.

'And the final total?'

'Seven and a half million,' she replied calmly.

He nodded vigorously. 'Have you seen to everything? Nothing must be overlooked. Are all arrangements in place?'

'The flight plans have been filed. Air traffic control has given a green for noon. I will personally supervise the smooth departure of your guests.'

'Excellent. And see to it that they breakfast well.'

'Champagne all the way,' she said, stepping closer to the side of his bed.

'And the girl, Emily?'

Ursula's mask-like face betrayed no emotion. 'She will be brought to you as soon as the last helicopter has departed. I thought it best to keep her out of circulation. She has been in her room throughout the sale.'

'Good. The less she sees, the better, perhaps.' He spread his legs apart and brought his gloved hands up to grip the brass bed-rail behind his pillows. 'Emily. She is well?'

'Fit as a fiddle,' Ursula whispered.

'Now that I find most curious. Fit as a fiddle. Surely it is the fiddler who needs to be fit, not the instrument he plays upon?'

'Calm yourself,' she soothed, brushing aside his semantic quibbling as a nanny would hush an excited child. 'Relax.'

'I will see her soon, you say?'

Ursula scooped up his shaft and encircled it firmly within her enclosed fist. 'She'll be under your whip before sunset.'

His shaft thickened at her words, twitching within her squeezing grip. Ursula closed his eyes with her fingertips and began to pump him rhythmically.

'She was not bored, unoccupied, during her confinement to quarters?'

'She was not bored,' Ursula murmured, 'or unoccupied. Just relax.'

He surrendered to her, inching his buttocks up from the bed as she thumbed his glistening glans.

Moments later he opened his eyes. 'Will it rain today? Is the forecast set fair? The helicopters—'

'There will be no precipitation today,' Ursula murmured, her pumping fist becoming a blur.

He gasped, slumping back into the pillows, the pitter-pat of his squirting semen breaking the silence of the still, cloudless dawn.

The Hong Kong twins were not twittering or giggling. They had not made a sound since midnight. Blindfolded, gagged and bending across their double bed, bellies squashed into the duvet, they kicked their heels helplessly as the titled Portuguese – kneeling before their bare bottoms – plied a silver dildo into each tightened cleft.

Out on the terrace the peacocks shrieked again. The

Portuguese nobleman looked up briefly, fancying the shrill screams to be from his victims' lips. No, not yet. In a moment, perhaps. Yes, in a moment. Then they would give full tongue to their torment. Gazing back down upon the prostrate forms of the svelte twins, he perused their neat bottoms. Pert boyish little buttocks. Yes, he nodded, dragging his lower lip down with three firm fingers. Extremely boyish buttocks. He returned to his task, driving a silver dildo ruthlessly between both pairs of clenched cheeks. Four heels kicked up in protest. The peacocks – charmingly on cue – screeched again. Across the bed, the boyish buttocks writhed.

Susie, bringing the peeled, dripping mango up to her exposed slit, levelled the shiny fruit then pressed it to her labia. Her bare bottom ground down against the edge of the scrubbed pine kitchen table as she juiced her flesh.

The mango was a special order for Ayani. Ayani, the kohl-eyed, red-lipped Lebanese. Susie imagined the kohl-dark eyes closing in concentration as the red lips parted wide, to guzzle the wet mango flesh. Susie jerked her hips, peeling her soft buttocks away from the pine table and rasping her clitoris into the fleshy pulp. She squealed softly, and savagely raked her slit with the fisted fruit. The image of Ayani bringing her red lips to Susie's slit became deliciously confused, melting illogically into the sensation of the oozing mango buried into her pink wetness. Ayani's lips. The pulpy flesh. Both firm, supple and pliant. All became one as Susie, buttocks tightening, started to come.

Pung. The large silver toaster disgorged six slices of blackened toast, and the kitchen quickly filled with an acrid smell. Susie grinned, more burnt toast for the peacocks. She closed her eyes, spread her soft buttocks against the edge of the table, and orgasmed.

Between the seething kettles spitting on the Aga, the abandoned blue tea towel crinkled up and shrivelled beneath an orange flame.

Like a lioness crouching over a freshly slain lamb, Ayani knelt over Emily's sleeping body. Lowering her face, she kissed then sucked gently at the sleeping blonde's right nipple. Emily stirred, and brushed her pubic bush gently with the knuckles of her left hand. Ayani, buttocks straining up, eased her bosom down and buried the blonde's upturned face beneath their warm weight. Emily stirred again, mumbling her lips into the thickening nipple. Ayani squeezed her thighs together as a silvery bubble shimmered at the crease between her recently shaven lips.

The cry of a peacock down on the terrace, instantly echoed by the ragged chorus of several more, broke the spell. The Lebanese sat back on the bed, content with the thought that back in Beirut this sleeping English rose would be hers, all hers, to awaken. To prune. To pluck.

Rising from the soft bed, Ayani carelessly wrapped her nakedness in pure silk. It rasped inaudibly at her peaked nipples and lapped at her shaven delta. Belting the silk tightly, she left the bedroom, intent on seeing the noisy peacocks down in the garden below.

The bell was shrill and continuous. So shrill, it made the cobwebbed bottles of vintage port tremble deep down in the dark cellar.

The bell sang fiercely. The Russian opened his eyes in alarm. A sharp elbow woke his oily-haired assistant into silent alertness by his side. The shrill bell spoke an international language they both instantly recognised and understood. Abandoning their bed of black satin sheets and assorted rubber implements for pleasure and restraint, they scrambled, clumsy in their nakedness, and bounded for the door. Mikhov turned, eye's wild with a bully's cowardice, and snatched up a Picasso and a small Matisse.

Dr Stikannos pushed Ursula's fingertips away from the second puddle of silver semen soaking the dark hairs on his chest.

'Help me,' he cried, twisting on his bed and jabbing a straightened gloved finger at his wheelchair. 'Help me!' Terrified of fire bells and the ravishes of fire since his experience and ordeal in the Swiss hotel, he begged for assistance.

But Ursula had gone, the bedroom door wide open after her.

Emily crawled out of the pit of her unconsciousness just as she had collapsed into its dark depths, with a shrill bell ringing in her ears. She shook her blonde mane and stretched. Her entire body ached. Her eyes blinked, then stared around in alarm. There was a bell ringing harshly. A continuous, sonorous moan.

A fire bell!

Naked, she slipped from the bed and dashed to the door. The pungent smell of smoke greeted her outside in the corridor.

The master. Where was Dr Stikannos?

She raced along the sumptuous stretch of crimson carpet, desperately trying to remember the location of his bedroom. Downstairs. Yes, of course. On the ground floor. She took the stairs three at a time, stumbling painfully as she missed the bottom step and floundered, face down into the cold marble floor. She sniffed at the warm trickle from her bloodied nose.

His shouts – in response to her cries – brought her quickly to his open door. There was little smoke but an all-pervading stench. Masked, gloved and naked, he had managed to scramble from his bed and was staggering towards his wheelchair.

Plucking up a snow-white towelling robe she covered his nakedness and eased him down into the leather seat. He was shouting. He was frightened and confused. His gloved fists smashed down upon the control panel. The chair veered sharply to the left then skidded to the right, almost toppling over. The engine whirred in protest.

The smell of burning grew stronger. Shouts and cries filled the corridors. Cursing, and sweeping Emily roughly aside, Dr Stikannos thumped the controls impotently: blind panic gripping him and divorcing him from cold reason. The wheelchair jerked, stuttered across the carpet and slued to an abrupt halt. He shouted in an agony of dread.

Calming him and soothing him, Emily returned to his side, knelt and fiddled frantically with the controls. They had jammed, the circuits shorted. The chair remained stubbornly still, useless and inert.

She sprang into action, quickly taking stock. The seat of the fire, she decided, could be anywhere between the bedroom door and safety in the grounds outside. The house was a vast maze. She didn't even know where the rear entrance was, and the front steps lay beyond stretches of corridor.

'No, wait,' she squealed as he rose up, uncertainly, and staggered towards the open door. 'This way.'

Slamming the bedroom door shut, she raced across to the French window. Grabbing at an Adam chair she hurled it at the sheer pane. With a shattering splinter the priceless chair sailed through the glass and smashed into pieces on the stone terrace beyond.

'No, not yet,' she warned as, in his panic, Dr Stikannos stumbled towards the frame of jagged shards. 'Wait, the glass.'

It would have ripped to shreds the soft white towelling robe, and the crippled flesh inside. Picking up a lighter chair, an exquisite little Hepplewhite, she raked the legs up and down the inner doorframe, ridding it of the dangerous splinters.

'It's okay,' she whispered, cuddling and guiding him

through the void to safety. 'It's okay now.'

Out on the terrace, stepping gingerly through the splintered glass, they were met by a pride of curious peacocks still awaiting their toast. Emily steered her stumbling master down onto the lawn.

The Lebanese approached them, her golden sandals silent as she ran across the grass. Emily left Dr Stikannos in her care.

The Holbein. Leaping back into the mansion through the smashed French window – ignoring her master's shouts to keep out – she ran to the foot of the stairs and dashed up. There was no smoke at all on the first floor, but the bell was still ringing violently. She slackened her pace, concentrating. Yes, there, the door to her original room. She ran in. Yes, the right room. The William & Mary four-poster. On the pillow, the Holbein – the delightful portrait of Anne Corderey.

The bell snapped into silence, leaving a strange, still calm ringing in Emily's ears. She trotted back down the staircase, hugging the Holbein to her naked breasts. Anne Corderey's lips pressed up into her left nipple.

Out in the sunshine she saw Dr Stikannos waving his arms and shouting. As she emerged on the front stone steps he staggered up and cried out his loud relief.

Emily surveyed the lawn.

The Russian and his assistant stood side by side, each holding a painting. Mikhov nursed the Picasso, his silent assistant clutched the Matisse. Several feet away Ursula cradled a painting protectively. It had been hurriedly wrapped in a white sheet, and much of the sheet trailed down on the green grass. Beside her, Chloe vainly tried to hide a smaller, uncovered painting behind her back.

All eyes turned to the stone steps. On them, looking distinctly sheepish and ashamed, Susie stood, a charred tea towel dangling from the point of a carving knife angled up from her right fist.

'Sorry,' she called out, her impish voice bright and far from apologetic.

Behind her, led by the impeccably dressed Portuguese nobleman – carrying lavender gloves and a clouded cane in his raised left hand – shivered the two Hong Kong twins: tethered together, blindfolded and utterly naked. As they shuffled obediently in the nobleman's mincing wake, a silver dildo slipped out from both their boyish bottoms.

Laughter greeted the tableaux, and those on the steps paused, uncertain and bemused.

A pistol shot cracked sharply. The short crisp bark scattered screeching rooks from nearby elms. All eyes – including these of the tethered twins who rapidly removed their blindfolds – turned to Mikhov. He was brandishing a 9mm Browning automatic. Up above, the rooks continued to wheel in the bright sunlight. Down below, kneeling before the Russian, Ursula was just completing the task of placing her palms upon her head. A Picasso, identical to the one Mikhov had rescued from the threat of fire, winked on the grass before her. By her side, Chloe shivered. At her knees, an identical Matisse.

Emily guessed the truth immediately.

The Russian looked stupid in his angry confusion. He waved the pistol in an all encompassing arc. Emily slipped her hand into the gloved hand of her masked master. The dark hole of the pistol stared directly into her gaze. She tensed. Dr Stikannos squeezed her hand protectively and pressed his thigh against her trembling flesh.

The pistol, aimed directly at the heart of Dr Stikannos, quivered in the angry Russian's hand.

'You dare to cheat me?' Mikhov raged. 'Me?'

Dr Stikannos released Emily's hand and spread out his gloved palms expansively. The pistol barked. Emily screamed, dancing aside as the bullet kicked up a clump of lawn between the feet of her master. Dr Stikannos did not flinch. Emily gasped, truly sensing his strength and power.

Behind the metal mask, she knew, was a dominant spirit that was incapable of even the slightest gesture of surrender or submission. The metal mask. It was their only chance. A calculated risk, but she took it. Reaching up she quickly snatched the mask away from his damaged face. Audible gasps greeted the twisted features as Dr Stikannos, cursing, was suddenly exposed to the sun.

The Russian grunted and stepped back, the pistol momentarily useless in his flabby hand. Emily dashed forward and, before the metal mask hit the ground, punched the pistol out of Mikhov's lifeless grip. Quickly stooping she snatched it up and aimed it directly into the stupefied Russian's open mouth.

Breaking into a sweat, Mikhov managed to curse Dr Stikannos for the cheat he thought him to be.

'No,' Emily whispered, lowering the gun and, to the Russian's astonishment, replacing it into the hand from which it had been snatched.

'But…' Mikhov spluttered.

'There,' Emily said, pointing to where Ursula and Chloe cowered on the lawn. 'There are your cheats.'

Mikhov stared down at the pistol in his hand, tossed his head back in both anger and exasperation and then pocketed the gun. Emily turned again. Like hers, all eyes were on the unmasked face of Dr Stikannos.

Chloe squirmed as Ayani pressed the pale bambusa at the nape of her neck. Stretched face down across the vaulting horse in the hi-tech gym, the naked girl whimpered. Ayani tenderly smoothed the long tresses of raven hair down along Chloe's face, leaving her neck and shoulders deliciously exposed. Arms stretched out before her, wrists tightly bound, Chloe lay utterly helpless beneath the quivering bambusa. Ayani was protracting the pre-punishment preparations, deliberately pacing the pain-of-mind building up in the nude's anxious imagination.

Dr Stikannos, supported by Emily, crossed the sheen of the polished wooden floor slowly, pausing at the scuffed hide of the horse. Steadying himself, gloved hands upon the leather, he grazed Chloe's soft thigh with his leathered fingertips. Chloe squeaked and shrank from the cold leather at her flesh, and Emily watched the girl's buttocks ripple and bunch as she writhed.

Taking a step back from the vaulting horse and remaining arm in arm, master and slave watched attentively as Ayani palmed the upturned cheeks she proposed to punish with the cruel bambusa cane. As Emily gazed down, she knew that Chloe's nipples would already be painfully peaked and pressed hard into the hide. She studied the nude's fear-tightened cleft now almost invisible between the clenched cheeks. Soon, Emily knew, the shivering girl's dark pubic snatch, rustling softly as it kissed the leather, would become wet and shiny: as would the horse with the ooze of the caned nude's feral juices.

It was a beautiful bottom, Emily reflected. The pale ivory skin taut across generously sculpted peaches. As Ayani continued to smooth the crowns of both cheeks with her skimming palm, the curves depressed slightly beneath her dominant touch. Pliantly submissive, the peach-cheeks submitted to the punisher's supremacy. Ayani raked her curved thumb across the buttocks, and Chloe yipped as her soft hillocks wobbled deliciously.

Yes, Emily thought, Chloe had a beautiful bottom. Her throat tightened as she yearned to crush her face into the perfect cheeks. Crush her face down into their satin softness, to kiss then slowly bite them.

Ayani positioned herself at the horse, judging the distance carefully with the levelled cane across the cheeks. Grunting softly, the Lebanese shouldered her cane. Down across the horse, the naked buttocks tensed in a spasm of fearful dread.

'Chloe,' Dr Stikannos growled. 'Before you receive your stripes, the stripes you have earned by your deception and betrayal, I wish you to know that I have no anger in my heart for you. No anger, just sadness and disappointment. You have hurt me, Chloe. Yes, you have hurt me, as severely as the cane is, I trust, about to hurt you.' He pointed his gloved index finger down to the base of her spine and, dividing her soft cheeks dominantly, raked the velvet of her warm cleft. 'Suffer, beautiful Chloe. Suffer your stripes.'

He stepped back and took Emily's hand in his. Together, united in the pleasure of another's pain, they watched closely as the Lebanese severely caned Chloe's bare bottom.

The thin wood whistled down, lashing the upturned cheeks and leaving a line of livid fire across their punished swell. Chloe squealed and jerked across the hide. Jutting out at the far end of the vaulting horse, her naked feet danced in the empty air.

Ayani drew a second crimson weal an inch below the first stripe with her cane. Emily squeezed her master's leather glove firmly as Chloe sobbed.

The third stroke… a sudden, vicious fourth. Emily saw that all four had bequeathed painful pink weals that deepened into a cruel crimson. Chloe's naked feet were drumming the air wildly as, writhing into the hide, she cried out in exquisite anguish.

Ayani paused, lowered the length of pale bambusa against her right leg and lowered her face to the whipped cheeks. Emily instantly drew her master's gloved hand to the heat of her prickling pussy as she saw, and heard, the Lebanese licking Chloe's striped buttocks. Dr Stikannos grunted softly as he drove his knuckled fist firmly into Emily's soft warmth.

A shriek from the far side of the gym reminded Emily, and her master, that Ursula was being whipped by Mikhov: but master and slave only had eyes for the bare-bottomed nude stretched across the vaulting horse before them.

Ayani slowed the administration of the caning, taking longer and longer pauses between each deliberate, cruel cut. It was, Emily thought, so pleasurable, so arousing, so delicious to be a witness to the punishment of another. Not to be the punished – that was a dreadful delight. Not to be the punisher – though that too was a darkly disturbing joy. No, to witness the bare-bottomed caning of a beautiful naked girl. She rose up on tiptoe as the gloved knuckles of Dr Stikannos brought her to her first climax. No, not to punish or be punished, but to watch, intimately and at very close quarters, the suffering of a beautiful girl beneath the bamboo.

Chloe was moaning a tuneless song, her lips trembling into the sour tang of the hide. Jerking her belly and hips into the horse in response to each blistering stroke, she was approaching her own vicious orgasm. Ayani spotted the signs. Snarling, she flexed the bambusa then probed the whippy wood between Chloe's belly and the wet hide below. Chloe arched her buttocks up – and was immediately rewarded with a searing swipe across her straining cheeks.

Emily cried out in joy and, twisting sideways so that her pubis ground into her master's hard hip, came furiously. Dr Stikannos remained motionless as she hammered into him, just as he had remained impervious to Mikhov's 9mm bullet.

Bathing and luxuriating in his cool indifference, Emily tumbled helplessly into her adoration of her master. She slid slowly down the length of his left leg, crushing and raking her wet seethe into him. At his feet, she hugged him, her blonde mane spilling over her eyes as she kissed his feet in total submission and surrender.

A gloved hand gently taloned her hair and dragged her back up on unsteady feet.

Ayani lashed Chloe's bare bottom harshly. The whipped nude squealed.

The gloved hand slowly drew Emily's trembling fingers to the proud erection. It jerked upwards as she encircled the rigid flesh and squeezed.

Ayani aimed the cane devilishly, striping Chloe's ripe outer curves with a vicious stroke. Chloe screamed and writhed, causing her punished cheeks to splay wide and reveal, briefly, her dark cleft.

Emily, boldly shy, started to gently masturbate her master.

The bambusa thrummed two evil notes from its song of sorrow, eliciting carnal grunts from the lips of the punished nude stretched and bound helplessly across the horse.

Emily, staring directly down at where the pale bambusa had just seared the proffered buttocks twice, sensed Dr Stikannos tense and stiffen. Her wrist became more supple as it quickened: bringing him up onto his toes.

Gasping aloud, he emptied his squirt of release. The quicksilver streaked up and spattered down across Chloe's whipped cheeks, just as Ayani whipped the cane down yet again.

The Lebanese tossed her bambusa aside then buried her face into the semen-silvered cheeks she had just mercilessly lashed. Emily stretched her fingers down to a small wet stain darkening the curved edge of the horse. A wet semen splash soaking into the hide. Dipping her fingertip into the shivering puddle of her master's warm release, she raised it to her lips. Closing her eyes tightly, she sniffed the smell of her master. Squeezing them shut even more tightly, she sucked, tasting his spilled seed.

'It was a clever little scheme. Neatly conceived and executed. Have you destroyed the fakes?'

'All three of them, yes,' Emily replied, raising her voice above the sudden chatter of a helicopter. 'The important thing is that your name, your reputation, isn't.'

Dr Stikannos nodded, then jerked his thumb up at the shattering din above.

'The Portuguese taking the Hong Kong twins with him,' she shouted as the Lynx clattered above the elms before peeling away over the rolling Wiltshire hills.

'Are you absolutely sure they only substituted three fakes?'

Emily nodded, patting his shoulder reassuringly. 'Chloe

was most forthcoming under Ayani's cane. She spilled the beans along with her tears.'

Yes, it had been a neat little scheme. Ursula had acquired passable copies that would not have been spotted after the careful post-sale switch, until the wraps were taken off in Moscow or Beirut. Selling Emily into bondage had been a little bonus, netting her the dollars and the pearl. They planned, Chloe had sobbed as the cane lashed her cheeks savagely, to desert Dr Stikannos that evening, disappearing with the three stolen paintings.

'Several million pounds,' Emily concluded, 'though of course they would have been lucky to achieve a million for the lot. Fine art is difficult to fence.'

'For some, perhaps,' he conceded.

Hand in hand, her soft pink fingers gripped by his dark leather, they crossed the floor of the gym to the wall bars. The master trod the polished wood cautiously, steadied and supported by his slave. Halfway across, Emily paused and stood aside.

'I think she's been keeping you in that chair on purpose. I'm sure your legs are strong. Lack of use, that's all.'

'Do you think so?' he asked.

Emily nodded. 'You're out of her clutches now. It suited her scheme to keep you confined to the ground floor. Look what she almost got away with.'

'Almost, but not quite.' Taking tentative steps, unaided by his lovely blonde slave, he made it across the gym to where Ursula, naked and howling, hung suspended from the wall bars, while Mikhov gleefully punished her.

The Russian held two whips, gripping the long snaking length of oiled hide in his right hand and a viciously supple cat o' nine in his left. His method was brutally unsophisticated – two measured lashes of the cracking bullwhip across Ursula's flayed cheeks punctuated by a cunning flick of the cat up at her exposed breasts. Jerking in her bondage as she spindled down from bound wrists, the green-eyed woman was beginning to beg for mercy.

As Mikhov snapped the lash again across Ursula's striped buttocks, Emily stood next to the silent assistant who gazed in dumb devotion as his master plied the cruel thongs. Ursula, deemed by those she had attempted to dupe to be the architect and chief culprit, was being given a correspondingly more severe punishment, while across the gym Chloe squealed under Ayani's bambusa cane.

Mikhov paused to inspect the weals raised across the naked cheeks with his whip, then turned to Dr Stikannos.

'You wish to whip her for her treachery, no?' he suggested, surrendering both whips to the gloved hands.

'No,' Dr Stikannos murmured, drawing his gloved hands fastidiously behind his back. 'Though she betrayed me, I seek no revenge. She has sewn the seeds for her own sorrow, a sorrow she is to harvest soon enough. A bitter harvest.'

'A bitter harvest, doctor, as you say,' Mikhov grunted, thumbing his cat tenderly. 'That Lebanese, she is a devil. A dark-eyed devil.'

As she watched the Russian smoothing out each lash between his fat finger and thumb, Emily's throat tightened. She knew exactly what was in store for both Ursula and Chloe. In her pocket, her fingers found the small pearl and the roll of thousand dollar bills – the price Ayani had paid for Emily. But once the full extent of Ursula and Chloe's treachery had been uncovered, Dr Stikannos had compensated his guests royally, consigning Chloe into servitude in Moscow and Ursula into bondage with the cruel Lebanese.

'You,' Mikhov whispered fiercely, wiping the sweat from his brow. 'You like to punish the bitch, no?'

Emily accepted the smaller whip, thrilling to the tease of the nine short thongs against her right leg. It was surprisingly light in her grip but unpleasantly moist from the Russian's sweating palm. She stepped up to the wall bars and gently tapped the exposed soles of Ursula's feet with the trembling tips of the thongs. The bound nude jerked in a desperate effort to evade the impending pain. Shouldering the tails of the cat, Emily clambered up the wall bars, two at a time, bringing her eyes close to Ursula's tearstained face. Pushing out her tongue, Emily delicately licked the salt from the whipped nude's cheek, tasting at last her enemy's contrition and penance. Angling the cat o' nine down so that the short tails trailed over the swell of Ursula's whipped cheeks below, Emily deliberately teased and tormented the helpless, striped flesh.

'I'm not going to whip you,' she whispered, her lips wetting Ursula's ear. 'I too have no taste for mere revenge. For I have had a sharp taste of what it is that awaits you in Beirut.'

'No, no…' Ursula wailed, jerking in her bondage.

'Yes,' Emily hissed in triumph. 'Yes.' She licked the bound woman's face gently, savouring the glistening salt tears. 'You forced me into Ayani's clutches for one brutal afternoon, remember? So I know some of her tastes, some of her appetites. You, Ursula, will come to know them all. Eventually.'

Ursula jerked with renewed energy as Emily's words haunted her imagination – jerked and writhed in a paroxysm of torment.

'All useless,' Emily whispered, flicking the cat to steady and still the nude against the wall bars. 'You will go with Ayani as her slave, in my place. Go with her, as her slave and plaything, to be trained and painfully prepared for your duties. Your first duty, Ursula, will be to serve Ayani. Then later, you will serve her clients in her seraglio. It is an interesting little corner of hell, I gather. Did you know that Mikhov proposes to expand into Beirut? Hm? Oh, didn't they mention that? Yes, he's going to be paying you a little visit in the seraglio.'

Ursula turned her tear-brimmed green eyes to gaze pitifully into Emily's stern grey gaze. 'I beg you…' she whispered, the words barely audible from her parched lips.

'No,' Emily murmured, ignoring the pleading woman. 'I shall not whip you now. In Beirut you will learn the meaning of domination and submission. I pity you, Ursula. Yes, I really do, for I know what your future is to be. I will remember you in my prayers.'

Ursula sobbed, begging for mercy and release, pleading to be kept. Kept and punished, anything but Beirut. 'Do what you want with me, anything. Anything but that…'

Placing the whip between her teeth, Emily carefully descended the wall bars.

'My God,' the oily-haired assistant gasped, breaking his mute silence for the one and only time, 'what did you say to kindle such fear in her heart?'

Emily smiled as she returned the shivering little whip into Mikhov's impatiently outstretched hand.

Ducking down under the gently swishing rotors, Emily side-stepped the fat tyre and mounted the red and white striped steps up into the belly of the Allouette six seater. Registered for convenience in Finland, the helicopter knew no international boundaries, and was capable of whisking Mikhov from Murmansk to Malaga, or wherever he chose beneath the skies of Europe. The pilot, alien-like behind a tinted visor, turned.

'Keep clear,' he barked, 'take off in two minutes.'

'I'll only need one,' Emily shouted above the gathering whine of the starboard engine.

'Welcome aboard,' Mikhov bellowed, raising a chilled bottle of Krug to his lips. The gold foil rasped against his dark jowls as the spume trickled over his unshaven chin. Beside him, in a blue tracksuit, Chloe wriggled within the tight embrace of a safety belt that bit into the swell of her bound breasts.

'I want her,' Emily shouted; the port engine had just coughed and opened up into a full-throated whine.

'Want her?' Mikhov echoed, his mouth open, the Krug foaming his lips. He lowered the bottle and smiled, his piggy eyes screwing up shrewdly. 'But can you afford her, hmm?'

'Ninety seconds,' the pilot warned.

Emily held up the pearl. Its soft sparkle closed the Russian's mouth and opened his eyes wide.

'Da,' he nodded decisively, grabbing the pearl. Twisting, he jabbed a fat finger into the red release button: the safety belt slithered away.

Trembling, Chloe sprang out of her seat and, clutching Emily's hand, skittled down the red and white steps, seconds before they were swallowed up into the belly of the helicopter.

They stood in silence, bodies pressed tightly together, hair streaming and eyes watering, as the Allouette rose up, banked and chattered away into the gathering dusk, its tiny red and green lights winking brightly in the violet haze of the approaching Wiltshire night.

Chloe started to sob gently. Emily remained silent. Chloe continued weeping. Emily let the girl cry her fill. Still crying, though more gently, Chloe pressed her wet face into Emily's shoulder.

'You rescued me,' she whispered huskily. 'After everything, you set me free.'

'I bought you, remember. I bought you.'

Out in the darkness, beyond the shivering elms, a vixen barked.

The following morning, after breakfast, Ayani led Ursula, still shouting and sobbing until she was bound at the wrists and tightly gagged, up the three steps of a sporty little red helicopter.

'Getting her and the paintings onto the Lear jet at Gatwick will present me with no difficulties,' she assured Dr Stikannos. 'It will be so pleasant dining in Beirut tonight. Goat flesh is so sweet when done slowly over the coals.'

Dr Stikannos and Emily waved her off, shading their eyes into the late summer sunshine as the red helicopter skimmed the beech trees.

'And after the traditional desert meal of roasted goat,' Emily remarked as they turned back across the lawn, 'some traditional desert sweetmeats.'

'Just desserts,' chuckled Dr Stikannos, taking Emily's hand.

Nougat, sherbet, dates and rose-water ices, Emily thought. Then she shivered, despite the warmth of the sun, as she imagined Ursula, naked and bound, squealing under the bambusa of the hungry-eyed Lebanese.

'The peacocks,' Dr Stikannos sighed. 'What do we do with the peacocks?'

'Susie is so fond of them. Why not let her take them with her?'

He nodded, slowly recounting the thirty thousand dollars Emily had just given him in exchange for Susie's release.

'I trust she appreciates your generosity,' he whispered. 'This,' he continued, tapping the fat roll of thousand dollar bills Ayani had given to Ursula, and which Emily had appropriated along with the pearl, 'will cancel all debts. Susie is now free to go. She should be very grateful.'

'Very grateful,' Emily repeated softly as she went down to the kitchen to break the news to the lovely maid.

Two hours later, Emily emerged from the kitchen flushed and tingling. After zipping up her black pencil skirt, she drew her trembling fingers up to the buttons of her blouse. Susie had been very grateful – fully appreciative of Emily's generosity.

The venerable Bentley whispered to a halt beneath the trees in the secluded Mayfair square. A liveried footman snapped quickly into action, assisting the blonde onto the pavement then deferentially up the marble steps and through the golden double doors.

The lift was quieter than the Bentley, completing the ascent with little more than a brief sigh. Stepping out for the penthouse, from which all of London was visible, Emily turned as – swish – the lift doors closed. She paused, her fingers poised above the silver security panel.

Five digits away, she knew there would be a delicious lunch. Her finger remained an inch away from the silver panel, primed to tap in the code. Yes, a delicious lunch. Carefully cooked and served by Chloe. Chloe, her personal maid. Emily closed her eyes and shuddered with pleasure.

Chloe, pertly dressed in that trim black uniform, a tiny white rubber and lace apron tied tightly around her waist. Chloe, bending submissively to offer a chilled amontillado from a silver salver. Chloe, above the deliciously seamed black stockings the tight white pantied buttocks. Chloe, within the warmth of the tight white panties, the delicious rounded cheeks. Cheeks bearing four crisp cane cuts, the weals deepening now from pink to crimson. Emily had caned Chloe earlier that morning, caned her maid slowly and strictly for some petty misdemeanour. Or was it for some minor transgression? Emily shivered again with raw pleasure. Sometimes she caned Chloe without reason. Simply swished the raven-haired beauty's bare bottom until one, or both, of them came. Without reason, purely for pleasure. Emily had come to learn that no excuse was needed when you owned a personal slave.

She gently tapped in the code. The doors to her new world parted obediently. In the library her Holbein graced the far wall. Anne Corderey gazed down on Emily's happiness. In the master bedroom, curled up on a tray of beaten gold, the camel bull's penis. Just one stroke of the wicked little anal whip was still enough to make her climax on the spot.

Emily reviewed her day. During her chilled amontillado, before the breast of pheasant and bread sauce, she would instruct Chloe to bend and bare her bottom, allowing the caner to peruse the effects of her whippy wood across the naked cheeks of the caned.

Then lunch, and after she would be attending that important sale in South Kensington. In an embassy, wasn't it? Dr Stikannos would be bidding strongly – Emily had spent the last three days researching the catalogue carefully, advising him of the most important piece. And during the bidding he would suddenly remove his metal mask, as she had suggested, stun his rivals and secure the bid. Another trophy in his collection.

Collection. Emily fingered the studded collar at her throat. Touching it still made her pussy prickle. Yes, her labia always pouted and became pleasantly moist when she fingered her studded collar; touching it made her juices weep. But not as much as the little ring that Dr Stikannos had pierced her labia with one night. She cherished it as she would a wedding ring, and with it the solemn vow always to obey.

Exciting titles available from Chimera

* * *

All **Chimera** titles are/will be available from your local bookshop or newsagent, or direct from our mail order department. Please send your order with a cheque or postal order (made payable to *Chimera Publishing Ltd*) to: **Chimera Publishing Ltd., PO Box 152, Waterlooville, Hants, PO8 9FS**. If you would prefer to pay by credit card, email us at: **chimera@fdn.co.uk** or call our **24 hour telephone/fax credit card hotline: +44 (0)23 92 783037** (Visa, Mastercard, Switch, JCB and Solo only).

To order, send: Title, author, ISBN number and price for each book ordered, your full name and address, cheque or postal order for the total amount, and include the following for postage and packing:

UK and BFPO: £1.00 for the first book, and 50p for each additional book to a maximum of £3.50.

Overseas and Eire: £2.00 for the first book, £1.00 for the second and 50p for each additional book.

*Titles £5.99. All others £4.99

For a copy of our free catalogue please write to:

Chimera Publishing Ltd
Readers' Services
PO Box 152
Waterlooville
Hants
PO8 9FS

Or visit our Website for details of all our superb titles and secure ordering
www.chimerabooks.co.uk